SHADES
of
GRAY

SHADES of GRAY

a novel

Pamela Carrington Reid

Covenant Communications, Inc.

Cover image: *Woman Standing on Windy Beach*, photography by Trinette Reed © Getty Images.

Cover design copyrighted 2008 by Covenant Communications, Inc.

Published by Covenant Communications, Inc.
American Fork, Utah

Printed in Canada
First Printing: February 2008

13 12 11 10 09 08   10 9 8 7 6 5 4 3 2 1

ISBN 13: 978-1-59811-502-4
ISBN 10: 1-59811-502-2

To my family

Prologue

The path to the beach had become familiar over the last week while she'd been staying with her grandparents, and Samara walked it quickly. A cold, brisk wind was picking up, making a small piece of paper dip and swirl in front of her, and the dark gray sand lifted in erratic spirals, whipping against her legs. She shivered slightly and glanced up and down the beach. Since the sky had become overcast, there weren't many other people around, and she recalled her grandmother's words to her before she went out. "Stay close to the path, dear, and be sure that you don't talk to any strangers."

She murmured under her breath as the path opened out onto the beach. "Yes, Grandma . . . I won't talk to anybody strange . . . not that there's anybody to talk to and not that I ever would anyway."

Samara had spent most of her time over the last week at Sumner Beach reading, swimming, and taking walks. Every time she went out, her grandmother repeated the same warning, and every time she gave the same response, but the warning was usually accompanied by a warm hug and the security of knowing that her grandmother really did care about her safety.

Samara smiled as she thought about her grandmother. She was always doing things that she thought Samara would like, and yesterday she'd brought out a small camera for her to use. It was obviously old and not at all like the ones Samara had been staring at in the shop in Christchurch, but Samara touched the camera now tucked in her jacket pocket and smiled again. She'd only had to mention that she'd really like to do photography and her grandmother had tried to help her. Now, at least she could try and take some photos on her own.

It was getting late in the afternoon, so the setting sun was creating a silver haze over the water and sky and on the wide expanse of soft sand; the receding tide had left a glistening blanket that reached to the lapping waves. It was very different from the golden sands of the endless beaches near her home on the Gold Coast in Australia, and the temperature was definitely colder. She pulled her cotton jacket more tightly around her slim body and wished she'd worn trousers instead of her beige shorts.

There were only a few other people on the beach. Samara avoided them and walked along to her favorite rocky outcrop to sit and watch the beach and seagulls. She pulled her knees up close to her chest and wrapped her arms around them, and although it didn't do much to stop the cold, it still felt comfortable.

She sat there for only a few minutes before she noticed a man down by the water. He had a camera and was repeatedly lifting it to his eye then putting it down and shading his eyes to look around the beach. It was as if he were looking for something, and because she was the only other person on their section of the beach, she finally took a deep breath and began to walk down the beach toward him. She was quite close before he turned and noticed her, but he smiled immediately and nodded before looking back along the beach.

Samara hesitated for a second, but the sight of his impressively large, black camera spurred her on.

"Hello." She stood near but he didn't seem to hear. "Hello? Are you looking for something?"

"Oh, hi." She noticed his accent immediately as he looked back at her. It sounded like the American missionaries she often met at church.

"Hello." She suddenly hesitated as her grandmother's words reverberated in her head, but he had a kind face, and the camera looked huge and important. "You looked like you were looking for something. Can I help you?"

She noticed that he took a moment to respond, then he nodded as if giving himself consent to talk to her.

"Actually, you probably could help, but let me introduce myself first. My name's Adam Russell, and I'm visiting from Canada."

"I thought you were American." She always said what she thought.

"Close." He smiled, and she liked the way his eyes crinkled at the corners. "Look, I know you've probably been told not to talk to strangers, and I wouldn't normally talk to a young lady on her own, but seeing as you've already asked me if you can help . . . I do have a favor to ask." He raised one eyebrow as if waiting for her to object, but she simply stared straight at him.

"Tell me first." She kept her hands in her jacket pockets.

"Okay . . . well, I'm a professional photographer and I was trying to get some pictures of the beach, but I prefer to have a subject against a background and . . . I was wondering if I could get some shots of you sitting on that rock." He handed her a small business card with the black silhouette of a camera on one side. The name *Adam Russell* and an address were written in white scroll font against a steel gray background on the other side. "This will prove I'm legitimate." He spread his hand wide and waved it in a half circle toward the beach. "I was thinking your silhouette would look great against the different shades of gray right now."

Samara frowned as she stared at the camera, then she looked where he was pointing. Sure enough, the sand was now a dark gray against the lighter gray of the tide, and the sky had become layers of silvery gray. They seemed to blend into a very deep shade of purple-gray as a long, dense cloud spread itself across the entire sky like a roof over their heads.

"I've never noticed that before." She put her head to one side and studied his face for a moment, then she took the business card and studied it as well. "Can I see what it looks like through the camera?"

He seemed surprised by her request, but he nodded and slipped the strap up over his head and held the camera toward her. Curiosity got the better of her as she took the camera in both hands and held it up to her eye. As she looked through the eyepiece, he did something to the front of the camera, and the scene suddenly came into brilliant focus.

She gasped out loud and kept staring through the eyepiece as she slowly moved her body and the camera so that she was seeing the whole view. It was as if something magical was enabling her to see the same things differently.

"It's so beautiful like this." She slowly lowered the camera and stared at it, then she nodded decisively. "I'll be in your pictures if you show me how to use the camera." Her voice was quiet but firm, and he looked at her in surprise.

"Are you making a deal?" He smiled, but she wasn't looking at him.

"You show me how to take photos, and I'll be in them," she repeated firmly as she stared at the camera. "And I'll show you some cool driftwood and things that people don't usually notice farther down the beach."

He looked thoughtful, and when she finally looked up at him he nodded.

"It's a deal."

They worked at the photos for over an hour. Every time Adam set up a shot, he would show her how to frame it with the camera and then how to use the different settings. She happily posed in several of them but was soon preoccupied with looking around intently, searching for the next thing to photograph. He followed, and they walked and talked as the sun gathered specks of gold from the sky and cast them down as rays that reflected off the silver tide.

"So how old are you, Samara?" He stood up from where he'd knelt to capture a small pool formed against an arch of bleached driftwood.

"Nearly fifteen," she answered confidently, then blushed as he stared at her. "In about fifty-one weeks. So how old are you?"

He smiled at her immediate response, then shrugged.

"Oh . . . nearly twice that. In about forty weeks."

She nodded briefly at this information, then kept walking with her hands in her pockets. Occasionally she would reach up and pull her long, silky black hair back from her face and twist it into a knot at the back of her neck. It never stayed there for long, but she didn't seem to notice how often she did it.

"My parents gave me this trip to visit my grandparents for my birthday." She pointed back in the direction they'd walked. "I actually live on the Gold Coast, over in Australia."

"Ah . . . I thought your accent was a bit different." Adam nodded and then stopped as he noticed a patch of tussock grass blowing in the wind; a faint mist of sand swirled around it like a miniature tornado. In a second, the scene was captured on film.

"My brother, Terry, came over last year for his birthday." She pointed at a shell lying half hidden among the slim strands of grass, and he nodded.

"So you're pretty close to your brother?" He focused the camera.

"Yes, he's my best friend," she answered in a matter-of-fact way, and he grinned.

"A lot of girls don't feel that way about their brothers."

"Do your sisters feel that way about you?" She seemed to be able to ask him questions about anything.

"I don't have any sisters . . . or brothers." He rested his hand on the top of the camera and noticed that she immediately copied his movement with the small camera he had given her to use.

"Do you have parents?" She seemed without guile, and it fascinated him.

"Not really." His answer was evasive, but she seemed to accept it. "What about you . . . what are your parents like?"

"My mum's cool. She runs a motel, and that keeps her pretty busy. We live there, so I sometimes have to clean and stuff if we get busy."

"And your father?"

She nodded and spread one arm out wide.

"He drives a huge truck all over the Australian outback, and sometimes we're allowed to go with him if we're on vacation." She nodded. "He's really clever . . . like, he fixes the truck if it breaks down, and he could survive anywhere with hardly any supplies. Sometimes it's not so good because he can't come to church and activities with us, but Mum always takes us." She dropped her voice a tone. "She says the gospel is the constant in our lives."

"So your father's away a lot?"

"Heaps." She stopped and picked up another small piece of driftwood, studied the curves of the knotted wood, then threw it back down onto the ground. "But that's all right because one day he'll take my mother to the temple, and then we'll be sealed to them for eternity, so his being away now doesn't really matter that much."

He took a minute to absorb what she'd just said, then he began to walk backward as he questioned her so he could watch her face.

"So what do you think eternity is like?"

"I think it's like being the happiest you could ever be all the time," she answered immediately, and her face lit up. "When Terry and I were really little we'd see if we could be happy all day so that we could get an idea of how it would be. Sometimes we'd make ourselves laugh and laugh even if there was nothing to laugh at, but by then we were hooked on laughing."

"I'd think that would be tiring." He smiled as he took a quick photo, but she didn't seem to notice as she nodded.

"We figured that out after awhile, and then Terry decided one day that being happy wasn't about laughing all the time; you could be silent and still be happy."

"So did you practice that?" He quickly took another photo as she shook her head.

"I decided that I was happiest when my dad was home. He made my mum happy, and that made us all feel good."

"So you love your father?" He asked the question with a different emphasis, and she noticed immediately.

"Don't you?"

"Pass." He turned around to walk beside her, and she held up her right hand. There was a very slim gold band on her little finger.

"My father gave me this so I'd never forget him when he was away." She shrugged. "I told him I loved him too much for that, but I still wanted the ring."

"That was very practical." He smiled as he glanced up at the darkening sky. "You know, I think we'd better turn back or your grandparents will be sending out a search party."

"Yes, we probably should," she agreed immediately, then held up the camera. "But I've thought of a few more questions."

"And so have I." He laughed as he stopped deliberately and swiveled in his tracks so that he was facing back the other way. "I want to know what your church thinks about what happens after you die."

She screwed her face up and looked at him as if he were slow-witted. "Don't you know?"

"Um . . . sort of." He held up his hand. "But I want to know what you think."

CHAPTER ONE

"I wonder who she's found today." Samara Danes stopped beside a small, red Nissan car and glanced back up the path leading to the university. She knew from past experience that it would be at least ten minutes before her friend Jackie arrived, and that she'd probably be talking to an unknown male.

Samara checked her wristwatch and toyed with the idea of getting a book out to read, then lifted her face to the sun. Even at three thirty in the afternoon the relentless Australian sun was still powerful, and its radiant heat just invited a body to relax and enjoy its warmth.

"I give in," Samara murmured as she walked over to the shade of a twisted gum tree. She moved a few pieces of the torn peelings of silver-gray bark and leaves and then sat down, her legs outstretched as she rested against the tree trunk. A few tiny flies immediately began buzzing around her head, and she unconsciously brushed them away with her hand and pulled her beige cap farther down over her face.

Her whole body was just beginning to relax when she heard Jackie's signature giggle and then some deeper male tones. Samara opened her eyes and watched her friend walking down the concrete pathway from the lecture block with a man on each side of her. Jackie Novelli's face was shining with her usual beaming smile, and one hand held books while the other constantly brushed back her mass of bleached-blonde curls. Her tanned arms and legs were attractively offset by long khaki shorts, a crisp white cotton shirt, and tan leather sandals.

Samara glanced down at her own worn jeans and the simple pink, checked shirt. Both items had flecks of white where the color had been bleached out by chemicals. She rubbed at one new spot, then, in an almost defiant gesture, she took off her cap and brushed the thin strands of her shoulder-length black hair back behind her ears with one hand.

"Sam! Come and meet Ben and . . ." Jackie neared the car and glanced at the tall man on her right. "I'm sorry . . ."

"Mark," he obliged with a nod and broad smile. Both men had light brown hair that had been blonded on the ends by hours spent in the surf and sun. Samara suppressed a smile. There was such a pattern to the type of people that Jackie befriended with her bright personality.

"But then they try for more than just friendship." She would give a resigned shrug and another wide grin. "They don't understand that I'm only trying to help them recognize their divine potential."

Samara looked at both men standing in front of her and quickly evaluated them. *I wonder if either of these guys has divine potential. Ben . . . no. Mark . . . possibly.*

"I've invited Mark and Ben to come on the young single adult hike and barbecue on Saturday." Jackie smiled as she unlocked the car door and waved a piece of paper at the men. "I've got your numbers, so I'll call you with the arrangements tomorrow, okay? Now we must rush. Poor old Sam always has to wait."

"So where did you find them?" Sam gave a desultory wave at the two men as they drove out of the parking area.

"Oh, they've been assigned to my marketing tutorial group. They're such nice guys. What did you think?" Jackie leaned forward to judge the stream of traffic then quickly moved out onto the highway.

"Are we talking divine potential?" Samara grinned. "If we are, then I think I'd go with Mark."

"Mmm . . . I agree." Jackie nodded. "Mark is a bit shy, but he was the first to agree to come on Saturday. Now I'd better make sure everything goes really well. I asked Leon to organize the barbecue, but I haven't checked with Rick about the hike yet. Has he said anything to you?"

Samara gazed straight ahead. "No . . . I haven't really spoken to him this week."

Jackie quickly glanced sideways. "Where exactly are you two at? I thought things were going well between you."

"They are . . . I've just been busy."

"Samara, what is wrong with you? One of the nicest guys in the stake worships the ground you walk on, and you're too busy? I swear I don't know about you."

"Don't swear," Samara answered mildly, which she knew would only infuriate Jackie more. After being close friends at church and school for nearly eight years, there wasn't much they didn't know about each other. The fact that they were so completely different had been a source of contention at the beginning when Jackie's family had moved to the Gold Coast, but they had discovered a lot of common interests as well and had become firm friends.

"So what is happening?" Jackie leaned forward as she pulled out to pass another car.

Samara stretched her arms and shrugged. "I have to concentrate on my assessment at the moment, and Rick has gotten a new job at Currumbin Sanctuary in addition to all his studying. We're just . . . busy."

"Rubbish!" Jackie frowned. "I mean, I can see you're busy, but . . . Rick's been home nearly six months, and I thought . . ."

"Like everybody thought?" Samara shook her head. "That we'd get married as soon as Rick got home?"

"Well, you did write to him his whole mission, and you were dating before he left."

"I know . . . and I do really like Rick . . ."

"Like? I thought you loved Rick."

Samara stared out the window at the high banks of yellow clay topped with stands of gum trees. "Jackie, I just don't know how I feel about Rick anymore. He's the only guy I've ever dated, and that wasn't a whole lot."

"But you wrote to him regularly for two years."

"And I loved writing to him, and he writes great letters. I just loved hearing all about Japan and the culture and his missionary work."

Jackie nodded knowingly. "So he's not that interesting now that he's not in an exotic land?"

Samara turned in her seat to face her friend. "That's the problem . . . I just don't know. I definitely like Rick . . . but I don't know if I love him, and I don't have anything to compare it with."

"I told you to go out with other guys while he was away." Jackie tapped her fingers on the wheel. "You've always had some excuse not to."

"Jackie, I'm just not interested in nonmember guys, even if they have divine potential, and the guys at church seem to just want to get married, or they just go to church because it's expected." She clenched her fist and rubbed it along the car seat. "And I want to do more than just get married. I want to see the world first and experience exciting things."

Jackie took awhile to answer, and when she did she was surprisingly serious.

"You know what, Sam . . . I hope Rick does go out with somebody else. Maybe that will help you come to your senses."

* * *

Samara stood with her hand poised above the doorbell for several seconds before she finally pushed the button at Rick Jamieson's front door. He only lived around the corner from her house, so at Jackie's request to find out about arrangements for the hike, Samara had gone there before going home. She folded her arms and listened to the tune of the bells echoing through the house until a small figure came and pushed itself against the glass door while reaching up to pull on the inside door handle. A tiny ginger kitten was also getting pressed tightly between the boy and the glass, and Samara grinned as the door finally opened.

"Hi, Sam. D'you like my new kitten? Rick got it for me." The little boy adjusted the thick-lensed glasses he was wearing with one hand while holding the door open with his foot.

"Hi, Toby." Samara reached down to rescue the kitten, which was now being dangled at arm's length in her direction. "I love your kitten. What's his name?"

"*Her* name is . . ." Toby corrected her solemnly, then frowned and put his finger to his head. "I don't quite remember . . . yes, yes I do. Her name is Melody."

Samara knelt down and held the kitten against her chest while she gave Toby a hug with the other hand. His white-blond hair was spiked up with gel so that it tickled against her cheek.

"Melody?" She paused a moment, then nodded. "That's a pretty name. Did you think of that?"

"No, Rick did. He said it should be something musical 'cause her singing kept him awake all night." Toby turned and gave Samara a tight squeeze around the neck, then held out both hands to take the kitten. "Rick'll be home soon."

"Who said I came to see Rick?" Samara smiled as she gave him the kitten and stood up. "I came to see my best friend Toby."

She was rewarded with a wide grin that showed one missing bottom tooth.

"Do you want to see the house Rick and I made for Melody?" Toby led the way inside and into the lounge where a large basket filled with a bright green cushion sat on a low table. He dropped the kitten onto the cushion and began to stroke her firmly so she couldn't move. "Mum already had the basket, but Rick sewed the cushion and I stuffed it."

"Rick sewed the cushion?" Samara raised one eyebrow as she knelt beside Toby again. "I didn't know Rick could sew."

"Rick can do anything." Toby stopped stroking Melody and looked directly at Samara. "Are you going to marry Rick?"

"Umm . . . I . . ." Samara stammered as she concentrated on the kitten. "I don't . . . I mean, he hasn't asked me," she finished lamely.

"What if he asks you?" Toby persisted as he leaned against her, resting his elbow on her knee. "Rick likes you."

"And . . . I like Rick." Samara felt the blood beginning to rise up her cheeks.

"Well, that's nice to hear." A deep voice sounded behind her, and Samara turned quickly, lost her balance, and fell against the lounge suite. Toby immediately chuckled and pretended to fall down as well. "Does this mean you've finally fallen for me?"

Rick walked into the room and sat down on the floor next to Samara and Toby. He had to bend his long legs to fit beside them, and his knees still reached above the table. The next instant, the kitten jumped and landed on his chest, sinking its claws into his shirt.

"Ouch!" Rick eased the claws out, then let the kitten rest against him. It immediately began purring.

"Well, at least the kitten likes you." Samara liked the warmth of his arm against hers but she still felt flustered.

"It likes my chest." Rick grinned as he used one finger to stroke the kitten's back. "It slept on it most of the night. It kept coming into my room."

"I thought it slept in its own bed." Toby climbed up on top of his brother's knee and balanced with both arms out. "It was there this morning."

"That's because I put it there before I went to work." Rick stretched out to put the kitten back onto the cushion, then he sat back and rested his arm along the couch behind Samara. For the briefest second she felt his head rest against hers. "So, to what do we owe the pleasure of your company, Samara Danes?"

"I . . . actually I came to ask you about the hike on Saturday." Samara swallowed. Somehow she always felt comfortable with Rick, but it was almost as if it was too comfortable. She moved slightly away as she looked sideways at him. "Jackie said she needs to know the details. She's asked some guys from school to come along."

"Ahh . . . some more blond-haired surfing guys with divine potential." Rick laughed as he shook his head, then he held out his other hand to steady Toby as he wobbled on his knee. "How does she do it?"

"I really don't know." Samara clasped her arms around her knees. "This time it's Ben and Mark. Mark seems the nicest."

"Does Jackie like Mark?" Toby gave up balancing and slid down to lean against his brother's leg, resting his elbows on Rick's knees.

"Who knows who Jackie likes." Samara shrugged and smiled as she reached out and touched Toby's cheek. "She likes the whole world . . . just like you do."

"Which is kind of a nice way to be," Rick agreed as he dislodged Toby and stood up. "I wish I could be like that."

Samara looked genuinely surprised as she glanced up at him. He seemed extra tall from where she was sitting. "But you are. You're just a bigger version of Toby. Everybody loves you and Jackie."

"Everybody?" Rick responded quickly as he held out his hand to help her up. She knew that he sensed her hesitation before she took it and stood up quickly, but when she tried to pull her hand away, he held onto it lightly. "Does that include present company?"

"Of course Toby loves you." Samara deliberately stared at the bookcase behind him. The pressure of his hand on her fingers was distracting so she tried to change the conversation "So how is your new job at the animal sanctuary going?"

"My job is going fine." Rick squeezed her hand slightly before he let it go and lifted Toby up instead. "You should come and visit some time. You could bring Toby."

"Can we Sam?" Toby immediately looked at her hopefully. "Tomorrow?"

"Not tomorrow, Toby." Samara still couldn't look straight at Rick. "Maybe we could go next weekend . . . after I've finished my assignments for school."

"Promise?" Toby pushed his glasses back onto the bridge of his nose. The simple movement seemed to make him appear so much older than his four years. "Double promise? Cross your heart?"

Samara laughed out loud as she finally looked up and used her forefinger to trace a cross over her heart.

"Double promise."

"Cool!" Toby held up his hand to give her a high five as Rick squeezed his little brother tightly.

"How about you ask her if she'd like to stay for dinner?" He deliberately avoided looking at Samara. "You seem to be better at this than I am."

Toby took a second to stare at his brother, then he nodded as if he understood and looked back at Samara.

"Can you stay for dinner, Sam?"

"Not tonight, Toby." Samara shook her head. "I'd like to, but I'm going over to Sister Patterson's to set up a new darkroom for my photography."

"Okay." Toby took a deep breath, then he slid down from his brother's arms and pushed him on the leg. "I guess Rick will just have to walk you home then."

* * *

"You really didn't have to walk me home." Samara noticed how Rick shortened his stride to match her smaller steps as they walked down his street.

"It's fine. I need to fill you in on the details for the hike."

"Well, it's probably better if you give Jackie a call." Samara held her bag against her chest. "I'm not sure that I'll even be going."

"You mean you'll be doing more schoolwork?" Rick walked with his hands in his pockets.

"Perhaps." Samara shrugged. "But mainly, Mum said she'll be needing help with the cleaning in the morning. She's had another cleaner leave this week."

They walked in silence until they were standing outside the driveway to a small two-level motel. The neon sign out front flashed now and then, giving both of their faces a yellowish hue.

"Can't Terry help her out?" Rick leaned against one of the poles holding up the sign. "He's not working, is he?"

"No, Terry's not doing anything." Samara answered briefly as she stared at the motel windows, suddenly reluctant to enter the world that was her home. Now that she was here, she could visualize the scene inside the tiny lounge room that adjoined the motel reception area. Her older brother, Terry, would be lying on the couch flicking through the television channels while her mother sat at a small, round dinner table that would be covered in accounts and bills.

Samara lifted her chin defiantly as she turned to Rick. "You know, Terry used to be my best friend when we were growing up, and now it's like . . . he's like a stranger, and he won't do anything. My father isn't ever here to do anything because he's away on the truck, and my mother seems incapable of even wanting to try right now." She attempted a slight smile. "And that's why I must do something . . . something on my own."

"That sounds pretty definite." Rick folded his arms. "Like a future being all mapped out?"

"I wish it were as simple as that." Samara found she couldn't look at him. "I know what I'd like to do, but sometimes . . ." She hesitated.

"Sometimes people get in the way?" Rick asked quietly, and she felt the meaning that he put into the question.

"Sometimes." Samara barely nodded, then she spread her arms out from her sides. "It just seems like there's a whole world out there that I've never experienced, and if I want to make it as a photographer I feel like I should do some exploring."

"So you need to go and visit all those exotic places around the world?" Rick leaned forward slightly to look at her face. "You'll never be happy until you do, will you?"

"I . . . I don't think so." Samara suddenly felt as if her heart was beating out of control, and tears were close to the surface. "Rick . . . I'm sorry . . . I . . ."

"Hey, there's nothing to be sorry about." She found herself gathered up in a tight hug, and her tears began to wet his shirt. She felt the slightest pressure of his chin against the top of her head, then he held her away from him. "I did want something to happen for us, Samara. I really enjoyed getting your letters while I was on my mission, and I prefer your company to any of the other girls, but I'm not stupid . . . I know you haven't really been feeling anything . . ."

"It's not that I haven't . . ." She began to protest, but the look on his face stopped her. "I just don't know right now."

"And that's okay." Rick put his hands into his pockets. "I want whatever's best for you, Samara, but I'm not prepared to play second fiddle to a passport and camera."

There was a moment's silence, then Samara took a deep breath. "That makes me feel kind of selfish when you put it that way."

"Not selfish." Rick shook his head and smiled. "And I didn't mean it quite that way. I just know that when I get married, I want a wife who's right there with me, not someone's who's always wondering if there could've been something or someone better."

"You want the ideal?" Samara found herself trying to smile back.

"The ideal is good." Rick nodded and grinned as he rested one arm along her shoulders. "Let's say we'll be ideal friends . . . until something better comes along."

"That sounds ideal." Samara rested her head briefly against the familiar weight of his arm until they both drew away. She took a few steps up the driveway before she turned.

"Rick . . . thank you for understanding."

She saw him swallow before he shook his head slightly.

"I never said I understood, Samara. I said I only wanted the best for both of us."

* * *

Her brother wasn't lying on the couch, and her mother wasn't sitting at the table. There wasn't even the usual pile of bills and documents on the dining table.

"Mum?" Samara glanced around the room with a frown beginning to settle on her face. "Mum, are you home?"

"She's upstairs." Terry walked in from the small kitchen with a sandwich in his hand and a drink in the other. He was wearing the same T-shirt and jeans that he'd worn for the last two days, and his dark brown hair looked as if it hadn't been cleaned or brushed in an even longer time. "Where've you been?"

"Over at Rick's." Samara answered briefly as she set her bag down by the door. She didn't usually spend a lot of time talking to her brother anymore, mainly because he seemed unable to have a conversation without finding fault with her. "And I'm going out again in a minute to Sister Patterson's." She pointed at the table. "Why is everything so tidy?"

"Why does anything get tidied around here?" Terry sat down on the couch, balanced his drink on the arm of the couch, and picked up the TV remote.

"Oh . . . when does he get back?" Samara asked quietly.

"Maybe tomorrow . . . maybe the next day." Terry shrugged. "You know Dad."

"I know that much." Samara ran a hand along the edge of the dinner table. "Did Mum say she was going out tonight? She's supposed to be taking Sister Patterson to Enrichment class at the chapel."

"Yep, she mentioned something about it." Terry chewed on his sandwich and waved it in her direction. "Are you staying in later? Because I'm going out."

Samara stared at her brother. A few months ago he had been an easygoing, thoughtful youth whose natural shyness only served to make him more conscientious in his engineering studies. Then he'd become friendly with another student from out of state and begun attending parties and staying out over the weekends. In the last few months, he'd not only dropped out of school, but he'd become almost antagonistic toward his family and friends and now spent most of his time sleeping in the morning and staying out late.

"Yes, I am." Samara turned toward the kitchen, and she didn't attempt to keep the sarcasm out of her voice. "I hadn't expected that you would be home. You always seem to have something important going on lately."

She walked through to the kitchen and stood looking at the food lying all over the kitchen counter. With a deep sigh she began to put things back in the fridge.

"Sam, is that you, love?" Tracey Danes appeared in the kitchen doorway adjusting a pair of earrings. She was dressed neatly in a skirt and blouse with her shoulder-length brown hair pulled back into a bun. Samara couldn't remember when her mother had looked any different . . . always neat, tidy, and tired looking.

"Are you going over to Sister Patterson's?" Tracey smoothed the front of her skirt.

"I'm going right now." Samara walked over and kissed her mother on the cheek. "I thought I'd check in to tell you that I'll be home to go on duty while you go to Enrichment."

"Umm . . . yes." Tracey hesitated. "I was wondering about that. Your father called . . ."

"Terry said," Samara interrupted as she leaned against the bench. "And you are still going to go out, Mum. Dad didn't say when he'd be home. It could be anytime over the next three days."

Tracey put her hand to her cheek. "I just like to be here when your father gets home."

"When he gets home . . ." Samara tried to keep the cynicism out of her voice. "It might be nice for him to be waiting for you for a change."

"Oh, Sam . . ." Tracey looked at her daughter, and her shoulders slumped slightly. "I wish you got on better with your father. He does love you."

"But he has a different way of showing it." Samara nodded as she leaned forward to hug her mother. They had had this conversation so many times before she could almost repeat it verbatim. "I do love

Dad, Mum . . . in my own way. I just have a hard time liking what he does . . . to you."

"He's fine to me, Sam." Tracey relaxed against her daughter's shoulder. "Our marriage works better this way."

"It works better for you to be apart most of the time?" Samara shook her head. "I guess I haven't come to grips with that one, Mum."

"People love differently, Sam." Tracey bit her lip. "You'll find out someday."

"Well, I intend to have a husband that I can be with . . . who'll actually raise his children and be there for me." Samara took an apple from the bowl on the bench and turned toward the door. "I'll be home before six so you can get away on time."

Tracey watched the empty doorway for several minutes after her daughter left, then she stared at the ceiling, tears forming in her eyes.

"And I hope you do find what you want, Samara. You deserve it."

Chapter Two

"Hello? Sister Patterson? It's Samara here. Hello?" Samara knocked hesitantly on the door. As it opened under her touch, she stepped in and glanced around the kitchen. Two trays of freshly baked cookies covered almost the entire surface of a small table, and she breathed in the warm chocolate smell, bending closer to the cookies to get the full impact.

"Why don't you help yourself? I baked them for you."

"Oh!" Samara jumped as Naomi Patterson walked into the kitchen through another door. "Hi, Sister Patterson." She laughed and pointed at the table. "I was just beginning to feel like Goldilocks sneaking in and being tempted to sample things. These smell so good."

"Except that you've got lovely, shiny black hair instead of yellow curls." Sister Patterson slid two cookies off the tray and onto a thin china plate delicately patterned with tiny pink roses. "It's a shame you can't model for your own photos."

Samara self-consciously tucked her hair behind her ears as she bit into the moist warmth of the cookie. "You know, I thought it was a total blessing finding a darkroom. I didn't realize it came with cookies and flattering company as well."

Sister Patterson smiled and sat down at the table. "Oh, I mean it, and I think it's wonderful that you're using the old darkroom. Its just been sitting there for so long." She sighed. "As for the cookies and company . . . you're the blessing to me, my dear. I finally get to bake nice things for somebody else and to talk to someone other than the cat."

"Well, I'm more than happy to help out." Samara picked up the bags she'd placed on the floor and held them out, one in each hand. "I think I've got all the materials I need. My professor was really helpful and gave me all sorts of bits and pieces."

"Then let's get you organized." Sister Patterson led the way through a lounge that was always tidy and smelled faintly of roses, just as she always did. She hesitated as she opened a narrow door leading out into the garage. "Please excuse the mustiness, dear. I hardly ever come out here anymore."

She led the way through the garage, past a small car with a tarpaulin stretched over it and into a small room tucked away in the corner of the garage. She flicked the light switch and the room became illuminated with a soft yellow glow.

"It makes me feel good just walking in here." Samara glanced around at the stainless steel benches, the open shelving stacked with yellow trays and gray canisters, and the upright pinboard sheets that held rulers and scissors. She moved across the room and gently touched the solid frame of an enlarging machine. "It makes me feel like I can really produce some professional images."

"Well, I'm expecting to see some great pictures." Sister Patterson nodded as she looked around. "Peter was so proud of this room. When our first grandchild was born he decided to make photography his hobby so he could have this wonderful record of our posterity. He went to classes, then he bought a book on how to construct a darkroom." She chuckled. "He spent weeks doing little scale drawings of the room and planning where everything would go . . . the wet side and the dry side. I really think he got more fun out of actually building the room than doing any photography."

"Did he do much?" Samara pulled some slim yellow boxes out of her bag and stacked them neatly on the shelves.

"Oh, at first he was quite prolific . . . until the children began to cry every time they saw the camera." She chuckled, then pointed to a metal stool with a green plastic seat. "That was my seat. I used to come down and watch while Peter was developing the pictures. I had to be very quiet and stay out of the way, but I just loved watching the images appear. It was like magic."

Samara glanced around. "Would you like to watch when I'm developing? I'd appreciate any suggestions."

Sister Patterson clasped her hands in front of her. "Oh . . . I would like that." She looked hesitant. "As long as I'm not in the way, dear."

Her green eyes almost twinkled in the dull light, and she held her hands to her chin like a small child so that Samara wished she had her camera with her. Impulsively, she put her arms around the woman's frail body and hugged her tightly.

"Thank you so much for helping me with this, Sister Patterson. You're helping make my dreams come true."

The time passed rapidly as Samara determined the best layout and organized the bottles and papers. Sister Patterson sat on the stool, and they chatted easily as she worked. Finally, she placed her hands on her hips and looked around the small room.

"I think we're ready to go." She glanced at her watch. "But I'm going to have to start the developing tomorrow. Mum needs help at the motel tonight. I said I'd stay on duty so she could go to Enrichment."

Sister Patterson nodded and eased herself slowly off the stool. "Then I must get ready as well. Tracey said she'd take me with her." She smiled. "Your mother is such a lovely lady. Since she became my visiting teacher, she's taken me to church and activities. It's just lovely."

Samara nodded as she picked up the bags. "I think it works both ways. She hadn't been attending church very much at all until she met you, and now you've given her a reason to do things. She needs company."

"The Lord does work in mysterious ways, doesn't He?" Sister Patterson paused as she went to turn off the light. "All these years and I've never really spoken to your mum and now . . . it's like we've been put together."

"Well, I'm really grateful you have. I couldn't believe it when Mum came home from visiting you and said you had a darkroom I could use. That was almost too weird. I was hesitant to even mention it to her because I knew it was just going to be an extra expense."

"And I was wondering what to do with everything. How perfect." Sister Patterson laid a gentle hand on Samara's arm. "I guess we were both saying our prayers."

Samara nodded thoughtfully as she remembered the silent pleas she'd offered over the last few weeks to be able to finish her studies.

Her mother had no extra funds, and her father didn't consider fine arts as "useful," and so he wouldn't help her at all. It had felt as if her dream of becoming a professional photographer would always be just that . . . a dream.

"Do you mind me asking, dear?" Samara felt the gentle pressure on her arm again. "What made you want to be a photographer?"

"Oh . . . it's always been in my mind." Samara nodded as she rested the bag strap over her shoulder. "At least, since I was about fourteen." She glanced down, suddenly shy. "I was on holiday in New Zealand with my grandparents, and we were staying at a beach. I went for a walk and watched a man taking pictures, and he asked me if he could take some of me."

"Oh, dear . . . was that wise?" Sister Patterson put her hand to her lips. "He might've been dangerous."

"I remember thinking that, but there were a few other people around." Samara nodded. "And right then I was only interested in the camera he was holding. It was black and silver and it looked so . . . professional." She shrugged. "And no one had ever wanted to take my picture before."

"So, did he take your picture?"

"Mmm . . . quite a few." Samara warmed pleasantly at the memory. "But he also told me what he was doing and why he was trying different exposures to get different amounts of light in the photos. It was all so fascinating."

"And it sounds like he really was quite a nice man."

Samara smiled. "He was a very nice man. He actually made me feel like a grown-up." She stared at the ceiling. "He even told me about all the places he'd been around the world taking photos. That's why he was in New Zealand."

"And so you've wanted to be a photographer ever since." Sister Patterson smiled sweetly. "I get the feeling you'll be a very good one, dear. Maybe you will be a famous international photographer and I'll be able to say that you got started in Peter's darkroom."

Samara sighed as she turned to the door.

"Wouldn't that be wonderful?" She hesitated with her hand on the door handle, then her fingers tightened on the brass knob. "No. It *will* be wonderful."

* * *

Adam Russell stood for a few minutes outside the stake president's office, then, when no doors opened, he sat down on one of the chairs in the waiting area. Several Church magazines sat neatly on a small side table, so he picked up the closest and searched the cover briefly.

"*New Era* art contest." He read one of the captions quietly. "Let's see what the younger generation is producing."

He flicked through the magazine until he found the pages of photographs and paintings and began to look them over with a practiced eye. Most of them got a nod of appreciation, but on the last page, a stark black-and-white photo grabbed his attention.

The picture was of a very young boy with bright blond hair concentrating on the dandelion flower he was holding directly in front of his face. He was trying to blow the fairy-like seeds of the flower, but he was mainly blowing upward, making the wispy hairs on his forehead stand up. A few of the seeds had lifted into the air and were contrasting starkly with the black background in varying tones of white and gray.

"Very good." Adam murmured as he held the photo at a different angle. "Excellent light. Great subject."

He looked down at the caption below the photo.

"*Wonder* . . . by Samara Danes. Gold Coast, Queensland." His fingers suddenly tightened on the page. "Samara . . . Samara Danes." He repeated the name quietly as one of the office doors opened and his stake president came to stand in front of him.

"Adam . . . it's good to see you. Sorry to keep you waiting." President White stood beside Adam's chair with his hand extended. "Come on in. I'm always fascinated to hear what you've been doing."

The men shook hands, but Adam held onto the magazine with his other hand, then rolled it lightly as he followed President White into his office.

"So what have you been up to the last few months?" They both sat down on chairs in front of the desk. "Or is it years?"

Adam gave a half smile as he settled back into the chair.

"Not exactly years, President." He tapped the magazine against his knee. "But it has been awhile."

President White studied his face carefully. "I hear you've been up in Alaska . . . or was it Greenland?"

"Alaska, then Greenland . . . but I've been to Russia and Mongolia since then," Adam corrected mildly as he rubbed his beard. "Just visiting the cold places for this assignment."

"Mmm . . . I thought the beard was a new addition." President White nodded thoughtfully. "I guess you didn't get to church very often in those places."

"Not often." Adam smiled broadly, and his even, white teeth showed through his sandy colored beard and moustache, which was tinged with gray. "Is that what this interview is about, Stan?" Adam dropped the formality and addressed the man who had been one of his best friends since he had joined the Church.

President White took his time answering, then he stared straight at his friend. "It's funny, but all the time I've known you, I've never known why you joined the Church."

Adam met his look directly, then he shrugged. "I felt it was right." He nodded slowly. "I still do."

"And yet you travel around the world and hardly ever go to church. You haven't held a temple recommend for nearly six years, and to my knowledge, you haven't had a regular calling for at least seven."

Adam nodded and gave a wry grin. "You've been doing your homework. I could use you on my research team."

President White took his time responding, then he leaned forward.

"I'm serious, Adam. Since your marriage broke up, you've turned into even more of a wanderer. I know you have a testimony or you wouldn't keep coming back to church . . . but I'm just not sure what you have a testimony of."

Adam stared past his friend's shoulder and out the window. A brilliant ray of sunshine suddenly lit up the glass, and he turned his face slightly away.

"You asked me why I joined the church, Stan. Would you believe me if I told you it was because of a young girl's testimony?" He stared up at the ceiling. "I've never told you and Jane this, but . . . years ago I met a young girl at a beach . . . in New Zealand. She was watching me take photos, so I asked her to be in some of the shots."

"How old was she?" President White asked quietly.

"Fourteen . . . nearly fifteen." Adam smiled. "In eleven months. Anyway, she was fascinated with my camera and so I showed her how things worked, and then we just talked."

"You'd probably be accused of something inappropriate these days." President White leaned back in his chair.

"I know . . . but then . . . I found she was like a sponge, soaking up all the things I could tell her about my travels and everything."

"A good audience is great for the ego," President White interrupted wryly. "But what has this got to do with your joining the Church?"

Adam hesitated and tapped the magazine against his knee again.

"I asked her why she was in New Zealand . . . she'd said she was from Australia . . . and then she started telling me about going to church. She was so confident about it, and she had an answer for lots of things that I'd wondered about . . . God or a Higher Being." He shook his head. "It really impressed me that she was so young, and yet she had answers that wise old men I'd met on my travels didn't have."

"So you came back here and joined the Church?"

"Not immediately." Adam shook his head. "I actually went to church in several countries on my way back to Canada . . . and it impressed me that things were always the same wherever I went." He rubbed the back of his neck. "The organization was the same, but more importantly . . . I kept feeling the same . . . spirit." He looked straight at his friend. "She said I would feel the Spirit . . . and I did."

President White glanced across his desk at a framed photo of his family.

"My goodness, I hope my fourteen-year-old daughter can have that sort of testimony." He nodded slowly. "I wonder if that child realizes what an effect she had on you."

"I'm sure she has no idea." Adam loosened his grip on the magazine so it unrolled in his hand, then both men sat silently for awhile until President White stood up.

"Adam . . . don't waste that testimony. You have a lot of potential, and not just as a photographer." He held out his hand. "Shall we arrange for another interview soon . . . for the temple?"

Adam took his time answering as he shook the other man's hand, then he nodded. "Maybe in awhile . . . I've got another trip to make first."

"So where are you off to this time?" President White walked him to the door.

"Actually . . . I'm going to Australia." Adam gave a brief salute with the magazine and smiled. "I've got some unfinished business in Queensland."

CHAPTER THREE

"Yes! We have our resident photographer," Jackie called out to the group of young single adults gathered in the car park before she gave Samara a quick hug. "And just in time. Rick said he thought you might not make it, so we were going to leave."

Samara glanced around at the assembled cars and vans. She couldn't see Rick's distinctive orange-colored Tarago van.

"I didn't think I could, but my mum managed to get another helper today. You'll never guess who."

"Who?" Jackie managed to sound interested while still counting the number of vehicles and people.

"Sister Patterson." Samara put her backpack down. "Apparently she loves cleaning and company, so she's going to be Mum's reliable substitute if she has problems."

"Well, that should take some pressure off you." Jackie noted the numbers in the small, worn notebook she always carried. "You've been the reliable substitute for way too long."

"Mmm . . . it does feel nice to walk away from it all." Samara nodded. "So who do you want me to travel with?"

Jackie glanced sideways at her friend.

"I had put you in Rick's van, but I put Cassie in there when I thought you weren't coming. Is that okay?"

Samara leaned over to pick up her bag, and she tried to shrug nonchalantly.

"It doesn't worry me." She tightened her grip on the backpack strap. "Rick and I sort of called it quits last night."

"No way." Jackie actually stopped and stared. "As in . . . permanently?"

"I guess so." Samara nodded. "We're still friends . . . only . . ."

"Only you can't see a good thing when it hits you in the head," Jackie interrupted briefly before she leaned over and gave Samara a quick hug. "I sure hope you know what you're doing. I know at least three girls who'll be ready to swoop in now that you're out of the picture."

She turned, and in the next second was distracted as another car drove into the parking lot with the men she'd met earlier that week.

"Oh my, Ben and Mark did come!" She turned back to Samara. "Remember, you need to fill me in later on what happened, but right now I think we should travel with these guys."

* * *

The air was remarkably still and clear, and Samara took her time getting out of the car as she appreciated the view at the park. It almost seemed a shame to spoil the stillness, but with twenty young single adults noisily spilling out of cars, the moment soon passed. Jackie jumped into her organizing mode as she maneuvered Ben and Mark into a group while Samara wandered off to the edge of the picnic area. Without thinking, she reached into her bag and began checking that she had all of her camera gear, but when Jackie's laugh suddenly rang out, she quickly turned to take some candid photos of the group. She had the camera to her eye when a hand obliterated the picture.

"You know that when you do have children they'll have an identity crisis." Rick spoke from behind her, and she slowly lowered the camera.

"How's that?" She took her time looking up at him.

"Well, at school they'll be asked to draw a picture of their mother, and they'll draw a camera with two legs." He grinned. "Although I'm sure it'll be a fancy camera and a great pair of legs."

"Very funny." Samara smiled as she put the lens cap back on the camera. She had been dreading seeing him again, but she already felt at ease. That was so like Rick to make her feel better.

"Thank you." He gave a half bow. "I thought you weren't coming today."

Samara shook her head. "I wasn't, but then Sister Patterson offered to help Mum at the motel so I escaped."

"It's a pity you didn't escape sooner." Rick ran his hand over his face. "I had to spend the whole ride up here listening to Cassie prattle on about everything that is unimportant. How that girl can know so much irrelevant information is beyond me."

Samara laughed, then she stood awkwardly, not knowing what to say next.

"So will you make this hike more bearable and walk with me?" Rick pointed toward the pathway without looking at her. "If you want to, that is."

"Why wouldn't I?" Samara decisively put the camera back into the bag and swung it over her shoulder as she began walking. "Someone has to save you from Cassie, and I haven't done any other good deeds today."

"So you're going to make me a charity case?" Rick fell into step beside her.

"No . . . you'll owe me," she retorted with a grin. After the last few weeks it felt good to have this kind of conversation with him. They walked in silence for a few minutes, then Rick suddenly swung in front and began to walk backward, facing her.

"I was serious about staying friends, Samara."

"I know." Samara looked at his shoulder and swallowed hard. "And I'm glad. I know we said that but . . . I wasn't sure how it would be today."

"Sometimes it's different when you wake up." Rick was still walking backward, and he stumbled slightly so that she instinctively reached out to catch him. He stopped walking and faced her. "That's why I wanted you to know that I meant what I said."

"Come on, you two. You're blocking the path!" Jackie's voice sounded behind them, and they both stood aside as she strode past with Mark close behind. "We'll swim as soon as we reach the water-fall." She flashed a knowing smile back at Samara, then began to sing out loud as she walked on. "'There is beauty all around, when there's love at home.'"

* * *

"So what exactly is happening with you two?" Jackie sat down beside Samara on a wooden platform overlooking the natural pool where the rest of the party was relaxing. Most of the boys were swimming while the girls were lying in the sun on some of the large rocks surrounding the pool.

"Nothing exactly." Samara responded immediately. "We're still good friends, but we're . . . giving each other room to move."

"You mean Samara wants room to breathe and Rick is going along with it?" Jackie crossed her legs and adjusted her cap lower over her eyes.

"He's not just going along with it." Samara turned her face up to the sun. "He said he wants a relationship where there's commitment on both sides, and I'm not at that point yet."

Jackie sat quietly for awhile, then she rested back on her hands and stared ahead.

"I wonder what it is about your family . . . about commitment."

"What do you mean?" Samara looked at her quickly. "What has my family got to do with it?"

"Probably everything." Jackie answered bluntly, and for the first time her shoulders slumped slightly. "It's obvious Terry is finding it difficult to commit to anything. He's always been there for everything . . . since we were young . . . but when I called him the other night to see if he'd come today, he wouldn't give me a straight answer."

"The way Terry is right now, it's better he didn't come." Samara shook her head. "I really don't know what's going on in his head. He's always been quite serious, but he had a neat sense of humor and he was always reliable, but now . . ."

Jackie nodded. "But now he's different. I've really noticed it lately."

There was something in the tone of her voice that made Samara look at her intently.

"I thought you only noticed those with divine potential."

"You don't think Terry has divine potential?" Jackie answered quickly, still staring straight ahead.

"Umm . . . I guess so." Samara looked puzzled. "I mean I've never really thought about it. He's my brother," she said, as if that explained everything. "Besides, he only seems to annoy me these days. He seems to waste so much time."

"You don't think that maybe he has a problem?" Jackie asked quietly.

"Of course he has a problem." Samara frowned. "He's turning into a couch potato with no ambition."

"No, Sam . . . I mean, do you think he has a real problem?"

It took a minute for Samara to realize what Jackie was saying, and she finally folded her arms across her knees and rested her forehead against them. She didn't speak for quite awhile, then she slowly raised her head.

"If you're saying what I think you're saying, then . . ." She hesitated and took a deep breath. "I wouldn't be surprised and I don't know why I haven't thought of it before."

"You have been a bit preoccupied." Jackie smiled, then she stared out at the pool. "Why wouldn't you be surprised though?"

Samara hunched her shoulders and closed her eyes.

"My mum uses prescription drugs . . . lots of 'pick-me-up' and 'get-to-sleep' stuff. It's the only way she copes." She shook her head. "And I know my dad drinks."

"Even when he's driving?" Jackie looked surprised.

"No, I think he's more careful than that." Samara glanced sideways. "It's this agreement my parents have. He'll go and drive big trucks across the outback and get drunk for days in-between then come home occasionally and be nice to Mum with no drinking allowed. He knows she hates him to drink."

Jackie took awhile to answer.

"I knew they had an unusual relationship. I didn't quite realize it was quite like that."

"Oh yes." Samara bit at her lip. "Dad's not abusive or anything . . . I think he loves us in his own way, and Mum loves him, too."

"But it's not surprising that Terry might try . . ." Jackie hesitated.

"Drugs or drink?" Samara sighed. "I wouldn't be at all surprised, but if it is that . . . then I have no idea what to do about it. I can't see Mum helping."

"Maybe you underestimate your mum." Jackie rested a hand on her friend's shoulder. "I've noticed quite a change in her lately. She's been coming to church much more."

"Mmm . . . she has." Samara turned back to face the pool. Rick and several of the boys were gathering in a group, and she could see by the way they were pointing that they were considering diving under the waterfall. She knew it was a reasonably dangerous stunt, and yet somebody always tried it. "You seem to be noticing quite a bit about my family."

Surprisingly, Jackie's cheeks colored instantly as she drew an invisible shape on the wood.

"You have an interesting family. Mine are quite boring in comparison."

"Your family is not boring. They're wonderful." Samara thought of Jackie's father who had just been released as their bishop, her mother who was an accomplished artist and musician, and their six children. "I think you take them for granted."

"No, I don't." Jackie smiled. "I love them to bits. I just happen to love your . . . family as well."

Samara stared. Jackie had been her close friend for so long it had never occurred to her that she might have feelings for her brother. They had grown up together.

"Terry?" She felt her eyes grow wide as Jackie nodded without looking at her.

"Why not?"

"But . . . you could have anyone . . ." Samara almost spluttered. "Terry . . . really?"

"You said yourself he used to be so lovely." Jackie retraced the shape with her finger. "I think I fell in love with that Terry a long time ago . . . that's why I've really noticed the change, but I don't know what to do about it either."

"Oh, Jackie, I'm sorry."

"I don't want you to be sorry, Sam." Jackie straightened up. "I want to know what to do about it. Terry truly has divine potential, and I'm not prepared to see him go to waste!"

She spoke so strongly that Samara didn't know how to respond. She looked down at the pool where most of the boys were now standing around the edge, peering into the water. It seemed as if a hundred thoughts were racing through her mind. Why was her family different? Why did people like Rick and Jackie have to rescue them?

Why couldn't they help themselves? What was she going to do about Terry . . . about herself . . . about Rick?

"Jackie . . . Samara!" Urgent voices suddenly penetrated her thoughts as she became aware of some of the boys running toward the waterfall. "Rick hasn't come out!"

When she thought about it later, it amazed Samara how instantly the confusion had disappeared as she responded to the yells and raced with Jackie down to the waterfall. The relentless flow of water continued at the same speed, oblivious to their fears as they stood waiting.

"He went down with Ian and Mark."

"He should be back by now."

Samara heard the voices, but her gaze was fixed on the waterfall.

"Someone go down and check."

"You won't be able to see anything. You'll have to go back around."

Somehow her legs began to move, and she started to work her way around to the back of the fall. Rick? Not Rick! Her ears and head pounded with his name.

"Samara!"

"Rick!" Samara stopped, and her hands went to her mouth as she watched him appear from behind the wall of water. He was holding his right arm up, and his other hand was clenched tightly around a large gash. Blood flowed from the wound, mixing freely with the water running off his body.

"I had a little bit of an accident." He tried to smile, but his face was white, and he staggered slightly. He managed a lopsided grin as he saw the look on Samara's face. "Did you miss me?"

* * *

The hospital waiting room was quite full, and more people seemed to arrive by the minute as Samara and Jackie waited for Rick to be attended to. New patients of all ages came in sporting a wide variety of injuries and illnesses.

"I never realized you could be hurt in so many different ways." Jackie turned to watch a man being pushed in a wheelchair with his foot out in front. A small blond boy running in through the sliding doors narrowly missed hitting the man's foot before his mother caught him by the hand.

"Sam . . . where's Rick?" Toby demanded as soon as he saw her across the room. "Is he hurt bad?"

Sister Jamieson hushed him, but her concerned look spoke volumes as she looked at the girls.

"Rick's fine." Samara stood up and hugged Toby, then his mother. "He lost quite a bit of blood, and the cut is going to need a few stitches, but you know Rick . . ."

"Yes, I know Rick." His mother smiled and shook her head. "How that boy has survived to this age is beyond me at times."

"Did Rick's arm fall off?" Toby tugged at Samara's hand.

"No, his arm is okay, Toby." Samara smiled. "But you might have to write things for him for awhile."

"That's okay. I know my letters." Toby nodded importantly as he turned to look around the waiting room. He was the first to see his brother as Rick walked into the room with his heavily bandaged arm in a sling.

"Rick!" Toby was by his side in a second, jumping up to see inside the sling.

"Whoa there, fella!" Rick expertly turned and swung him on the other arm, but even that movement seemed to make the blood drain from his face. He raised an eyebrow and leaned against one of the chairs. "Wow, head spin."

"Well, just take it easy, Rick." Sister Jamieson was immediately by his side, and Samara noticed again how alike the two were. Both were tall and slender with thick brown hair, while Toby was stocky and blond.

"I will as soon as I can get out of here." Rick grinned and wrinkled his nose. "Everything smells hurt."

As they filed out to the parking lot, Jackie and Sister Jamieson swung Toby between them over the curbs while Samara walked quietly beside Rick.

"You really did have us worried." She finally spoke without looking at him.

"Us, or you specifically?" Rick asked easily. "I was quite impressed with the look on your face when I came out of the waterfall."

Samara glanced sideways at the sling. "I guess some people will do anything for attention."

"Ah, but they wouldn't have to do anything if they got attention in the first place." Rick countered quickly, then his expression changed. "Samara, I may be completely out of line saying this, especially after the other night, but . . . when I got sucked down under the waterfall . . . I really thought I'd had it and . . . well, you were all I could think of. I wanted to be able to see you again."

The headlights from an oncoming car blurred as Samara fought back the tears that had been threatening all afternoon, and she nodded quickly.

"I know, Rick. I felt the same way . . . when I thought you were lost."

Chapter Four

The opening hymn was already starting when Samara and her mother slipped into the back of the chapel. A few people smiled and nodded in greeting as they made their way to the pew where Jackie was making room for them. Samara sat down and quickly looked over the seats to where Rick and his family usually sat. She could see Brother and Sister Jamieson and Toby and his two sisters.

"He stayed at home. The anaesthetic wore off," Jackie whispered as she saw Samara leaning forward.

"Is he all right?"

"His mum said he's fine, but the doctor said to keep his arm up for a day or two." Jackie sang a few lines then whispered again. "How come you're late?"

"Dad got home early this morning," Samara muttered. "One argument down . . . ten or so to go."

"Who was arguing?" Jackie started, but the hymn finished and she stopped talking.

Samara sat back and tried to relax as one of the young priests began to bless the sacrament. She closed her eyes and tried to let the events of the morning wash off her.

Eddy Danes had gotten home at four o'clock in the morning, which was not unusual, but he had preceded Terry by only a few minutes. Terry's arrival had been the main cause for upset when his father realized that he was not behaving rationally. The ensuing argument had finished with her mother sobbing, Terry locking himself in his bedroom, and her father fuming about things going to rack and ruin while he was gone.

Samara shook her head at the memory as she opened her eyes and watched her mother sitting very still beside her with her eyes tightly shut. Instinctively, Samara reached out to put her arm around her mother and briefly rested her cheek on her thin shoulder.

The strange sensation of being watched finally made her turn around and look straight at a man sitting two rows behind them. He was unashamedly staring right at them, and Samara smiled politely, but she frowned as she turned back around.

"What's wrong?" Jackie whispered again as the bishop announced the first speaker.

"Nothing . . . just the new man back there." Samara gestured back over her shoulder.

"With the beard?" Jackie asked quietly as Samara nodded. "I don't know who he is, but I heard him talking in the foyer . . . he's American or Canadian."

Samara shrugged as she concentrated on the speakers, but she had the lingering feeling of being watched through the whole program. As soon as the closing hymn finished, she stood up but was immediately met at the end of the row by two little girls who grabbed at her hands.

"We're ready, Sister Danes!" The tallest child spoke first.

"We've done our assignments!" The smaller girl pulled a piece of paper from her bulging pink handbag. Several crayons fell out, but she kept talking as she bent to pick them up. "I know all my four generations!"

"That's wonderful, Anna." Samara rested her hand on the little girl's head. She had been called as the CTR 7 teacher only a few weeks previously, and she was already enjoying the children's enthusiasm. "Would you and Esther like to help me get the chairs ready for class? I'm running a bit late today."

As the little girls walked off quickly, Samara turned to her mother, but she was already talking to Sister Patterson, and Jackie was at the center of a group of young single adults. Instead, she found herself looking straight at the man from the back row. He seemed to be waiting to speak to her, so Samara smiled shyly.

"Welcome to our ward. Are you visiting us today?"

The man hesitated slightly before he nodded and smiled back.

"I am visiting." His accent was distinctive, and his voice was very deep. Even as he spoke, Samara felt a stirring of recognition.

"You've been here before?" She looked at him uncertainly. "You seem familiar."

"We haven't met here." The man inclined his head slightly and pointed at a rolled-up magazine at the ground. "But we did meet a long time ago."

"I'm sorry?" Samara frowned, and yet she could feel her brain working hard, trying to remember.

"In New Zealand." He unrolled the magazine and held it out. It was opened to the page where she immediately recognized her black-and-white photograph. She stared at the photo, then her mouth fell open as she looked back up at him. The dark suit and pale blue shirt and tie could have belonged to anyone, but the sandy colored beard, green eyes, and wavy, light brown hair curling slightly on his collar were exactly the same.

"Mr. Russell." She barely breathed the name, but she saw relief replace the doubtful look in his eyes.

"That's right . . . I really didn't think you'd remember." He smiled again. "Only it's Brother Russell now."

"Brother . . . ?" Samara hesitated. "You mean you . . ."

Adam Russell nodded. "I joined the Church some months after we met." He held out both hands. "I was so impressed with your testimony that I decided to find out more and . . . here I am."

"Here you are . . . oh, my goodness." Samara put her hand to her throat. "But why are you here?"

"Actually, I came to find you . . . en route to an assignment up north." He shrugged. "I saw this photo back home and realized it was probably yours so I decided to investigate this budding new talent."

"Oh . . ." Samara was at a loss for words, then she blushed as she thought about how many times she had rehearsed their conversations over and over in her mind through the last nine years. "I don't think you realize how much of an influence you had on me back in New Zealand. I'm studying photography at university now and . . ." She pointed to the magazine. "I'm specializing in black-and-white photography."

"Ahh . . . coming to grips with those shades of gray that are the essence of the shot." Adam looked at her closely. "It's funny how we influenced each other in different ways, isn't it?"

There was a moment's silence as Samara caught his eye. There was the same intent look that she remembered after all these years, and it made her smile.

"Samara . . . your class is waiting for you." She felt a slight touch on her elbow, and she turned to one of the Primary presidency waiting behind her.

"Oh, my goodness . . . I completely forgot." She turned to Adam. "Umm . . . I have to go and teach my CTR class . . . I—"

"I'm fine." Adam touched the rolled-up magazine to his forehead. "The bishop has already filled me in on where classes are." He raised one eyebrow. "Shall we catch up afterward?"

"Umm . . . yes, of course." Samara half turned, then she looked back and shook her head. "It is so amazing to see you again."

She knew she was smiling as she left the chapel, but it wasn't until she reached her classroom that she realized how much.

"You look really happy, Sister Danes."

"Who's that man you were talking to?"

"Why are your cheeks so red?"

Samara closed the door and sat down, and suddenly she realized that she hadn't really been breathing as she consciously inhaled. She looked around at the group of six-year-olds watching her curiously and put her hands to her cheeks. They were hot.

"Actually, I just met a very old friend."

"He is quite old." Anna nodded and folded her arms. "But he looks kind."

"Yes." Samara stared at Anna without really seeing her. "Yes, he was kind."

* * *

"Hello . . . and when are you going to fill me in on this new acquaintance?" Jackie took Samara's arm and led her back into her classroom as she came out of Primary at the end of the block. "You looked like you'd been hit by a truck when you were talking to him."

"It did feel a bit like that." Samara clasped her scriptures against her. "I can hardly believe it's him."

"But who is 'him'?" Jackie leaned forward and studied Samara's face. "Spill it now before we go out there. He's out talking to your mother right now."

"My mother!" Samara looked up quickly.

"Yes, and they were chatting like old friends." Jackie nodded. "So fill me in, please."

"Umm . . . there's not much to tell, really." She shrugged. "I met Mr. Russell when I was fourteen. I was on holiday with my grandparents in New Zealand, and he was taking photos at a beach. He took some pictures of me in return for explaining how the camera worked. It really fascinated me, and he was really kind. We talked a lot and even about the Church." She paused and smiled. "It was the first time an adult had ever really talked to me."

"And you fell in love with him." Jackie nodded knowingly. "First love."

"No . . . it was nothing like that," Samara denied vigorously. "He just really made an impression, and that's what influenced me to keep doing photography."

"So he was a member, then?"

Samara shook her head. "That's the weird part. He said that my testimony had a real effect on him, and he joined the Church when he went back to Canada."

Jackie gave a low whistle.

"Wow . . . that's quite a conversion story." She raised one eyebrow. "And now he's come back to find you?"

Samara waved one hand. "Sort of. He said he's going north for an assignment but saw the photo in the *New Era* and decided to look me up."

"Crazy." Jackie stood back from the doorway. "Then I guess you'd better go and catch up with your mentor."

"He's not my mentor." Samara walked past her. "He's just a visitor."

There were several people standing around Adam when Samara and Jackie walked into the foyer, and they were all laughing at something he had said. He stopped as soon as he saw them and raised his hand in greeting. Tracey Danes immediately turned to her daughter and pointed to Adam.

"Brother Russell has been explaining how he met you. Isn't it exciting? I've invited him over to dinner."

"To dinner?" Samara felt her stomach knot as she thought about the performance in their home that morning. "Are you sure?"

"Yes, I'm sure." Her mother was unexpectedly decisive. "It will be fine. I have plenty of food."

"But Dad's home." Samara reminded her quietly. "And Terry."

"That's right." Tracey gave a firm smile, although Samara caught a flicker of hesitation. "It's only right that you should get a chance to spend time with Brother Russell. This is a very special visit."

* * *

It wasn't until she was home and putting her books away in her room that Samara suddenly remembered that she hadn't talked to Rick's parents or inquired after him. In fact, she realized that she had hardly thought about Rick at all during the whole morning. Even during Primary she had often found herself reliving her first meeting with Adam. She could even visualize the way he had held the camera, hear his voice as he explained the settings, and she saw how his slender, tanned hands had moved when he directed her for posing in the pictures.

Samara sat down on the edge of her bed and stared at the ceiling. She hadn't realized how much of an impression Adam Russell had made on her, and now he was here . . . and he'd come looking for her.

"On his way to an assignment up north," she reminded herself bluntly and reached for the phone beside her bed. She hesitated for a second before she punched out the numbers and waited for the ring. Then, just as abruptly, she hung up again and made her way downstairs. "Later . . . I'll talk to him later."

As she reached the bottom of the stairs, she heard her father before she saw him.

"Why did you invite him over to dinner? I've only just got back. I want to relax in my home, not entertain some guy I've never even met."

"He seems like a very nice man." Her mother's voice was quieter, but quiet usually meant that she had made up her mind. There was none of the slightly whining tone that usually accompanied her conversations with her husband. "And he'll only be here a few days."

"Fine . . . a few days and I'll be gone. Invite him over then."

"Oh, Ed . . . he was kind to Samara. The least we can do is to show him some hospitality in return."

"Kind to Samara?" Samara waited outside the door to hear her father's response. "It sounds like he's the one to blame for this stupid obsession of hers with art—or whatever it is."

"It's photography, and it's not just an obsession. Samara is a very good photographer. She won that Church competition."

"For all that's worth! Why she couldn't train to do something practical that'll actually earn her some money?"

Samara clenched both fists and took a deep breath. It was always the same when her father came home. He was so outspoken about her decision to study photography, but he didn't realize that his objections only made her more determined to succeed.

"What time is Brother Russell coming over, Mum?" Samara walked into the kitchen and straight past her father on the way to the fridge. She deliberately opened the door between them and bent to look inside. "Do you want any help getting dinner ready?"

"You could do some potatoes, dear." Tracey's eyes flitted between her daughter and her husband. They were a lot alike in many ways. Samara could be just as stubborn as her father. "I think Terry will be here for dinner."

"Does anybody actually know what Terry is doing?" Eddy leaned against the kitchen bench and shook his head. "For that matter, does Terry know what he's doing?"

"He's taking time out of school right now." Tracey turned to busy herself at the sink peeling carrots. "He's not sure he still wants to do engineering."

"Trace . . . he can't look me in the eye, and he's got a totally vacant expression on his face when he's watching television. It's like he's on another planet." Eddy looked at Samara. "So what do you think about your brother?"

Something in his tone made Samara take a deep breath, and she clenched her jaw. It was so like her father to walk in after being away for weeks and want everything to be exactly as he wanted it. She stared straight at him now and lifted her chin defiantly.

"Actually, I think he's doing drugs, but that's only my opinion, and that doesn't seem to be worth much around here, so I won't say any more."

She heard her mother drop the peeler in the sink and knew without looking that she was staring at her. Her father looked straight at her for a second, then shook his head again. For a long time nobody spoke, then Samara closed the fridge door and moved to the sink. She bent forward and picked up the peeler and began removing the skins from some potatoes. She made no attempt to elaborate on what she had just said.

"I see . . . so I presume that's your last word on the subject." Eddy was staring at his wife now. "And are you of the same opinion as your daughter?"

"I . . . I really don't know." Tracey stammered uncertainly.

"Yet you see him every day!" Eddy practically yelled, and his wife flinched slightly. "I noticed something the moment he walked in the door."

"And what have you done about it except yell at him and yell at us?" Samara looked steadily at the potato in her hand. "It couldn't possibly be that you're just as afraid to suggest what it might be as we are?"

There was another long silence, and Samara felt a sickening tightness in her throat as Eddy took some deep breaths then closed his eyes briefly as if searching in his mind for something to say. She put the peeler and potatoes down and wiped her hands on a towel. It felt almost symbolic—as if she was washing her hands of them both.

"Yes, Dad . . . I have watched the way Terry looks, and I've watched that look getting worse, but what's worse for me is that it's the same look I've seen when you're drunk and when Mum's taken too many of her antidepressants." She folded the towel mechanically and set it on the bench. "You don't know what to do about Terry, but I don't know what to do with any of you. I pray and pray for all of you, but . . . now I'm just scared that one day I might end up like you all, and it scares me!"

She felt the tone of her voice rising and fought for control as she moved toward the kitchen door. Neither of her parents tried to stop her. It was as if they were both incapable of movement.

Samara managed to get through the door and into the reception area before her legs and hands began to shake, and she sat down heavily on the high stool at the desk. It seemed as if even tears were beyond her as the things she'd just said played over and over in her mind—things that she hadn't even admitted to herself before. But it was all true. Her whole family had some form of addiction, so it seemed like only a matter of time before it would happen to her. She rested her elbows on the desk and ran her hands through her hair, letting it fall forward over her face.

"Hi!" She recognized Adam's voice at the same moment as the doorbell sound jingled behind her. Her fingers tightened their grip on her hair as she squeezed her eyes shut and mentally willed him to go away. After another moment, she hitched a smile onto her face and went to open the door.

"I thought I'd come a bit early and see if I could help . . . with anything."

Samara heard the slight hesitation in his voice, and she looked up quickly, suddenly grateful that her eyes had refused to shed the tears that sat heavily behind them.

"Well, you are early but I think we're all right in the dinner department." She amazed herself with how bright she sounded. She also felt her heart do a complete flip as Adam smiled and set down a khaki canvas tote that bulged with objects hidden in numerous pockets. He had changed from the pale blue shirt, a tie, and the dark trousers he'd worn at church into a light green polo shirt and beige casual trousers that reflected the color of his eyes—eyes that were now studying her intently.

"I can come back later." Adam gestured vaguely toward the door.

"No . . . no . . . I'm glad you came early." Samara stood up quickly. "I feel like I have a thousand questions running around in my head."

"All for me?" He pointed at his chest and grinned. "I was only planning to stay a few days."

"Then we'd better hurry." She glanced at her watch. Suddenly she was curious to see what sort of façade her parents would put on when their emotions had been so recently raw.

"Mum! Dad! Adam's here!" She wondered what made her dare to call him by his first name. "We're in the lounge!"

CHAPTER FIVE

Her father came through from the kitchen first, and as he stood in the doorway in his black shorts, blue T-shirt, and bare feet, with a glass of beer in his hand, Samara had to admit that he wasn't one to hide his feelings. He stood and stared at Adam before nodding briefly and moving to the well-padded brown armchair that was automatically his to sit in whenever he was home. Before he sat down, and almost as an afterthought, he extended a hand to Adam.

"Eddy Danes. My wife will be in shortly."

Samara watched as Adam showed no reaction at all to her father's brusqueness, but she did notice that he took his time setting his bag down on the floor before he reached out a hand in response.

"I'm pleased to meet you, Eddy. Your family was very kind to invite me over."

The two men shook once firmly, looking each other straight in the eye as they did so. Eddy was the first to look away and, as he sat down, he roughly gestured toward the chair beside him.

"So tell me why you've come to Australia. My wife says you're going up north."

"And I came to catch up with your daughter." Adam pointed to Samara. "She's a very talented photographer, and that's my line of work."

Eddy dismissed the comment with a grunt. "So why are you going up north?"

"Uh . . . I've got an assignment to shoot some crocs." With a knowing look at Samara, Adam sat back in his chair. She managed a brief smile in response. "With a camera, of course."

"Plenty up there." Eddy nodded. "You don't want to get too close. A young kid got caught just awhile back. His friends escaped up a tree, but the croc dragged the boy under the water while they watched."

"That's terrible." Adam nodded, seemingly without any emotion. "But it's all just meat to the crocs, I guess. They have no concept of mercy . . . it's all about survival." He shook his head. "I've seen a few nasty things with lions in Africa."

"Africa?" Samara noted her father's surprised reaction. "Now, there's one place I'd like to go to. What were you doing there?"

She could see that he was now genuinely paying attention to their guest, and she sat quietly as Adam explained some of the assignments that had taken him around the globe: to the Sahara Desert, the Nile River, the Congo. She sat quietly as her father kept asking questions, and Adam answered them easily, taking them both into another world with his stories. She had no idea that her father was interested in the things that she found so fascinating. Within minutes, the tension that had existed when Eddy had first walked into the room had dissipated.

"I'm sorry I took so long. Terry called to say he'd be late." The quiet voice from the doorway almost came as a surprise. Tracey Danes stood in the doorway, and Samara noticed that her mother had changed into a pale floral summer dress and put on makeup. There was no sign of the distraught woman who'd been crying in the kitchen a short while before. "Dinner will be ready in a few minutes." She walked across the room and held out her hand to Adam as he stood up to shake her hand. "I'm so pleased you could come over, Brother Russell."

"Please, call me Adam."

"Adam's been telling us about some of his trips to Africa," Eddy interrupted from his chair as his wife sat down beside Samara on the couch. "Now that would be a great place to do some long-haul driving."

"Is that what you do, Eddy?" Adam sat down on the edge of his chair and directly faced Eddy. It seemed to Samara that he had the ability to make each one of them feel he was exclusively interested in them. It certainly seemed to be working with her parents.

Eddy nodded and gestured over his shoulder as if that one small movement encompassed the whole Australian continent.

"I've been driving for twenty years . . . big trucks . . . mainly north to Cairns and over to the west." He nodded. "I used to do central Australia. Every trip's an adventure."

"So tell me what it's like." Adam sat back again. "I might get some ideas for a new project."

"How about we talk over dinner?" Tracey had barely sat down before she stood up again and gestured toward the table. "Samara, if you'll give me a hand we'll have it all on the table in a few minutes."

Samara could hardly believe the change that came over her father as they sat down to dinner and then as they ate. He became animated as he began to describe his journeys through the outback and as he described encounters with snakes, racing giant red kangaroos, and time he spent with the indigenous Aborigine people. She watched his face light up and his hands move more. She had never heard him speak about his trips before, but the way he described everything she was able to visualize it all. Even her mother seemed to be spellbound, as if it were a different person telling the stories.

"You know, Eddy . . . I'm beginning to think there is a picture journey in all of this." Adam had listened quietly all through the meal. Now he leaned back in his chair, and Samara could see by the slight frown on his face that he was thinking and planning. "What's the possibility of riding with you on a trip up north?"

The question was so unexpected that Samara heard her mother gasp. Almost as interesting was her father's reaction. He stared at his plate for a long time before looking sideways at Adam, then he began to nod slowly as if weighing up the possibility.

"It's possible." He shrugged. "I'm going up in a few days. Would you be ready?"

"Born ready." Adam smiled and glanced at Samara. It was the first time he had even really looked at her throughout the whole meal, and she felt the color rise immediately to her cheeks as he gave her the tiniest wink. "I live out of a suitcase."

"Sounds familiar." Eddy grinned. "I live out of a truck cab."

"Well, I run a motel." Samara turned as her mother spoke out confidently beside her. "And I insist that you come and stay here as our guest until you leave with Eddy."

* * *

"Do you take that bag everywhere you go?" Samara frowned happily as she walked beside Adam. When her parents offered to tidy up, she timidly suggested that she and Adam take a walk along the beach just a street away. He'd responded by immediately getting his bag from the other room and swinging it over his shoulder as they made their way through the motel parking lot and onto the path down to the beach.

"Just about." He smiled as he swung into step beside her. "You never know when the perfect shot might come along. Haven't you discovered that yet?"

"Oh, yes." Samara laughed, and she knew her voice was a little higher than normal. "My friend Jackie calls me the resident young adult photographer because I always have my camera at activities, and my other friend says that one day my children will draw a picture of me and it'll be a camera with legs."

Somehow the mention of Rick made her speak more quietly. Once again she hadn't thought of him the whole time Adam had been visiting.

"So who is your other friend?" He didn't seem to miss anything she said.

"Umm . . . his name is Rick." Samara glanced at him quickly. "We've been friends since high school. He served his mission in Japan," she added, though it seemed irrelevant even as she said it.

"I see." Adam nodded as they stopped at the edge of the road to let some cars go past. "I like Japan, especially in springtime."

Samara started a little as he suddenly touched her elbow to guide her across the road during a break in the traffic. The faint touch seemed to send shivers right down her back. She didn't speak until they'd crossed the road, then she shook her head.

"You know . . . I feel as if someone's going to pinch me soon and I'll wake up and find that you're part of a huge dream."

"Why's that?"

She knew he was looking at her, but she kept watching the pavement as it began to blend into a sandy track. She stopped to take off her sandals.

"Well, this morning I was battling with my parents and again this afternoon before you came. My father doesn't like my doing photography . . ." She dropped her voice several octaves in a mock imitation of her father. "It's not practical. It won't earn me any money."

"Maybe I should show him my bank account." Adam walked with his hands in his pockets. "The money may be erratic at times, but it can be substantial."

"Yes, but that's you," Samara responded quietly.

"I'm sure it could be you too." Adam stopped and looked out at the expanse of beach lying in front of them. "I think you have a great ability."

"But you've only seen one picture!" she protested immediately.

"But it is an excellent picture, and I'm obviously not the only one who thinks so." He shrugged. "Besides, after you've shown me more of your work, I'll be able to give you a more accurate opinion."

She had a sudden mental image of him studying her work and seeing all of the possible flaws. Samara shivered at the thought and especially at the idea of working in close quarters with him. Adam Russell had been part of her memories and her dreams so long that it was difficult to see him as part of her reality.

"Are you cold?" Adam glanced at her as she trembled slightly again and rubbed her forearms.

"No." Samara shook her head and smiled without looking at him. "I was actually getting nervous at the thought of you seeing my work. All of a sudden it doesn't seem good enough at all."

"I hope you're going to let me be the judge of that," Adam responded briefly before pointing out toward the ocean. "Now tell me what sort of exposure you would use to get a really moody sunset."

They walked for nearly an hour with Adam choosing random scenes or objects and encouraging Samara to use several of the cameras he had in his bag to describe the angles and processes she would use for each picture. After awhile it became a game and they alternated, Samara asking him to describe a new image she'd selected. The beach was endless, the possibilities were endless, and Samara felt as if she wanted to keep walking forever.

"It's getting pretty dark." Adam finally stopped and looked up at the string of apartment buildings and hotels that stood as concrete and glass sentinels along the beachfront. In the gathering dusk they had become beacons of light that glowed against a deepening blue-black sky. He looked at his watch. "I think my body's time clock is a little bit haywire still. I've been awake for nearly thirty hours and I'm not even tired."

"Oh my goodness, I forgot you've been traveling. I'm sorry." Samara folded her arms and traced a line in the sand with her toe. "I was enjoying myself too much."

"And so was I—which was why I'm not feeling tired." Adam put a large camera back in the bag and clipped it shut. "And our walk has only confirmed what I was feeling all along."

"What's that?" Samara felt her breath catch in her throat.

"I think you have great perception as well as technical and creative ability." Adam touched her elbow again as they turned in their tracks back toward the motel. It was a simple courteous gesture, but she couldn't help the sensation of warmth that seemed to radiate whenever he touched her. "I insist you show me your portfolio." He smiled. "And I also insist that you show me in front of your father."

"My father?" Samara practically squeaked out the words and she gave an embarrassed cough then shook her head. "He's not even interested in my work, and I'm certainly not interested in listening to his negative comments."

"Samara." He said her name gently, and she loved the way he pronounced it with his accent. "Do you want me to help you?" Adam stopped and stared directly at her.

"I . . . yes, of course." She tried to laugh. "Why wouldn't I want the master to help me?"

"Then be a good student and let me decide." He folded his arms. "I think that once you get your father on your side . . . you'll fly as a photographer."

"But . . . why . . . how?" She knew she was stammering and it made her cheeks flame. "He's only ever ridiculed me."

"People often ridicule the things they don't understand." Adam persisted quietly. "Our job is to help him understand . . . and appreciate your work."

"But . . ." Samara started, then stopped as Adam held up his hand to silence her.

"Samara . . . you heard your father at dinner. Did you hear his descriptions of all those things on his travels? If he ever bothered to write anything down he'd be a great writer. If he'd ever bothered to take photos he'd be a great photographer. He has amazing perception and creativity and he's passed it on to you."

"My father?" Samara actually stared in amazement. She had never thought of herself as having anything in common with her father.

Adam nodded. "Why not? It has to come from somewhere."

"Yes, but I had managed to convince myself that I was adopted into this family." She gave a slight smile, but she couldn't disguise the pain in her voice. "Sometimes it helps to think of myself as just a visitor here."

There was a long silence with the only sounds being the distant noise of cars, of people living, and of the faint washing of sea onto sand. Samara swallowed hard as tears threatened to surface. Then she suddenly felt herself enveloped in a hug that was firm yet gentle. It was so unexpected that it was instantly comforting. She barely reached Adam's shoulder and her face pressed against his shirt as she began to cry quietly, silently surrendering to years of pain and doubt.

He didn't speak when she finally drew away, but a large, folded handkerchief suddenly appeared before her face. Somehow it made her laugh and she gratefully pressed both hands against the handkerchief to soak up the tears and hide her swollen eyes.

"There's a nice cool breeze coming up off the water. How about we face into it for a few minutes?"

Samara nodded without speaking and they retraced their footsteps toward the beach and stood facing the surf that was barely discernible in the evening darkness.

"I'm sorry." She tried to keep the quiver out of her voice but her whole body seemed to tremble as soon as she spoke, and she wrapped her arms around her body.

"There's no need to be sorry." Adam stood with his hands in his pockets as he stared out at the ocean. "It's good to be able to share pain."

Something in his voice made her glance up at him, and in the evening light she could see his eyes shining.

"It is." She rubbed her arms self-consciously as she lifted her face to the breeze. "I just never expected to share it with you."

"Are you sorry you did?" His voice sounded uncertain for the first time and she shook her head immediately.

"No. . . never."

* * *

"Well, you're back!" Eddy looked up from the newspaper he was reading as they walked into the lounge. Tracey was nowhere to be seen. "I thought we were going to have to send out a search party for you."

"There's been lots of years to catch up on." Adam smiled easily as he sat down on the couch. "And we played at a bit of photography as well. Samara has finally agreed to share her portfolio."

"Hmm." Eddy grunted as he folded the newspaper and set it on his lap. "Playing all right." Samara recognized the sound of disapproval and she took a deep breath, but Adam spoke first.

"I think you might be surprised with what she has to show you, Ed. I think this daughter of yours has real talent."

Samara couldn't even look at her father as she felt him stare at her. He had never asked to see her work and she had never felt to share anything with him.

"Well, go on then." He gestured upstairs with a brief nod of his head. "But be quick. I'm about ready to turn in. It was a long drive this morning."

Even with Adam's smile to reassure her, it still took Samara several minutes of staring at the large, black folder filled with her work to summon the courage to actually pick it up. As she reached the lounge, she met her mother in the hallway.

"Oh, there you are, dear." Tracey gestured back to her room. "I didn't realize you were home. Rick was just on the phone."

"Rick?" Samara put her hand to her forehead. "I forgot to call him."

"Well, I told him we had a visitor and he said he was only calling to ask whether you wanted to go ahead with your visit to Currumbin Sanctuary this week. Seeing he's hurt his arm, he'll be on light duties and could show you around for your project." She hesitated. "I didn't even know he was working there now."

"Oh . . . yes, about a month now." Samara tapped her fingers on her folder. "That's nice of him to arrange for me to go." She looked at her watch hesitantly and then into the lounge. "Should I call him now? I was just going to show Dad and Adam my portfolio."

"Your father?" Tracey looked genuinely surprised then she patted Samara on the arm. "I think I'd wait to call Rick back. He said anytime over the next couple of days."

"Okay . . . I'll call first thing in the morning before I leave for school." Samara rolled her eyes. "Oh no . . . school!" She'd forgotten about school the next day as well as Rick.

CHAPTER SIX

"Wouldn't you say your daughter has talent?" Adam leaned forward in his chair, resting his elbows on his thighs. He held a photo in each hand toward Eddy. "These would make it into any reputable photography magazine."

Samara sat silently, trying not to look overwhelmed by what Adam was saying. When she had first opened the folder she had haltingly explained that most of the photos were working prints while the finished prints were on display at school. Almost appearing to ignore her explanation, he had been painfully silent as he picked up each photo and examined it critically. He had even made two piles in which he placed the photos after he studied them. An occasional comment on the quality of the print was all that indicated his reaction to them, and she felt her throat constrict each time he added to the piles.

"Hey, I'm no expert. I don't know what's good and what isn't." Eddy shook his head and held up both hands.

"Then what impression do you get when you look at this?" Adam held up a rearview picture of a mother and a young toddler walking hand in hand. The little girl wore a pair of her mother's high heels and was looking up at her mother with a radiant smile on her face.

Eddy thought for a second, then he nodded. "It reminds me of Tracey and Samara when Samara was little. She was always trying to copy her mum . . . especially getting into her shoes."

"I did?" Samara frowned. "I don't remember doing that."

"You were only little." Tracey's smile was wistful. "Shoes were the favorite, although you were pretty determined to get my lipsticks as well."

Eddy chuckled.

"I remember once when I came home from a trip and Tracey had put her makeup on and you paraded out with lipstick from ear to ear and everywhere in between."

"Including your hair." Tracey smiled as she nodded.

"I never realized." Samara spoke so quietly she could hardly be heard. "You've never told me about anything like that."

There was an awkward silence, then Adam coughed and picked up one pile of photos.

"I think these are your best work and it looks like there's a common theme to most of them."

"Children." Tracey pointed to one of a little boy eating an ice cream and trying to lick the melted treat off his hand. "This is my favorite. It could be one of those calendar shots."

"I agree." Adam nodded. "You seem to be able to capture the essence of children."

"I . . . I do enjoy working with them." Samara stammered, still uncertain how to respond to Adam's words. "I'm actually going to do my end-of-year exhibition about children and sanctuary animals."

"Oh, is that what Rick was calling about?" Tracey looked up from the photo she was studying. "Is he going to help you?"

"Umm . . . yes." Samara suddenly felt uncomfortable talking about Rick in front of Adam and her cheeks began to feel warm. "I'd asked him if I could take some of my CTR class to the children's park where he works."

"So, Rick works at an animal sanctuary?" Adam placed the photos back in the pile. "That must be interesting work."

"Well, he's only working there part-time." Samara swallowed as her throat became drier. "He . . . he's actually pursuing a veterinary science degree."

"Oh, I thought he was going to be a doctor." Tracey looked surprised. "I'm sure his mother said that."

"He was . . . that is, he was going to, but then he decided to go this way. He really loves animals."

"Well, at least there should be some money in that." Eddy grunted as he sat back in his chair. "There are plenty of cats and dogs that need fixing."

"Actually, he's more interested in wild animals." Samara felt a need to elaborate. "That's why he's working at Currumbin."

"So he will be working for nothing." Eddy raised an eyebrow. "Wild animals don't pay you to fix them."

"No, but concerned people pay you to look after them." Adam nodded his head as if he was agreeing with Eddy, but he was also contradicting him. "I met a guy in Africa who was doing vet work on a reserve. He was from England and he was working for an international wildlife organization. He was paid well."

"Mmm . . . sounds fair enough. At least it'd be exciting." Eddy shrugged grudgingly. "But I'll be blowed if I can understand it though."

Adam smiled and gave Samara a surreptitious wink. It was the tiniest thing, and yet it made her feel as though he understood what she was going through—as though she wasn't alone in her own home.

She looked at her parents, and they were both listening again as Adam began to describe some effect she had used in one of the shots. They were actually studying the picture intently and her father was nodding. Her mother was smiling as well, but more at Adam than the photo. Samara looked up at the clock on the wall. Adam had been in their home for less than four hours and he'd already managed to get them looking at her work and listening and talking about things that none of them had ever mentioned to each other before. She thought about the number of times she had prayed, especially in the last few months, that her parents would understand how she felt about her work. Was this an answer to those prayers?

"What do you reckon, Samara?" She heard Adam's voice from a distance and she stared at him blankly.

"I'm sorry . . ."

Adam smiled and she felt her heart lurch as it seemed to do when he looked at her like that, as if she were the only person there.

"I was asking if it would be okay for me to come to the sanctuary with you." He lifted one eyebrow. "I could watch you in action and offer a little professional assistance . . . if required." He waved his hand to indicate the photos. "Not that I think you need much at all."

Samara's mouth dropped open slightly, then closed again as she thought about Adam and Rick in one place. At the moment she couldn't quite comprehend that.

"Umm . . . I guess so." She faltered. "I'll have to ask Rick . . ."

"Oh, I'm sure he won't mind, Sam." Tracey smiled happily. "I think it's a wonderful idea."

Samara stared at her mother. She seemed in an unnaturally happy mood.

"Oh, I'm sure, too." She nodded and took a deep breath. "Let's do it, then. I'll call Rick later and confirm it."

"Why don't you call him now, Samara?" Tracey smiled brightly. "He said he'd be home all evening." She touched Samara's arm with her hand as she turned to Adam. "The poor boy had an accident on a youth activity yesterday and hurt his arm badly."

"It wasn't a youth activity, Mum. It was young adults." Samara avoided looking at Adam as she stared at her mother. Somehow her mother's words made her feel very young, and she was suddenly shocked to realize that Adam was actually close to her parents in age. At least, closer to them than to her. "Umm . . . I'll go and call Rick." She practically mumbled as she quickly stood and walked to the kitchen. But the instant she had the door closed behind her, she leaned back against it and drew a long deep breath, her body quivering as she closed her eyes and slowly exhaled.

The problem was that as soon as she closed her eyes, Adam's face seemed to project itself onto a screen behind her eyelids, smiling and winking . . . just at her.

"Oh, my goodness." She put her hand against her mouth as she recalled the feeling of being held close to him while she cried. "He was being kind. Adam is kind."

She muttered the last sentence slowly, directing it back into her thoughts.

"Adam is very kind and he is trying to be helpful. He can help my career." Samara pushed herself away from the door and walked over to the phone. She automatically dialed Rick's number and waited as it rang twice.

"Hello."

Samara recognized Toby's voice as soon as he answered.

"Toby? It's Samara here."

"Hi, Sam. Are you coming over?" Toby's request was immediate. "My kitten can do tricks now. You should come and see."

"I'd love to Toby, but we have a visitor." Samara couldn't help smiling. "Maybe I can come over tomorrow. Can I talk to Rick right now, please?"

"Okay, I'll get him, but can you really come tomorrow?" Toby's voice had a pleading sound to it.

Not wanting to disappoint her young friend, she offered, "I might be late but I'll try, Toby."

"All right." He sounded happy. "I'll get Rick."

While she waited, she thought about a schedule for tomorrow. School all day and then . . . Adam would be home in the evening. Why had she promised Toby she would visit?'

"Samara? Are you there?" Rick's voice suddenly broke into her thoughts.

"What? . . . Yes!" She stood up from leaning against the bench. "Yes . . . Rick . . . sorry, I was daydreaming." She ran a hand over her head and coughed. "Um, we'd . . . I mean, I . . . no actually, we . . ."

"I'm not sure if I'm following this conversation." She could hear the smile in Rick's voice. "Have you developed a split personality since yesterday?"

Possibly. Samara bit at her lip as the thought raced through her mind. Then she forced a laugh.

"No . . . what I was trying to say is that I would love to come to Currumbin, but that we have a guest here from Canada who is a photographer, and he said he'd help me with the project, so I wondered if it's okay if we both come?" She took a slight breath. "He could help me with the children as well."

"That's fine." There was no hesitation in Rick's voice. "Mum said you had a visitor from overseas. She said he came looking for you."

"Goodness, news travels fast on the ward grapevine." Samara's hand tightened on the telephone.

"Actually, it was your mum who told her." Rick hesitated. "She said she seemed really excited that this guy had found you . . . that you met him years ago in New Zealand or something."

Samara hesitated before she nodded.

"That's right." She swallowed. "He was the first person to show me how to take a photo. I guess it's all his fault that I became obsessed with it."

"So, your mum seems happy enough. How is your dad handling it . . . having him there?"

Samara lifted her head as she heard her father chuckle out loud, followed by her mother's shrill laugh.

"Actually, they're both getting on really well with him." She shook her head. "It's all a bit strange really. Everybody seems to love him. Dad's been telling stories about his trips and Mum is hanging off every word they both say." She stared up at the ceiling. "He even made me show my portfolio to them all."

"And . . ."

"And what?"

"How did they react?" Rick's voice was softer.

"Umm, they were fine." She shrugged. "Even complimentary. I don't quite know how to handle it."

"Just enjoy it." Rick paused. "So when do we do our Currumbin thing with . . . what did you say his name was?"

"Adam," Samara answered quickly. "Adam Russell."

"Okay . . . with Adam Russell."

"Umm . . . how about Wednesday after school . . . so I can arrange things with the children's parents?" Samara thought ahead. "Dad is going to take Adam up north on one of his trips at the end of the week, so we'll need to get it done soon."

There was a brief silence before Rick responded.

"So he's really fit right into the family."

"You could say that." Samara nodded. "He certainly seems to get on well with everyone."

"Well, that's good." Rick sounded genuinely pleased. "I'm looking forward to meeting him. Wednesday, then?"

"Yes . . . or maybe tomorrow." Samara hesitated. "I told Toby I'd come over and watch the kitten do its tricks."

"Ahh, we do have a very gifted kitten." She heard him chuckle. "I think you'd get some once-in-a-lifetime photos."

"Then I'd better not miss it." Samara smiled in spite of herself. "I'll see you tomorrow."

She still had a slight smile on her face as she walked back into the lounge, and Adam noticed immediately.

"I take it from the smile that we're good to go?" He was carefully putting the photos back into the folio.

"Oh, Samara is always happy around Rick." Tracey bubbled happily as she waved one hand in front of her and crossed two fingers. "They're like this; they're so close. They have been since they were children."

Samara felt her stomach clench as she stared past Adam and straight at her mother. Why was she acting like this?

"Well, it's great to have lifelong friends." Adam responded easily as he put the last of the photos away. "I can't say that I have many because I travel so much."

"Oh, I'm sure a nice person like you must have lots of friends." Tracey leaned forward and patted him on the shoulder, and Samara flinched as she watched. She glanced up and saw her feelings reflected in her father's eyes as he watched his wife. There was definitely something unusual about her mother's behavior and she felt sickened by it.

To her relief, the doorbell from the motel's reception area suddenly rang from the connection in the lounge.

"I'll get it." Samara jumped up before her mother could speak and walked quickly out of the room. She almost collided with Jackie as she turned the corner. One look at her friend's face and her stomach knotted.

"Jackie! What's the matter?"

"Oh, Sam!" Jackie stopped and took a deep breath as she leaned against the wall. "It's Terry. He came over to my place and . . ." Tears welled in her eyes. "He's out of it! I heard the doorbell, and when I answered it I found him leaning against the wall. He looked okay. He gave me that silly smile, but when I opened the door he just slid down and fell in a heap on the step."

"What's wrong with him?" Samara felt her chest tighten. "Is he hurt?"

By the way Jackie looked at her, she knew immediately that Terry wasn't hurt, but her brain didn't want to accept it.

"He's out of it, Sam." Jackie spoke very quietly. "He's really out of it."

"So where is he?" Samara almost snapped the words.

Jackie pointed behind her.

"He's outside in the car. He's sort of drifting in and out . . . of something. Nobody was home at my place so I managed to move him enough when he was capable and get him into the car. I wasn't really sure how your parents would react but I didn't know what else to do."

Samara pressed her hand to her head as she glanced back over her shoulder.

"Umm . . . you did the right thing. I guess we'll find out how they're going to react. They'll have to help us get him upstairs." She took a deep breath. "Adam's here, so they might not be too bad."

"Adam . . . your man from Canada?"

"Yes, Adam . . . but he's not *my* man," Samara snapped as she turned away. "I'll go and get them."

Her father was still talking with Adam as she walked back into the lounge, but they both stopped and looked at her as she stood in the doorway. She found herself looking directly at Adam rather than her father as she gestured back over her shoulder.

"Jackie's here . . . with Terry." She bit her lip. "We're going to need some help to get him upstairs."

"Help?" Her father's eyes narrowed but he didn't move. "Why does he need help?"

"Probably because he can't walk." Samara barely kept the cynicism out of her voice. "Can you please help us?" She turned and walked back through the doorway without waiting for a response. Jackie was still waiting in reception area as Samara came around the desk. She put her arms around Samara and gave her a tight hug.

"I'm sorry, Sam."

"There's nothing for you to be sorry about." Samara stood still. She lifted her arms briefly to acknowledge the hug then dropped them as she heard Adam's voice behind her.

"Where is he, Samara?"

"He's out in my car." Jackie answered as she stood back. "He collapsed on my doorstep."

"How entertaining for you." Eddy spoke briskly as he moved past them all and roughly pulled the front door open.

Adam ushered both girls in front of him as Eddy reached the car. Eddy stood still for a second, staring in through the front window.

Samara watched his jaw clench as he pulled the back passenger door open. Terry was sprawled across the backseat and his arm dropped down as the door opened. His head had been resting on his arm and it rolled back, his mouth falling open.

"Great!" It was more of a growl than a word as Eddy reached inside, grabbed Terry under the arms, and began to lift him out. The muscles on his arms bulged as he strained to pull him out, and Samara noted in an abstract way how leathery-brown and worn her father's arms looked. She felt as if she were watching a movie scene as Adam moved to help and both men managed to drape one of Terry's arms over each of their shoulders and lift him until his feet dragged along the ground. Eddy glanced at Adam and nodded toward the stairs. Then they both bent and lifted Terry's legs. As they lifted him, Terry's head rolled back again and Samara quickly put her hand up to support him.

"What's going on? You all just disappeared. Why is everybody . . ." Tracey walked out of the reception area with the same bright smile that had been glued to her face all evening, but as she saw Terry her features suddenly contorted. Samara watched in disbelief as her mother put both hands to her face and bent down from the waist as if she'd been stabbed. It was a silent, grotesque movement that seemed to happen in slow motion until it was followed by a high-pitched scream that pierced the neon-lit darkness.

* * *

"Are you going to be all right, Sam?" Jackie stared straight ahead as she drove through the steady stream of traffic on the highway.

"I'm fine." Samara answered briefly as she kept her gaze equally fixed on the rear window of the red Toyota in front of them.

"I wasn't sure you'd want to come to school this morning." Jackie tightened her hands on the steering wheel. "That was quite a night last night."

"I'm only sorry you had to go through it." A muscle tightened in Samara's jaw. "My family put on quite a display, didn't they?"

"It was understandable." Jackie responded quietly. "I'm glad Brother Russell was there though. He seemed to keep everyone reasonably calm."

"Reasonably." Samara raised one eyebrow. "If you can call Mum having a hysterical fit, Dad putting his fist through the wall, and Terry throwing up all over his bedroom reasonable." She gave a wry laugh. "You're sort of used to us, but Adam . . ." She shook her head. "Brother Russell sure got more of a dinner invitation than he bargained for."

They drove in silence for some time until Jackie glanced at her friend.

"I think it was a good thing he was there."

"Who?" Drawn from her thoughts, Samara started slightly.

"Brother Russell." Jackie smiled. "Adam."

"Oh." Samara lifted her chin at the tone of Jackie's voice. "Yes . . . it was good. Everybody likes him." She frowned. "He has Mum and Dad eating out of his hand."

"Does that annoy you?" Jackie sounded surprised. "I thought you liked him."

"I do." Samara answered quickly. "I mean, he actually got my parents to look at my portfolio, and he talked about photography like a real job so that even my father was sounding interested."

"Your mum was pretty impressed with him at church."

"Don't remind me." Samara put one hand over her eyes. "She was acting like a teenager all evening—all giggly and smiley. I felt so embarrassed."

"Maybe she was just happy." Jackie shrugged. "She doesn't have much of a life and she had your dad home as well as a new person to entertain."

"Oh, she really entertained, didn't she?" Samara didn't try to hide the bitterness in her voice. "I'm not sure who was more out of it . . . her or Terry." Even as she said it Samara closed her eyes and put her head back against the car seat. "Oh no . . . that was probably it." She moaned slightly. "She'd been crying when Adam came, and then she disappeared upstairs for ages and came down all made up and really happy. She must have taken a whole bunch of her pick-me-ups."

"So when she saw Terry it went the other way?" Jackie frowned. "She was sure upset."

"She did think he was dead with his head rolled back and all." Samara shook her head. "Jackie . . . I'm really sorry you had to put up with all the rubbish. I don't even know why Terry turned up on your doorstep."

Jackie took awhile to answer, and then she swallowed. "It's probably because I call him quite a bit."

"You call Terry?" Samara turned quickly. "On the phone?"

"No, I yell all the way from my place." Jackie gave her usual dimpled grin, and then she nodded. "We talk . . . and he's been over a few times lately."

"To your house?"

"Mmm." Jackie nodded. "He doesn't say much but I think he likes being a part of everything."

"He likes being with your family?" Samara stared at her friend. "Or he likes being with you?"

"Both . . . I hope." Jackie's cheeks actually colored slightly. "He's actually interested in a lot of different things. Matt and Lily love playing with him."

Samara frowned as she thought about Jackie's brother and sister—twins—who were about nine years old.

"But aren't your parents worried about how Terry behaves?"

"They are worried about him." Jackie tapped the wheel with a brightly colored fingernail. "In fact, it was Dad who first suggested that Terry might have . . . a problem."

"Your father did?" Samara closed her eyes. "Did the whole world know and we didn't?"

"My dad is hardly the whole world. Most people wouldn't have worried, but he's been Terry's bishop for six years." She shrugged. "He notices people he cares about."

Samara was silent and then her shoulders began to shake slightly. She put her hand over her eyes as tears began to slide down her cheeks.

"I can't believe this is happening."

"But it is happening, Sam." Jackie briefly rested her hand on Samara's shoulder. "And it's better it comes out in the open now . . . before it's too late. At least Terry knows we know now. I think he wants help."

"Well, I haven't got a clue what to do." Samara wiped her face with the back of her hand and gulped. "I felt so helpless last night . . . and so angry."

"I know." Jackie responded briefly. "But Dad knows what to do in situations like this and I'm sure he'll talk to your parents." She glanced at Samara. "I also get the feeling that Adam will know how to help. He really took charge last night."

"Mmm." Samara nodded. "After Dad hit the wall with his fist and disappeared downstairs, Adam totally took over." She managed a half smile. "It must have been crazy watching us all running around."

"I was too worried to think about it being crazy." Jackie glanced sideways. "I was trying to be all calm, but all I could think to do was hold on to your mother while you cleaned up the mess and Adam looked after Terry. He really was great."

"But he's only here for a few days." Samara couldn't keep the wistful sound out of her voice.

"Well, he's already had a big impact, and he may be just what your family needs right now." Jackie added quickly.

Samara sat quietly for the rest of their ride into the city, lost in her own thoughts. The previous night's experience had been terrible, with her family being as extreme as she'd ever seen them.

It was Adam who had been the unflappable constant through all of it—Adam, who made sure they were all fine, and Adam who had held her gently while she cried.

She closed her eyes and rubbed her forehead.

She was glad when, this morning, he was nowhere to be seen as she left for school. Her mother had calmed down enough the night before to give him the key to a motel unit and Samara assumed he had made his way there after she'd fallen asleep.

CHAPTER SEVEN

Samara took her time walking from Jackie's house after school. She had insisted on being let off there rather than at her home, stating firmly that she had promised to visit Toby and the kitten.

"The truth is that you don't want to see Adam or Terry or Mum or Dad." She muttered to herself as she neared the end of Rick's street. "The truth is you're a coward."

She clasped her bag tightly against her chest.

"But I also need to keep my promise to Toby."

She walked quickly to the house and pressed the doorbell before she could change her mind. Nobody answered so she made her way back up the driveway.

"Now there's no more excuses." She found it better to coach herself as she walked, willing her feet to take her the last few meters to her home. "Time to face everybody . . . time to go on with living."

She took a deep breath as she walked in through the reception area, the bell sounding and surprising her mother, who had her back to the door.

"Oh, Sam . . . you're early!" She put her hand to her heart. "Goodness, everything keeps taking me by surprise today."

"I didn't mean to give you a shock." Samara frowned. "But I'm not early. I usually get home about now."

"Yes, I know, but Jackie called and said you were at Rick's, so I thought you'd be awhile."

"There wasn't anyone home." Samara responded quietly. "Why did Jackie call? Did I leave something in the car?"

"No . . . no, she called to see how we all were . . . after last night." Tracey pressed her hand to her cheek. "She was so nice and, of course, she really wanted to know about Terry. She's such a good young adult rep. So thoughtful."

Samara stared at her mother. Did she honestly think Jackie's interest was solely because of her calling? She shook her head. It was probably better that her mother keep thinking that way.

"So where is Terry?" She asked casually as she walked around the desk. "Has he surfaced yet?"

"Yes." Tracey took her time tapping the handful of cards she was holding into a neat pile. "He got up just after lunch."

"And . . . ?" Samara leaned against the desk.

"And he doesn't really remember much . . . at all." Tracey straightened the pile again. "He knew he was at Jackie's, but after that . . ." She wiped the side of her eye. "I don't believe he has any idea of the pain he caused us all last night."

"So where is he now?"

"Actually, he went for a walk with Adam, down to the beach." Tracey pointed behind her. "Adam came in after Terry had some lunch and I introduced them, and then I had someone check into the motel so I left them to it." She shrugged. "I got back after about twenty minutes and they said they were going walking."

"No way." Samara frowned. "Terry doesn't just go walking with strangers."

Tracey shrugged as she shook her head. "That's what I thought, but as they left they were talking about some engineering project."

"Terry was?" Samara looked genuinely surprised. "He hasn't talked about engineering for ages."

"Well, he wasn't doing much talking, but he was definitely interested in what Adam was saying—something about a bridge in Brazil."

"So what did Dad have to say about that?" Samara leaned against the desk and rested her bag on it.

"I don't know what your father has to say." Tracey shook her head. "He was gone when I woke up and I haven't heard from him all day."

"So he's out somewhere drinking." Samara made it a statement rather than a question.

"I wouldn't be surprised." Her mother finally put the cards away and picked up a pen. "You mustn't be too hard on your father, Sam. He got an awful shock last night."

Samara stared at her mother is disbelief. "He got a shock? We all did, Mum, but he didn't have to react that way. What would have happened if Adam hadn't been here?"

Her mother was silent for a long time as she drew tight little squares on the desk pad until there were thick lines on each box.

"I really don't know, Sam. I only know that I'm grateful that he was here."

Samara slowly took her bag off the desk and let it drop to her side as she stared at her mother. Then she walked to the door.

"Mum?" She didn't turn around.

"Yes."

"Were you on your drugs last night? More than usual?"

She waited for a long time before her mother spoke so quietly she could hardly hear her.

"Yes, I was, Sam."

"And now Dad's out drinking." Samara pushed the lounge door. "Do you wonder that Terry is doing it too?"

"But things have been so difficult lately, Sam. I wanted to make a good impression." Her mother's voice trailed off as Samara turned.

"Oh, you made a real impression, Mum." She felt the weariness in her own voice. "It's one I'll certainly remember for a long time."

* * *

Samara's bedroom was on the second level overlooking the motel parking lot and the front entrances of all the units. Sitting at her desk she could see right down the track that led to the beach, and although she tried to keep her mind on her assignment, her gaze drifted frequently to the window.

The sun was still shining warmly at four o'clock in the afternoon and there were the usual groups of tourists still making their way to and from the beach with towels and swim gear that were distinctive to the boutiques around town. At this time of day there were also groups of children and teenagers newly released from school, running down to the sand, clutching their surfboards.

Samara looked at her blue swimsuit, hanging on a hook, along with her towel decorated with multicolored swirls. She twirled her pencil between her fingers as she stared at the suit and felt a growing resolve to go swimming.

"A few minutes in the surf might clear my head." She murmured to herself as she stood up and stretched, still watching the beach track. Within minutes she had her swimsuit on and a matching sarong tied around under her arms. She was slipping her feet into her sandals when the phone rang. For a second she hesitated. Her mother would answer the house phone down at the desk if it kept ringing.

"Hello?" She stifled a sigh as she picked it up.

"Samara?" Rick's voice sounded hesitant on the other end.

"Hi, Rick." She swung around and stared out of the window. "You caught me just before I went for a swim."

"That sounds like a great idea." His voice sounded more confident. "I wish I could join you but this stupid arm has to be kept dry."

"How is it?" Samara felt annoyed at the slight sense of relief at his words.

"It's fine. I'm a quick healer." There was the slightest pause. "Umm . . . I'm wondering if we're still on for Wednesday."

Samara heard the hesitation in his voice again.

"As far as I know." She tried to make her voice sound casual. "Unless you want to change plans."

"No . . . not at all." Again she heard the uncertainty in his voice. "I just wasn't sure if . . ."

"Rick, have you been talking to Jackie?" Samara switched the phone to the other hand.

"I . . . actually, yes." His voice was even quieter. "She was worried about Terry . . . and your family."

"So who else knows?" Samara folded her arms across her chest and struggled to keep her breathing even. "Who else in the ward knows about the dysfunctional Danes family?"

"Samara . . . that's not fair. Jackie was concerned about you all and she knew we were supposed to be doing your project tomorrow. She thought it better for me to call you . . . just in case." Rick's voice was more definite.

"Just in case . . . just in case I wasn't capable of doing my work because my brother's a drug addict and my parents flipped out as well." Samara clenched her teeth to stop the tears and swallowed hard.

"No." Rick pronounced the single word strongly. Then he spoke very precisely. "Just in case other things had cropped up that might require your being someplace other than a sanctuary."

Something in the way he said the word "sanctuary" suddenly broke down Samara's defenses. Suddenly she could visualize Rick standing there, a mirror image of herself right then, his arms across his chest and legs apart.

"Rick, I'm sorry." She barely whispered as she closed her eyes. "This place has been like a zoo."

"Then maybe you need to visit a real one to show you that yours isn't really that bad."

"I think that sounds like a great idea." Samara smiled and felt a sense of calm settle over her as she thought about something other than her family. "I've checked with my class and there are only two that are able to come . . . Anna and Emily."

"So why don't I bring Toby for the guy element?" Rick chuckled. "He still thinks he's a movie star since you took that dandelion photo of him."

"That would be great." Samara nodded. "Tell him I'll bring choco-late."

"I don't think chocolate is a problem right now. Our main worry could be convincing him he can't bring the kitten with him."

"Oh dear." Samara giggled. "That could make for some really interesting shots."

"Well, from what I've seen, you don't need a kitten to make inter-esting shots. You do awesome stuff." Rick sounded genuine and Samara smiled.

"Then you'd better get all those wild animals ready for us." She suddenly remembered the conversation from the night before. "Umm . . . one more thing. Is it still okay if A . . . if Brother Russell comes?"

"Absolutely." Was there a hesitation? "Jackie said he was great last night, helping you all."

"Yes." Samara answered briefly. "Yes, he was."

"So I guess I'll look forward to meeting him tomorrow." Rick paused for a second. "We'll be praying for you, Sam . . . and your family."

When he shortened her name like that and his voice deepened, she knew he meant what he said.

"Thanks, Rick, and I'm sorry I was so nasty." She stopped as he interrupted again.

"Nasty situations sometimes make for nasty reactions. You don't need to be sorry . . . just don't do it again."

She could visualize the smile on his face as he said that, and she smiled in response.

"Okay, I'll try. I'll see you tomorrow, Rick."

"See you, Samara."

* * *

Rick sat staring at the lounge wall for a long time after he finished talking to Samara. He turned the mobile phone over and over in his hand as his mind raced. Then he tapped the phone on the arm of the chair.

"What are you doing?" Toby walked into the lounge clutching his kitten against his chest, its legs dangling.

"Thinking." Rick smiled at his little brother, and he put down the phone, holding his hands out to take the kitten. "How about you hold her like this?" He cradled the kitten with one hand and supported its legs with the other. "I don't think she likes just hanging there."

"Okay." Toby nodded as he stroked the kitten's head. "Who were you talking to before?"

"Samara." Rick looked at Toby with his eyes half closed. "She wants you to do some more photos for her . . . with the animals at the sanctuary."

"Really?" Toby looked surprised, then he nodded. "That's okay . . . I know what to do now."

"She's bringing some of the girls from her CTR class as well." Rick grinned at his brother. "Anna and Emily."

Toby again looked thoughtful for a moment, then he nodded. "They'll be all right." He leaned forward to put his face close to the kitten. "Is she going to take photos of you?"

"I don't think so." Rick shook his head as he stroked the kitten's back. "Samara is going to bring another friend along, though. He's a photographer . . . from Canada."

"The man with the beard?" Toby poked his tongue out at the kitten's nose. "And the green eyes."

"I really don't know." Rick smiled. Toby had a unique ability to notice people and to evaluate them. "You obviously saw him on Sunday." He hesitated. "What did you think of him?"

Toby shrugged. "He looks okay but he doesn't wear a white shirt to church."

"Oh . . ." Rick nodded. Toby always insisted on wearing his white shirt and tie on Sunday and usually made sure that Rick dressed the same. "Did Samara talk to him much?"

"She kept laughing and smiling." Toby looked up at his brother. "Does Samara like him?"

"I don't know, Toby." Rick stroked the kitten more firmly as it stretched under his hand. "I think she's happy to see an old friend."

"Do you think she likes him more than you?" Toby frowned as he rested his arm across his brother's knee. "That wouldn't be good. Samara is your girlfriend." He put his head to one side. "Isn't she?"

"Of course, she's my friend." Rick answered easily but his brow creased slightly.

"She's my friend too." Toby sighed and stared at his brother. "But is she your girlfriend? Are you going to marry her?"

Rick took his time answering and Toby patted his knee.

"Are you going to marry Sam? Do you want to?"

"Hey, little brother . . . enough of the questions." Rick forced a grin as he picked up the kitten and handed it to Toby. "Especially about my love life."

"But do you want to?" Toby persisted as he carefully cradled the kitten. "I want you to 'cause then Sam would be my sister and I'd do photos for her whenever she wanted me to."

"Well, that's the important thing." Rick stood up and ruffled Toby's hair. "Are you going to do the gel thing with your hair for the photos?"

"If Sam wants me to." Toby nodded. "Can you call her and ask her?"

Rick stared at the phone. "Umm . . . I'm sure she wants you the same as last time . . . with the spiky hair thing happening."

"Okay." Toby struggled to his feet with the kitten in his arms, then automatically raised one arm toward Rick, his usual request for a good-night hug. Rick bent down, picked him up, and squeezed him hard. There was something about Toby that always made him feel good.

"You know what?" Toby squeezed him back, careful not to crush the kitten. "I could tell Sam you want to marry her."

Rick leaned back and took Toby's chin firmly in one hand.

"Toby, I want you to promise me that you'll do no such thing." He shook his brother's chin gently. "I'll ask Samara when I'm ready."

"So you are going to ask her?" Toby's eyes sparkled immediately. "She is going to be my sister."

Rick rolled his eyes as he let Toby and the kitten slide to the floor.

"Toby . . . go to bed so you'll be handsome for tomorrow."

He watched as his brother walked out of the room, but at the door Toby turned back. "Are you going to tell Sam so she doesn't like the other man?"

"Toby, don't worry about it." Rick waved his hand toward him. "She doesn't like the other man, so it's not a problem."

He waited until he heard Toby go into the kitchen. Then he picked up the phone and stared at the buttons for a long time. He finally dialed and then waited.

"That is . . . I don't *think* she likes the other man . . ." He sat down on the couch as he heard a voice answer. "Hi, Jackie . . ."

* * *

The wind had picked up slightly so there was a light breeze coming up the beach from the ocean when Samara reached the end of the path. There were still plenty of people swimming, jogging, and walking, so she made her way down to the edge of the dry sand and made a small pile with her towel, sandals, and sunglasses. A quick look around showed no sign of Adam or Terry, so she undid her sarong and dropped it onto the pile. The breeze suddenly picked up and she rubbed her arms to stop the chill as she walked to the water's edge.

"Watch out, lady!"

Samara instinctively ducked as a bright yellow Frisbee whizzed past her face and fell a few feet short of a young boy as he threw himself into the shallow waves to catch it. He stood up quickly, swung his head to get the water out of his hair, and lunged for the

Frisbee again. An incoming wave caught it and swept it to Samara's feet. She bent and picked it up to hand it to him, but he was standing waiting for her to throw it.

"Throw it, lady." The other younger boy who had thrown it the first time called out, so she turned to skim it to the bigger boy. It went directly to him and both boys hooted at the accuracy.

"You can play instead of him!"

"Not today." Samara laughed as she walked out into the waves, breathing more quickly as the cold water reached her feet. It was funny how a small thing like throwing a Frisbee could make you feel better. She laughed to herself, then began her usual countdown from ten before she ran into the water.

As she ran, the clear water splashed up onto her body, and she felt the pull of the deepening waves against her thighs. As she brought both arms up into a dive position she suddenly felt the water surge beside her as another large body lunged past and beneath the wave in front. Barely hesitating, she plunged under the cresting wave, pulling herself deeper with strong arm movements fighting the current before allowing herself to float up to the surface. Her face broke the surface and she instantly felt the warmth of the sun on her skin as she kept her eyes closed and inhaled deeply.

"I thought you weren't going to come up." Adam spoke close by and she swung around in surprise, swallowing a mouthful of water as another wave hit her from behind.

"Agh!" She began to cough and struggle for air as she treaded water until a strong hand held her arm and lifted her slightly with the swell of the next wave. Samara coughed and wiped the water off her face with her free hand.

"You gave me a fright!" She closed her mouth again to make the coughing stop, but it seemed to make it worse. The next moment, she felt Adam pounding her back, and she hiccupped.

"There . . . that fixed it." Adam swam in front of her while keeping afloat with wide, circular strokes, and she noticed a long, fine scar running down the middle of his chest, white against his tanned skin. "I seriously didn't mean to frighten you, though."

"Well, I . . ." Samara didn't know where to look. His green eyes were staring right at her and his body was disconcertingly close. "I . . . um . . ."

"You threw a mean Frisbee back there. Those boys were impressed."

"Where . . ?" She looked back at the beach where the boys were still playing.

"I was up by the bank." He gestured with his head. "Terry went back to talk to your mother."

At the mention of her brother, Samara screwed up her face.

"What's he like today?" She began to work her arms in a circle as he was doing, and she found the movement strangely relaxing.

"I guess repentant would be a good description." Adam smiled and she noticed how his smile made his eyes seem to glisten. "He doesn't remember much."

"No, Mum said he only remembers being at Jackie's. I thought that was pretty convenient." She didn't try to disguise the coolness of her voice.

"I think he's telling the truth." Adam nodded. "Drugs have a way of making you blank out."

"Did he happen to say why he did it?" Samara let her body drift with a large wave, then she floated back to Adam.

"I don't think there's any one reason." He shook his head. "He's pretty mixed up about everything . . . especially about your parents."

"That follows." Samara rolled her eyes. "I wonder where he gets it from."

"It's a shame you're a cynic at such a young age." Adam joked gently as the water rolled them closer together. He put out a hand to push her away as she frowned.

"It's funny . . . I don't feel young" She grimaced. "Quite the opposite at times."

"Then I hope I can help you regain your youthfulness." He swung around and pointed to a lady floating on a boogie board. "Race you to the board. I'll give you a head start."

"Who says I need a head start?" Samara began to tread water more vigorously, ready to propel herself forward, and then she was gone, pulling ahead with strong, firm strokes. She didn't even try to see if he was following but gave her body up to the familiar rhythm of swimming, rising, and falling with the swell as she pulled through the waves. When she stopped and looked around, the woman on the board was well behind her.

"I said go to the board . . . not to New Zealand." Adam pulled up beside her and they both took awhile to regain their breath.

"That was good." Samara nodded as she sunk her head back into the water and then let the water drain off her hair.

"It was." Adam nodded and they treaded water without speaking.

"How did you get Terry to talk to you?" Samara finally looked straight at him.

Adam stared down at the water and brushed his hand at a small piece of seaweed drifting past.

"I just talked about similar interests while he listened."

"But how did you know what he was interested in?"

He shrugged. "You learn a lot when you look at the walls in somebody's room for a few hours."

"You stayed with Terry last night?" Samara almost gulped more water.

"Somebody needed to." He answered simply. "And the rest of you were busy. I had plenty to read on the walls. Terry has achieved quite a lot, by the look of the certificates."

"That's what makes it so hard now." Samara shook her head. "He's always been a great student and a really good brother. I just don't understand what's happened. I can't even talk to him anymore."

"He knows." Adam frowned. "But right now he's caught between two worlds and doesn't want to be in either one."

"But how do we help him?" Samara heard the pleading in her own voice.

"We talked about that." Adam nodded back toward the shore. "I think he's ready to get help."

"But why would he listen to you and not to anybody else?" Samara slapped at the water with her hand.

"Maybe, because . . . I've been there and done that." Adam answered quietly.

"You've been on drugs?" Samara's eyes widened. "But . . ."

"Yes, a long time ago, but I hope I never forget how it felt when I realized what it was doing to me." He looked straight at her. "I was struggling with it when I met you in New Zealand. I'd already given up, but I knew I was still open to being . . . persuaded. Somehow, after I met you and learned about the gospel . . . it gave me the strength to stick with it. I realized then that everybody can tell you to give up, but there's got to be a moment when you find it inside yourself . . . when you want to change."

"So, do you think Terry is there yet?" Samara didn't even want to ask and she felt her heart sink as Adam shook his head.

"He's ready to be obedient but he'll be on thin ice for awhile."

Samara nodded as she gazed back in the direction of the motel.

"And what should I do?"

"Be there. Love him. Share your life with him." Adam smiled. "Listen to him. Don't lock him out anymore."

"That's what Jackie said." Samara took a deep breath. "I didn't even think I was locking him out. I thought he was doing it to me."

"It gets to be a bit of a catch-22." Adam nodded. "He hurts you, so you retaliate, then he goes quiet, so you go quieter." He looked straight at her. "And so it goes on until someone has the courage to break the cycle."

Samara stared down at the water, suddenly uncomfortable with the direction the conversation was heading. He seemed to be able to go straight to the point, requiring her to think about things she didn't want to think about.

Under the dark, clear green water, her hands were several shades whiter than the skin on her arms. She flexed her hands and put them half out of the water. Where they had seemed light and smooth, they were actually beginning to wrinkle. She twisted her hand to face Adam.

"I guess we've been talking too long. I'm starting to go pruney."

He held up his hand and it was starting to look the same.

"We'll just have to finish this conversation on dry land." He began to sidestroke lazily toward the beach. "Although, I could stay here forever. I love the ocean."

"Me, too." Samara floated on her back and kicked slowly, propelled by the swell of the waves beneath her. The brightness of the sun had faded so she could look directly up at the sky. There were no clouds—only a clear, deepening blue expanse. "When it's like this it's as if there's nothing between you and heaven. You're just floating." She smiled to herself. "I've always wondered if this is what it's like after you die."

She didn't see Adam watching her as she looked upward or see him turn onto his back as well. For a long time, neither spoke. Then as her hands propelled her, she felt a sudden shock as she drifted closer to him and touched his hand. She jumped but then felt Adam's hand squeeze hers gently and release it.

"Thanks for sharing your bit of heaven, Sam."

Then he was gone, pulling strongly away from her and disappearing in the swirl of white waves as they crashed near the beach.

Chapter Eight

There was no sign of Adam when she walked in from the surf, and she deliberately went the long way to her room to avoid passing his motel unit. She even took her time changing when she got back to the motel. It seemed that changing back into her regular clothes placed her firmly back into having to face reality—and her family. She changed twice, finally settling for a red, cap-sleeved shirt and beige cotton trousers, as she quietly sang a familiar Primary song to herself.

"Red is for courage to do what is right . . ." She kept humming as she finished dressing.

"But someone has to have the courage to break the cycle." Samara repeated to her reflection as she began to dry her hair with the dryer. She took her time brushing long, slow strokes as the warm air played against her scalp. "Someone to love and listen."

She could almost hear Adam's voice saying the words as she kept brushing.

"Someone to share." She turned the dryer off and faced her reflection. "Something that Jackie is so much better at than me."

Her hair shone as it hung straight, slightly turning up at the ends where it passed her shoulders. She reached into a small basket of cosmetics and quickly applied a layer of reddish lip gloss then, as an afterthought, a bit of mascara and blusher. As she placed the cosmetics back into the basket she stared at the hand that Adam had held, then she slowly raised it against her heart. The slight movement seemed to make her feel warm again, and she smiled at her reflection.

Red is for courage to do what is right. She hummed quietly as she opened the door to her bedroom and walked down the hallway to her brother's room, hesitating only a second before tapping on the door.

"Terry . . . can I come in?" She took a quick breath. "I need to talk to you."

She had to tap once more before a quiet voice called her in.

Somehow, because she was feeling much better and full of resolve, Samara expected to see a similar change in Terry, but when she walked in he was sitting on his bed with his legs drawn up to his chest and his forehead resting on his arms on top of his knees. He slowly lifted his head as she sat down on the bed, and Samara had to control the expression on her face as she looked at his pale cheeks and the darkened shadows under his eyes.

"Are . . . are you feeling better?" she asked quietly, and suddenly she noticed the strong smell of disinfectant in the room. She stood up and went to open the window. "You were right into redecorating this room last night."

She turned to see the slightest smile lift the corner of his mouth.

"Adam said I chucked up buckets."

"Well, don't look so proud of yourself." She chastised him gently. "Guess who had to tidy it up?"

"I don't remember." Terry answered briefly as he rested his head back on his arms. "I don't want to remember."

He didn't speak again, and Samara felt a growing desire to leave the room, but she took a deep breath.

"I went swimming with Adam today . . . after you left the beach." She pointed vaguely in the direction of the beach. "He said you were coming back to talk to Mum."

When he still didn't respond, Samara sat down on the bed again. "Did you talk to her?"

"A bit."

She could hardly hear him so she moved closer.

"Jackie called to see how you were." She watched him closely but there was no reaction. "She's such a good friend."

She watched the color in Terry's ears deepen to a darker red.

"I've made a total fool of myself . . . in front of Jackie . . . everyone . . . even a complete stranger."

"Adam?" Samara smiled as she twisted a button on the duvet on his bed. "He's the most un-stranger-like stranger I've ever met."

Terry lifted his head slightly and rested his chin on his arms.

"He talks a lot."

"Only when he needs to." Samara pulled herself further onto the bed and crossed her legs. "He's a really good listener as well."

"Mmm." Terry barely nodded. "He knows a lot about engineering."

"I think he knows a lot about everything." Samara rolled her eyes. "He's even had Dad listening and chatting about his trips. I never knew about most of the things Dad talked about last night." She shook her head. "It was like listening to a different person."

"That'd be nice." Terry rolled his head to one side and stared out the window. "I don't like the old person too much."

Samara nodded as she remembered the look on her father's face as he'd told the stories.

"It was nice." She shrugged. "He and Mum even talked about when we were little." She nodded. "It was really nice."

They sat in silence for awhile, but it wasn't uncomfortable, and Samara began to look around the room. She looked at the chair beside the bed where Adam must have sat the night before and turned to see what he would have looked at. On the opposite wall there were several framed certificates and two shelves with trophies of different sizes and shapes. Two photos showed a much younger Terry, one in rugby uniform and the other in tiny swim trunks with a medal around his neck.

Samara felt tears well in her eyes, but she swallowed hard to contain them.

Love. Listen. Share.

"Umm . . . I was wondering if you could give me a hand tomorrow." She looked at the duvet buttons again, but she was aware of Terry slowly lifting his head. He didn't say anything, but she knew he was listening.

"I have to do a project at Currumbin Sanctuary tomorrow. Rick has arranged for me to go and I'm taking photos of some of the children with the animals." She spread both hands. "They say it can be tricky working with children and animals, and I'm doing both, so . . . I wondered if you wanted to give me a hand."

Terry still said nothing as he dropped his head back on his arms. Then he slowly shook his head.

"I'll shout for orange ice cream." She added quietly, remembering Terry's favorite food. She was rewarded with a slight smile.

"I'm a bit busy right now." He lifted his head in a brief nod, but he was smiling. "Maybe another time when it's not so hectic."

She thought about the hours he'd spent on the couch or in his room over the last few months and how it had annoyed her so much she couldn't even speak to him. In that instant the image seemed to vanish. She stood up and rested her hand briefly on his shoulder.

"I'll hold you to that. We're having swimming races for our next activity."

Terry nodded slowly and rubbed his hand over his mouth as the muscle in his jaw began to pulse, and she watched him swallow hard. He nodded again and she knew it was time to leave. At the door, she stopped as he spoke.

"Thanks, Sammy—for asking."

As he whispered his nickname for her, Samara didn't do anything to fight the tears that began to stream down her cheeks. In a second she walked back across the room and held her brother tightly as they both cried.

"What happened, Terry?" Samara barely whispered as the tears finally subsided and they sat quietly beside each other. "What happened to my big brother?"

Terry took some time to answer, his hands shaking as they played with the corner of his bedsheet.

"Friends." He almost choked on the word, and he screwed the sheet tightly in his fist. "The wrong friends."

"Doug?" Samara asked quietly, suddenly remembering the name of the guy she'd seen only once when he'd waited outside the motel in his car for Terry. He had never made any attempt to come inside, but just watching him from the reception area, she'd had the impression he was brashly confident behind his black sunglasses.

"Doug . . . among others." Terry nodded. "He has a lot of friends."

"Like him?" Samara frowned as Terry shrugged.

"Pretty much, and they were all pretty loaded as well."

"How did they get their money?" Samara almost didn't want to hear the answer. "Were they rich kids?"

"Some . . . but they mainly got it off mugs like me." Terry's voice was bitter.

"But how did you get into it?" Samara's voice was barely a whisper. "You've always been so against drugs and drink."

There was a long silence as Terry rested his head in his hands. Then he stared up at the ceiling.

"It was after a session at home here with Mum and Dad and I just didn't want to hear them going at each other anymore. I'd been trying so hard to make excuses for the way they carry on, but all of a sudden I was just sick of it and so I went in to school to study in the library and Doug came along . . ." He took a deep breath. "It was a Saturday afternoon and we got talking. He said that no one should be studying then."

"Then why was he in the library?" Samara frowned.

"I don't know . . . maybe looking for people with no life, like me." Terry shrugged. "Anyway, I knew him a bit from a couple of classes we had together, so when he suggested we go to the beach, I figured, why not?"

"Why not . . . because it felt good to go against everything that was familiar and not much fun." Samara stated quietly and smiled as Terry glanced at her. "You're not the only one to have those feelings."

"Yes, but you didn't go with Doug." Terry shook his head. "Doug and his little friends."

"Little friends?" Samara looked puzzled, then she watched as Terry held his fingers to his lips. "Oh . . . little friends."

"We hung out at the beach for awhile, then Doug casually brought out his "little friend" and . . ." Terry hung his head and beat his fist against his leg. "I can't believe I got sucked into it."

"But you did." Samara added quietly. "It seemed to happen very quickly."

"Way quickly." He nodded. "At first it just felt good, and I began to wonder what all the fuss was about." His voice broke and his shoulders began to heave. Samara waited.

"After awhile, I found I was looking for Doug each day, and then I was starting to fall behind with classes because I just didn't realize the time . . . and then I didn't really care."

"So you knew what was happening?" Samara looked puzzled. "Why didn't you stop before it was too late?"

"Because I didn't know when too late was." Terry looked straight through her, and she could barely hear him as he repeated himself. "I didn't know when too late was."

* * *

Her father and Adam were sitting at the dining room table when she finally went downstairs. Adam looked up and smiled but there was a questioning look in his eyes and her heart began to beat more strongly.

"Your dinner's cold." Eddy barely glanced up at his daughter as she walked into the lounge. "We went ahead and ate awhile ago." He turned his attention back to the large map of Australia spread across the table and pointed a broad finger toward the northern part. "I usually travel this road."

Adam gave Samara another quick look as she walked past them toward the kitchen, then he turned his attention to the map.

"So what do you usually haul?"

"Oh, pretty much anything." Eddy waved his hand in the air. "Cattle, building materials . . . I did a load of camels a few years back." He chuckled. "Worst passengers I ever had."

"You took camels?" Samara stopped on her way to the kitchen.

"Yep . . . a trailer load." Eddy pointed at the map. "From here to the top. The guy took me for a ride on one of them when I delivered."

"You rode a camel?" She gave her father a puzzled look. "You never told us."

"You weren't interested." He responded briefly without looking at her.

"Maybe you never thought to ask if I was," Samara responded curtly. Then she caught the look on Adam's face and tried to smile. "I actually think camels would be great to photograph. They're so . . . snooty looking."

"They're mean." Eddy glanced up. "And they spit . . . right at you."

"I'll second that." Adam grinned. "I had one do that to me in Egypt."

"So I'm the only one in this room who hasn't ridden a camel . . . or been spat at." Samara rolled her eyes. "I find that so unfair."

Eddy chuckled and it sounded genuine but he didn't say anything else.

Tracey walked in from the reception area and Samara noticed that she avoided looking in her direction. "That was such a nice family that just checked in. They're going to stay for a week." She glanced at her husband and Adam. "So what's unfair?"

"Samara wants a camel to spit at her." Adam sat back in his chair and stretched his arms above his head. "So we'll probably have to go and find one."

"Aren't you going to the sanctuary tomorrow?" Tracey still didn't look at her daughter. "Maybe Rick could find you one there."

"I'm sure Rick could." Samara responded quietly. Why did her mother have to bring up Rick's name every time they were together? She glanced at Adam. "Do you still want to come tomorrow?"

"Yes, I do." He answered quietly as he watched her carefully and began to toy with a pencil lying on the map. "Do you think maybe Terry would like to come with us?"

Samara stared for a second, then she nodded with a slight smile.

"I already asked him but he said he'll pass this time."

"Like he passes on everything these days." Eddy muttered as he began to fold up the map. "The kid's useless."

"He's not useless . . . he's just made some wrong choices." Samara immediately leapt to her brother's defense and watched her father hesitate in his map folding. "I think he wants to change . . ." She faltered and fought to control the tremor in her voice. "But he doesn't know how."

"Well . . . that's a different tune from the other night." Eddy stared straight at her. "I didn't think you had much time for your brother."

"I . . . I didn't." Samara stammered, glancing quickly at Adam and then back to her father. "But I had a talk with him just now . . ."

"So he's able to talk?" Eddy curled his lip. "At least that's an improvement on last night."

"Well, he might have talked to you today if you hadn't been out . . . drinking." Samara responded quickly, feeling her jaw tighten at her father's remarks. She felt her control slipping and knew Adam and her mother were watching her closely. Taking a deep breath, she pressed her lips together and counted to five. "I'm sorry . . . I know it's been difficult for you . . . and for all of us, but Terry knows he's doing wrong and he wants help . . . our help." She stared down at her hands. "And I want to do everything I can because . . . I want my brother back."

The ensuing silence was so complete that the ticking of the clock on the wall began to feel as if it were synchronized with the pounding in her head. Her father simply sat and stared at the folded paper while her mother nervously twisted several papers into a tightening tube. Adam was the first to speak as he stood up and rested his hands against the back of his chair. He coughed and then tightened his grip on the chair.

"Umm . . . I don't wish to intrude in all this, but it seems like I've managed to in the last two days."

Two days. Samara glanced at him. He'd only been in their lives for two days and yet she already found herself waiting for him to take the lead.

Adam didn't smile, but he nodded thoughtfully as he rested his hand on Eddy's shoulder. "I think we need a plan of attack so that everyone knows how to respond to Terry. Right now he wants to stop using whatever he's on." He smiled wistfully. "And I don't think he's too bad at all. It's all been enjoyable until now, so he's not thought of it as a problem, but now his body is getting used to it so he wants more."

"Will he have to go through . . . withdrawl?" Tracey stammered slightly. "I know I've tried stopping my . . . medicine and . . . I couldn't do it."

"I've told you time and again to stop using that stuff." Eddy grunted. "You need to have more control. You give up too easily."

"Like you with your drink?" Tracey's eyes flashed and then clouded over.

"I drink for pleasure." He snapped back at her and hunched his shoulders. "I could stop anytime."

"Well, I take drugs so I can find some pleasure . . . in living." Tracey sat down suddenly on the chair beside her. Samara could see the muscles in her jaw working to fight back the tears, and she suddenly felt an overwhelming sense of pity for her . . . and for her father. They were as helpless in their own way as Terry was. She looked up to find Adam watching her, but if she expected to see sympathy in his eyes she was disappointed. He was actually smiling at her, or at least his eyes were, and under his gaze she became aware of a growing sense of her own determination.

She took a deep breath.

"Well, it looks like this plan will work all ways." She tried to sound confident but she could hear the quiver in her voice. "At least Terry will have our empathy. You'll know what he's going through and maybe it will help us as well."

"Speak for yourself." Eddy still would not look up.

"I am." Samara deliberately relaxed her shoulders as she looked at her parents. "Terry needs to give up drugs. Mum, too. And you, Dad . . . you could drink less. And I have to give up feeling like the victim . . . for being part of all this." She nodded. "I've been just as crippled as any of you."

"I'm not crippled by anything." Eddy objected immediately, but when his comment was met by silence he sat for a long time staring at the wall. When he finally looked up, there were tears in his eyes. "But I do want to help . . . somehow." His voice broke. "I know I've been mucking this family up for too long, but I don't know how to fix it."

Samara watched in total shock as her father's shoulders began to shake and he put his head into his hands. It was as if she was watching a silent movie play out when she felt the pressure of Adam's hand in the small of her back, gently pushing her out to the kitchen as her father sat and cried and her mother cried beside him, her head resting on his shoulder.

Adam guided her through the kitchen and out the door, and they didn't speak until they reached the path through the sand. As they stood staring out at the black expanse that was the ocean, Samara lifted her hands to her face, pressed her cool fingertips against her eyelids, and ran her hands down her throat. It was a strangely cleansing action as she lifted her face to the sky.

"I thought I would cry but there's nothing there," she observed softly.

"Maybe you've moved on." Adam stood slightly behind her, but she knew he was looking up at the sky as well.

"Moved on to what?" She blew a breath through pursed lips.

"To the next stage." He answered so quietly she could barely hear. "You could have moved sideways . . . but you've moved onwards." He hesitated. "And I get the feeling that you're bringing your family with you."

Samara nodded. Then, in an instant, it turned into a shaking motion.

"Oh, Adam, I don't know if I can." She half turned as her hands dropped to her sides. "It all seems too big."

"I know, Sam . . . it seems huge right now, but—" She felt the warmth of his arm briefly around her shoulders. "You can do this. One step at a time."

CHAPTER NINE

"So he thinks you can help everybody?" Jackie glanced at Samara as she drove, a smile hovering on her lips. They were halfway to school, and after awhile of driving in silence Jackie had finally asked how everybody was doing, which had led up to Samara's description of her walk with Adam.

Samara held up her finger and thumb and nodded. "Bit by tiny bit."

"That does make sense." Jackie nodded. "So have you talked to Terry?"

"No, we haven't talked to Terry about anything yet." Samara shook her head. "I think Mum and Dad have to get their act together first before they can really help Terry." She ran a finger along the dashboard. "I think you and I are going to have to be the ones to help Terry right now."

"That's sounds all right to me." Jackie smiled. "He called last night and we talked for quite awhile."

"So that's why he didn't come downstairs." Samara glanced at her friend and then turned sideways on her seat to face her. "I can't quite get used to the idea of you and Terry . . . my best friend and my brother."

"Why not?" Jackie shrugged. "Until a few months ago we did lots of things together."

"Yes . . . all of us." Samara drew a circle with her hand. "You never looked like—" She hesitated.

"I never looked like I was interested?" Jackie grinned. "You can fool some of the people some of the time—"

"But why would you suddenly come out and say that you like him when he's being rotten? Most people would run the other way."

"I know, and my mother was suggesting that." Jackie gripped the steering wheel more tightly. "I've always really . . . appreciated Terry, but he's always been more like a big brother and so it felt funny to think of him any other way." She hesitated. "When he started acting strangely it hurt me that he was doing it to himself and hurting other people as well. But then one night I spent all night thinking of him as he always had been and what he could be again and I knew that I had to do something. So I started calling him and inviting him to activities. I knew he wouldn't come but I wanted him to know that we—that I was thinking about him."

"And that was when he started coming over to your house?" Samara stared at the front window. "Did he ever behave strangely when he was there?"

"Not really." Jackie shook her head. "I think he knew the boundaries."

"Because there aren't any at our house." Samara shook her head. "Only examples of what not to do."

"Whatever, but he's responded to the friendship I've offered him, and it wasn't until the other night that he collapsed." She sighed. "I was terrified, but at the same time I was glad he felt comfortable enough to come to me."

"I'll bet you're glad your parents weren't home." Samara smiled weakly.

"I'll admit that the thought of them getting back gave me the adrenaline I needed to get him in the car." Jackie grinned. "He may look slender but he's heavy."

Samara nodded and lapsed into a thoughtful silence for some time. They were on the outskirts of Brisbane when Jackie spoke again.

""Sam . . . I have to ask . . . about Brother Russell." She leaned forward over the steering wheel. "He seemed very at home at your place. Did you say you only met him once before?"

Samara nodded. "Just once. Nine years ago, and it has been . . . quick . . . the way he's fitted in. Mum and Dad don't usually even have people come over, and Dad was really against it at first, but Adam . . ." She noted Jackie's quick look. "Adam seems to be able to relate to everyone, even Terry. They went for a walk yesterday." She frowned. "Terry and a total stranger. Dad and a total stranger . . . even Mum. She's was acting like a teenager for awhile . . . until Terry came home. Then everything went to pieces, and Adam has been the constant for everybody."

Jackie looked at her.

"And what about Samara?"

"What do you mean?" Samara stared ahead.

"I mean, how do you feel about Adam suddenly arriving on the scene . . . and in the middle of a crisis?"

Samara rested her arm along the window edge and leaned her head against her wrist. The pressure felt good against her throbbing head.

"I feel . . . grateful. I'm beginning to feel like he's here to help us all through this." She nodded and smiled. "He's a very kind person."

"He seems to be really nice, and he certainly doesn't look your parent's age." Jackie added quietly.

"But he's not." Samara responded quickly, catching the questioning look on Jackie's face. Her cheeks flushed instantly. "He's quite a few years younger."

"And you two have a lot in common with photography and everything." Jackie swung the car into the university parking lot. "That must be really fun . . . and a change."

"It is." Samara reached into the backseat to pick up her bag. "He makes me feel like a different person."

"Different to how Rick makes you feel?" Jackie switched off the engine and pulled the key out of the ignition.

She waited as Samara paused with her head down.

"Very different. He makes me feel very different."

"*Good* different?" Jackie persisted as Samara straightened up and clasped her arms around her bag.

"Yes!" She answered almost defiantly, tilting her chin up. "He makes me feel . . . important. Like the things I have to say and do actually mean something to him."

"So Rick doesn't make you feel like that?"

"Yes . . . I mean, Rick makes me feel good. He's a lovely person, but I . . ."

"Don't know if there's something else out there." Jackie quoted their previous conversation. "Or someone else."

"That's right." Samara almost mumbled as she gripped the door handle then looked straight at Jackie. "Adam seems to make everything make sense, and he makes me feel good about myself and what I want to do."

"And you really like him?"

Samara had difficulty swallowing as she nodded. "I really like it when he's around."

"But he'll be going away soon." Jackie smiled gently. "What will happen then?"

"I don't know." Samara shrugged as she opened the door. "Right now I just have to get through today." She hesitated. "Oh, I forgot to tell you not to wait for me because I'll be catching the bus back early. Rick is helping me take the children to Currumbin for the afternoon so I can do photos for my project."

"Okay, no worries." Jackie nodded, then she leaned back against her seat. "What's Adam going to do while you're working?"

"Umm . . . he's coming too." Samara answered quietly. "To give me advice."

"Wow . . . both of the men in your life helping you at once." Jackie rolled her eyes. "That could be every girl's dream come true."

"Or nightmare." Samara frowned slightly.

"That was my other thought." Jackie jumped out of the car. "Better you than me." She waved as Samara began to walk up a separate path from the one she was going to take. "Have a really exciting afternoon."

Jackie waited for a few minutes, leaning against the door of the car until Samara disappeared around a bend in the pathway. She had talked to Terry the night before, but she had also spent a long time talking with Rick on the phone, and most of his conversation had been questions about Samara . . . and about Adam Russell.

* * *

Anna and Emily from Samara's Primary class were waiting with their mothers in the motel reception area when she arrived home later in the afternoon. Both little girls were dressed in jean skirts and T-shirts but the similarity ended there as Emily's long, blonde, curly hair reached nearly to her waist, where Anna's straight, silky, blue-black hair was cut into a neat bob below her ears.

"I hope they'll listen to your instructions, Samara." Emily's mother laughed as her daughter swung on her hand, giggling nervously as she kept her lips tightly pressed together. She reached down and touched her daughter's cheek. "However, we did have a slight accident and Emily's not sure you'll still want her for the photographs."

"Why, what happened?" Samara looked at Emily but the little girl hid her face behind her mother's arm. "Are you all right, Emily?"

"Yeth." Samara could barely hear the whisper then Emily peeked out and smiled hesitantly, revealing a wide space where two front teeth had been on Sunday.

"Oh, my word." Samara bent down and looked her right in the face. "Did it hurt when they came out?"

Emily nodded. "Jothif puthed me," she lisped quietly.

"Her brother, Joseph, pushed her off the couch . . . it was an accident." Her mother quickly explained. "Do you still want her?"

"I think it'll be perfect." Samara stood up. "It'll add to the charm."

"Did you hear that, Em? Samara says it'll be fine." She smiled. "She could hardly sleep last night; she was so excited and worried all at the same time."

"It was the same with Anna." Anna's mother nodded in agreement. "And I had to wash and blow-dry her hair." She lightly stroked the fine, black strands. "I'd better get used to having a model in the family. She's decided that's what she wants to be now."

"Oops, I hope I haven't created monsters." Samara smiled at the girls and opened her bag. She pulled out a camera and bent down to show them some of the dials and buttons. "I have to use all these different settings to get very good photos, so it may get a bit boring."

"I won't be bored," Emily answered primly, swinging her arm out wide like a ballet dancer. "I can thit thtill for ages."

"Me, too." Anna nodded and looked up at her mother. "You'd better not wait up for us . . . we may be late."

They all laughed as her mother rolled her eyes. Then Samara watched the girls' attention suddenly focus behind her. Without turning, she knew Adam was standing in the foyer.

"Brother Russell, it's good to see you again. We met on Sunday in the foyer." Emily's mother held out her hand. "I didn't realize you were staying here."

"Not only staying here, but I believe I'm going to watch Samara turn your daughters into models." Adam answered easily as he shook hands with both mothers.

"Oh, you're going to Currumbin as well?"

Samara caught the slightest look pass between the two women, and it was obvious Adam had too.

"Brother Russell is a professional photographer, so he's going to help me with the shots," Samara explained as she held out her hands to the girls, who took hold of them eagerly.

"Oh, well that's lovely." Emily's mother smiled widely. "I must be sure to get some copies of these photos."

"And I'll be happy to do those for you." Samara swung the girls' hands as they giggled. "Toby is going to be coming with us as well." She looked up at the others. "And I thought we could get some dinner after we finish."

"Here's Toby now!" Anna interrupted with a squeal as Rick drove a large van into the driveway. "And Rick! Is everyone coming?"

"All of us." Samara felt her stomach churning as she watched Rick swing easily out of the van and help Toby jump out right behind him. He looked tall and athletic in his beige uniform shirt and shorts with the Currumbin Sanctuary logo. The white bandage on his arm looked bright against his tanned skin. She took a quick breath and smiled brightly as he and Toby greeted everybody.

"Hi, Rick. Hi, Toby." She waited until they both reached her, then held up her hand to gesture between the two men. "Rick, this is Adam Russell. Adam . . . Rick and Toby Jamieson."

"Hi. I'm going to be the male model." Toby immediately pointed at his chest. "Are you helping Sam take photos?"

"Hi, Toby. It's good to meet you." Adam's lips twitched as he bent down to shake Toby's hand. "And I'm coming to watch and learn while Samara takes the photos."

Toby nodded wisely as Adam stood up and extended his hand to Rick. There was no hesitation as Rick grasped the other man's hand and shook it warmly.

"It's good to meet an old friend of Samara's." Rick smiled. "I'm glad you set her on this path. She's an awesome photographer."

"And it's good to meet you finally, Rick, and I agree with you." Adam looked straight at Rick, and he nodded as he gave Rick's hand a firm pump. "I'm looking forward to seeing how this project develops today."

"Then let's get right on our way." Rick turned to Samara. "You're the group leader, ma'am. Tell us what you want us to do."

Samara smiled as her heart did a quick flip at the two men standing side by side. They were both the same height, although Adam was slightly broader across the shoulders, and the two seemed to dwarf her and the other two women and children. She gave a nervous laugh and shepherded the children in front of her.

"I'll sit in the back with the children and start giving them an idea of what we're doing, and you two can talk in the front." She felt like a coward as she waited for the children to climb into the van, but Rick and Adam were already talking as they climbed into the front seat. By the time they waved to the mothers and drove out of the motel driveway, she could hear Adam asking about Currumbin and Rick answering enthusiastically.

The children chattered incessantly on the twenty-minute drive, alternating between pointing out the window, describing their adventures at different places, and telling Samara and each other which were their favorite animals.

"I want to cuddle a koala." Anna wrapped her arms around her body. "My sister did it, and she said it was so warm and fluffy."

"Well my thithter thaid the wombat wath betht." Emily lisped as she nodded her head knowingly. "And it'th fatter."

Toby listened but he kept squirming in his seat and pulling on the seat-belt strap until he suddenly called to his brother.

"Hey Rick, am I allowed to tell them that we're going to hold the snake?" His eyes were wide as he breathed the word *snake*.

Samara heard Rick chuckle as he glanced in the rearview mirror.

"Gee, Toby . . . I guess we have to tell them now." He nodded. "But is there anybody who wants to hold the snake?"

There was a hushed silence as Anna and Emily looked sideways at each other.

"How . . . big is it?" Anna asked cautiously.

"It's huge!" Toby spread his arms wide and hit Samara on the shoulder. "Rick showed me a photo of him holding it." He wrapped both his hands around his throat. "It goes right around your neck . . . really tight!"

Emily swallowed and she looked at Samara. "Can I hold the wombat?"

"You can hold whatever you want, Emily," Rick answered for her. "We'll leave the snake stuff to Toby."

Happy with that solution, the girls chattered on while Samara watched the backs of the men's heads as they continued their conversation. She hadn't anticipated that they would get on so easily. In her mind they were two men whom she found attractive, and somehow they should be opposed to each other. She gave a slight start as Adam's deep laugh echoed in the van and Rick's hand moved in the air to demonstrate something he was talking about.

She closed her eyes and shook her head. It was going to be a very interesting afternoon.

CHAPTER TEN

"I thought we could take a train ride first and get the kids a bit excited about it all." Rick stood back to let them all through the front gate at the animal sanctuary, nodding at the girl at the kiosk as they passed. "And it'll give you a better idea of which animals to concentrate on." He glanced at his watch. "We can also catch the lorikeet feeding at four if you want to, and go to the play park."

Samara nodded as she held on to Emily's hand and stopped her camera bag slipping off the other shoulder as the little girl jiggled and danced on the spot.

"I think the train ride would be good." She looked back at Adam. "Any other suggestions?"

Adam held up his hand where he already had a camera open and was fitting a huge lens onto it. "I'm just following along." He nodded to Rick. "You're in charge."

"Okay." Rick took hold of Emily's other hand so that she let go of Samara. "I'll do child patrol while you concentrate on the pictures you want."

He led the way to the miniature red train and sat Toby next to him, with Emily and Anna in the next seat. Samara sat down and Adam swung in behind her.

"Do you mind if I make a few suggestions to start with?" Adam leaned forward and she felt her skin tingle slightly as he spoke close by her ear. Without thinking she glanced up at Rick, but he was busy pointing out something that was making the girls giggle.

"Anything at all." She picked up the camera hanging around her neck. "I'm ready."

"Okay, well like Rick said, watch the children and get their reactions before we visit the animals. I heard them telling you their favorites in the van, so work on those but also think about what kept you spellbound as a child . . . or even now. If you're fascinated, they'll be fascinated." He rested his elbow on the back of her seat. "What was your favorite animal when you were little?"

"Umm . . ." Samara tried to focus on the question. "Probably the kangaroo. I wasn't into cute and cuddly koalas . . . the kangaroo seemed more adventurous."

"Heading away across the outback?" Adam laughed, and she saw Rick look back toward them. "A bit like your father."

"A bit," Samara answered and looked down at her camera. "What else should I be thinking about?"

"Okay . . . children are natural actors, so let them perform—act like the animals or whatever. Don't push them into the shot that you think will look best."

"But there are certain shots that I've had in my mind for the exhibition." Samara frowned. "Shouldn't I be trying for them?"

"You can try for them but be aware that you might get a much better shot while you're waiting for the other." Adam rubbed his beard. "It's the serendipity concept. You know what you want in the long term but you need to be aware of what you might gain along the way." He leaned back against his seat. "You don't want to miss out on your best shot just because you're looking for something else."

There was something in the tone of his voice that made Samara look up quickly. He was watching her closely and she felt the color rise in her cheeks.

"Umm . . . so I let them get really engrossed in the animals first?" She looked down so her hair swung over her hot cheeks. "Then I watch for the shot I want but make sure I get lots of others along the way."

Adam nodded. "Try and see what the children see and not what you want them to." He pointed to the front as the train jolted and began to move forward. "I'll keep an eye out to see if I think you're missing anything."

She was grateful to turn and concentrate on the children as the train began to move around the roadways through the sanctuary. As they passed the different enclosures, she watched their growing excitement as they pointed and called out to each other, even though they were sitting right next to each other. She watched Rick leaning down and pointing and laughing as they responded. She smiled as Toby grabbed Rick's face between his hands and directed him to look up at something in the trees.

"Is your camera ready?" Adam spoke quietly behind her.

"Oh . . . no, I was waiting until the animals . . ." She pointed out at the enclosures but he interrupted her.

"Always be ready so you don't miss the important shots." He held up his camera. "There've been some beauties already."

Samara felt slightly chastised as she pulled the lens cap off her camera. Her hand shook slightly as she adjusted the settings.

You don't want to miss out on your best shot just because you're looking for something else.

She focused the camera on the children and began to watch their faces and actions more intently as Adam's words repeated in her mind.

* * *

"So how's it going?" Rick spoke beside her as Samara knelt to get a better view of Anna holding a large, gray wombat. The little girl was sitting on a low bench and had pulled the plump, hairy animal onto her lap with her arms secured tightly around its middle.

"Anna thinks she has a new baby." Samara smiled behind the camera as she focused on Anna, watching as the little girl's face crinkled when the wombat's tiny pointed ear twitched and tickled her nose.

"So does Emily." Rick chuckled as Emily leaned close to Anna and stroked the wombat's soft fur. She seemed mesmerized by the animal and suddenly planted a tiny kiss on the it's cheek. The animal turned and looked at her, and Emily's hand instinctively came up and touched its face. Samara moved slightly and her finger pressed downwards several times as she gave a small moan of delight.

"Oh, that was gorgeous." She looked up at Rick and her face was radiant. "Adam was right. I was looking at one thing and an even better thing was happening right beside it." She smiled at him. "Thank you for seeing that."

"Hey, happy to help." Rick grinned and shrugged. "Do you want to cuddle a koala now? That wombat's looking bored with all the female attention."

The koala seemed no less impressed with the children's embraces, but Emily seemed to be existing in a state of continual loving as she closed her eyes and cuddled her face against the koala's soft, gray fur. When it placed its paw on her shoulder, she smiled blissfully.

"It loves me," She crooned against its head as it lifted its wide, flat nose in the air. She looked up at Rick, who was standing beside her keeping a watchful eye on the animal. "I think it really loves me."

Samara felt a lump form in her throat as Rick leaned down and stroked the koala's ear. "I think it loves you too, Emily."

The child smiled and gave the koala another squeeze before it started to protest, and Rick took it quickly. Almost immediately, the koala looked up into his face and rested its paws against his shoulders as it touched its nose up against his.

"It loves you, too, Rick!" Emily squealed and clapped her hands in delight. "It's kissing you!"

"I'm just kissable." Rick deliberately crossed his eyes as he peered down at the koala. Then he lifted it up to rest in a nearby tree and grinned straight at Samara. "I just have a hard time convincing anybody else."

"Or anything else." She corrected with a smile as she took Emily's hand. "Shall we see if Rick can get a snake to kiss him now?"

Toby was beside himself with excitement as he watched Rick lift a large snake up around his shoulders and let the reptile ease its way around his neck.

"Feel it, Toby." Rick held the snake's body out on his hand. "Is it hot or cold?"

Suddenly tentative, Toby reached one hand out and touched the smooth, scaly skin. The snake moved slightly and Toby whipped his hand back against his chest.

"It's scary." Toby frowned up at his brother. "I think you should put it down, Rick."

"But Rick promised me he would kiss the snake." Samara lowered the camera. She knew she was taunting him, but it seemed to fit the lighthearted mood that had developed between them.

"Ah, but I only kiss ladies . . . and this is a man snake. It wouldn't be right." Rick grinned as he eased the snake's head toward her. "Maybe you should do the honors."

Samara stared at the reptile's face as it moved upward, and then she backed up quickly, putting the camera up in front of her. She stumbled slightly as she stepped back and immediately felt a strong hand grasp her elbow to steady her.

"So, what's going on in the snake den?" Adam spoke beside her as he released her arm, but once again she could feel the tingle on her skin where he had touched her. She coughed quickly and pointed back at Rick.

"The animals are under control but I'm not sure about the keepers." She straightened the bottom of her shirt and adjusted the camera hanging around her neck. "Maybe we should visit the kangaroos before we lose too much light."

* * *

"So which animal did you like the most, Anna?" Rick asked the question as he set a tray of hamburgers down on the table in the restaurant. Samara followed behind with packets of fries, and Adam balanced a tray of drinks as the three children slid themselves along the semicircular seat of the cubicle. As they settled in, both men stood back at either side of the seat to let Samara in first. She felt the blood rush to her cheeks as she fought instant feelings of indecision and pretended to make a fuss of getting her bag off her shoulder.

"Sit by me, Sam!" Toby moved a few inches as if to make room for her and she moved forward immediately, as if he were the deciding factor, brushing past Rick as he stood to the side.

"You all did very well, today." She began talking as soon as she sat down, pushing the bag along with her feet and ignoring Rick sitting down beside her. It was a reasonably tight fit with them all around the seat, and Rick sat slightly to the side with his arm along the seat behind her as she handed out the burgers and fries. Adam sat on the other side, making sure everybody got their chosen drink. "I feel really happy with all the photos."

"Can we see them, Sister Danes?" Anna asked as she delicately nibbled her way through a single fry.

"Yeth, can we thow our mumth?" Emily was trying to negotiate her hamburger but the gap in her teeth was still a novelty, and she giggled as she bit into the bread and nudged Toby to show him the bite marks. He responded by taking a giant bite and making loud chewing noises so that the girls giggled more.

"Easy does it, Toby." Rick leaned across behind Samara and touched his little brother on the shoulder. "Remember you're in the company of ladies."

Samara smiled as Toby chewed once and swallowed the huge mouthful in one gulp. "Sorr . . ." He looked up at Rick and began to cough as the food stuck, then his eyes grew wide as he began to choke. In a second he was fighting for air with his little hands hitting the table.

Samara felt Rick's body against her as he stood and lifted Toby bodily out of his seat and held him over his arm and began to hit his back. As the coughing lessened he stood him on the seat and lifted his arm up until Toby was drawing in deep gulps of air.

"Are you okay, Toby?" Emily's blue eyes had tears rimming them as she watched.

"Mmm." Toby nodded, then gasped as his breath caught again and he began to cough rapidly. Rick slid quickly into the seat beside him and repeated the arm movement and gently rubbed his back until the fit subsided. This time Toby leaned weakly against his brother's chest, breathing in through his nose with his eyes closed. His spiked blond hair was almost the same color as his pale face.

Samara looked up at Rick as he cuddled his little brother tightly against him, and she saw the concern in his eyes. She moved closer and reached out to pat Toby's leg but found her hand covered by Rick's as he drew her up against them both and kept her hand under his. Toby kept his eyes shut as he turned his head to lean against Samara's shoulder. She responded by resting her cheek against his head and within seconds she could feel his body relax against her and his breathing become more regular.

"Will he be all right?" Anna was still nibbling on her fries but her eyes were big with concern. "Can he breathe?"

"He'll be fine." Rick gently squeezed Samara's hand as she straightened up. Toby opened his eyes and coughed once more. Then he rubbed his face with his hand and looked down at the table.

"Oh no!" He reached out to pick up his burger. "It's cold!"

"Then maybe you'll eat it more slowly." Rick gave Samara's hand another squeeze as he moved to give Toby room. He didn't look at her, but she found the gesture oddly comforting, and her hand felt cold as he released it. Very quickly she turned her fingers upward and gave his hand another squeeze back. This time she looked up and saw him watching her over Toby's head and felt his hand respond. It was the briefest touch but it seemed to match the warmth in his eyes. And then he let go.

"It's not too bad." Toby took a much smaller bite of his burger and chewed carefully as he pointed to Rick's meal. "You can still eat it warm."

Samara laughed along with the others and looked over at Adam. In the last few minutes she had completely forgotten about him, but he didn't seem to notice as he turned his attention to Rick.

"You handled that well." He gestured toward Toby. "Almost like a professional medic."

Rick shook his head as he finished his mouthful. "Not really a professional medic . . . more like professional brother." He nudged Toby with his elbow. "This fellow's had a reflux problem since he was a baby. As soon as he gets excited his air passage seems to shut down, so we have to get things working again."

"I'm not as bad as Lisa." Toby put up his hand as he spoke. "She really stops breathing."

"My little sister gets asthma." Rick explained easily as he took a drink. Then he grinned. "The other siblings are pretty normal."

Adam watched him as he toyed with the paper around his burger. He shook his head. "That's something I've never had." He gestured between Rick and Toby. "Sibling interaction." He shrugged. "Or family interaction, for that matter."

"You don't have a family?" Emily frowned.

"How can you not have a family?" Anna stared at Adam. "Everyone has a family."

"Not necessarily." Adam tapped one finger on the table. "I was my parents' only child and they died when I was quite young."

"How old were you?" Samara felt her food stick in her throat.

"Sixteen." Adam nodded. "Young enough to miss them but old enough to not have anybody want the responsibility of me."

"So you've been on your own since you were sixteen?"

"Technically." Adam nodded. "But realistically . . . well before that. My father worked away from home a lot and my mother chose not to be part of the real world."

Samara stared as he caught her eye and inclined his head slightly toward her. No wonder he could relate to her family. It must have felt like his own childhood.

"Have you got children?" Emily put down her burger and held up six fingers. "We have thix in our family."

Adam smiled as he shook his head. "No, I don't have any children."

"Are you married?" Anna stared up at him.

"No, I'm not married, either." He smiled and raised one eyebrow. "But it was nice of you to ask."

"You should be married." Anna persisted. "In the temple," she added for good measure and began to open the paper surrounding her burger.

"Anna, your food will be really cold now." Samara felt a need to change the subject.

"That's okay, I like it cold." The little girl bobbed her head happily before she looked up at Adam again. "And it's okay because you can still be married in the temple and . . ." She pointed to her chest. "You can still have children because my mum is old like you and she just had a baby."

There was a long silence where Samara didn't know whether to laugh or cry as Adam stared down at Anna. It was difficult to read the expression on his face, and Samara found herself wishing he would look up and wink to show that he thought everything was all right. Then she watched his long, slender fingers as they rolled the edge of the napkin back and forth.

"Isn't it amazing the things kids come out with?" Rick suddenly spoke and began to stack the empty cartons and papers onto one tray. "I'm sure I wasn't as aware of things when I was 'thix.'" He deliberately lisped so that Emily looked up and giggled. Toby joined in straightaway and the three children were soon all laughing.

Samara looked at her watch and began to help tidy up.

"My goodness, I didn't realize the time. We need to get you all home. Then I have some serious work to do in the darkroom."

"How can you do any work in a dark room?" Toby looked puzzled. "You won't be able to see."

Samara smiled as she stood up and ushered him in front of her. "I do have a light but it has to be mostly dark so I can develop the photos."

"How do you develop photos?" Anna spoke precisely. "My mum goes to the shops and gets our photos out of the machine."

Samara picked up her camera bag and patted it. "I use a camera that uses different film. I have to develop the film so that I can get good black-and-white pictures."

"But why do you want black-and-white pictures?" Anna pulled at the sleeve of her pink T-shirt. "Why aren't they colored?"

Samara opened her mouth to answer, but she shut it again and shook her head.

Adam grinned as he helped Anna out of her seat.

"Why don't you wait and see the pictures?" he quickly suggested as she opened her mouth and frowned at the same time, looking as if she were going to ask another question.

"Answer a question with a question." Rick grinned as he kept his hand on Toby's shoulder. "I remember my mother doing that to me. I could never think what to say."

"Then let's go quickly while it still works." Adam smiled at Samara and bowed slightly to allow her to pass with Emily and Anna.

* * *

They dropped both of the girls off at their homes, and within minutes of waving good-bye to Emily, Toby had curled up with his head in Samara's lap and drifted off to sleep. After the children's constant chatter and giggling, the van seemed suddenly silent. Even Adam and Rick only spoke occasionally as they neared the motel, and their voices were quieter from not having to speak above the noise.

Rick pulled the van up outside the reception area and jumped out to open Samara's door. She got up carefully, easing Toby down onto the seat where he continued snoring peacefully.

"Someone's exhausted." Rick smiled as he held out a hand to help her out of the van. Samara hesitated, then she took his hand firmly and quickly stepped out.

"I am," she offered, although she knew he was talking about Toby. "I've never heard so many questions in so short a time, and my eyes are worn out from darting everywhere to make sure I got all the shots I could." She pretended to frown at Adam as he came to stand beside them. "I'll have you to blame for that. I'm paranoid about missing the unexpected now."

"You'll get used to it." Adam answered easily as he held out his hand to Rick. "Thanks, Rick. I really enjoyed myself."

Rick nodded thoughtfully as he shook the other man's hand.

"Same. I'm glad I got to know you." He pointed at Samara's camera bag. "I reckon I understand a lot more about photography now. It was interesting to watch you two in action."

Samara stared at the van's door handle as he spoke. Was he referring to just the photography? She suddenly remembered several times during the afternoon when Adam had been showing her different camera techniques and she had looked up to see Rick watching them. Her cheeks grew warm and she quickly turned toward the motel.

"It has been great, Rick. Thank you so much." She smiled brightly. "I'll see you . . . sometime."

"What about the young adult bowling activity on Friday night?" Rick slowly closed the van door so that it clicked shut.

"Umm . . ." Samara tried not to glance at Adam as she straightened the strap on her shoulder. "Maybe. I'll see how this project works out, first." She looked over Rick's shoulder. "Adam said he'll give me a hand with the developing, so I may get finished early."

Rick nodded slowly, then raised a hand in a brief salute as he walked to the driver's seat.

"Then I'll see you around. Good luck with the assignment." He climbed into the van and started the engine. "Bye, Adam."

Samara didn't stop to watch the van turn and go down the driveway, and she was already in the reception area when Adam caught up in a few long strides. They walked into the lounge in silence, but Samara stopped short by the door.

"I'm sorry . . . I . . . ." She turned her head almost into Adam's shoulder as he was right behind her and then looked back again as Terry and Jackie quickly moved apart where they'd been sitting on the couch. "We didn't mean to interrupt anything."

She watched in disbelief as Terry casually draped his arm along the couch behind Jackie's shoulders and smiled.

"You're not, now."

CHAPTER ELEVEN

"So, how was the picture taking at Currumbin?" Jackie asked casually as she watched Samara cutting up some vegetables. The knife was fairly flying through slices of cucumber and strips of carrot.

"Very busy." Samara concentrated on cutting the ends off another carrot. "Though not quite as busy as you've been, by the looks of it."

Jackie leaned forward and helped herself to a piece of carrot. She took a small bite and pointed the carrot at Samara.

"Would you like to look at me before you kill that carrot? I can't quite tell if you're smiling or not."

Samara paused and looked up. She took a deep breath then pointed the knife at Jackie.

"I'm sort of smiling . . . but it's kind of mixed with a surprised frown."

"Well, put the knife down when you say that and I'll explain." Jackie gingerly touched the tip of the knife blade and turned it away.

"You don't need to explain anything." Samara did smile as she finished slicing the carrot. "You and Terry . . . together . . . on our couch." She waved the knife again.

"Would you put the knife down?" Jackie grinned. "I'll feel a lot more comfortable."

"You looked very comfortable a little while ago." Samara put the knife down and looked straight at her friend. Then she began to laugh. "I wonder whose face looked the funniest when I walked in."

"Definitely yours." Jackie munched on the carrot. "Your mouth was so wide open—and then you turn and run right into Adam."

"Yes, but your eyes were huge!" Samara smiled. "Almost as huge as Terry's grin."

"He was . . . ?" Jackie's cheeks began to flush with color and she shook her head. "I can't quite believe it's happening."

"So what did happen?" Samara stacked the vegetables on a plate. "You didn't mention anything about coming over tonight."

Jackie shrugged as she sat down on one of the chairs. "Terry came over this afternoon when I got back from school. He said he wanted to apologize for the way he's been behaving. He started to get a bit emotional, so I suggested we walk over to the beach."

Samara nodded. "And . . . ?"

"And we walked for ages and talked about so many things." Jackie took a deep breath. "We even started reminiscing about all the things we've been doing over the years . . . all of us."

"Well, thank you for remembering me." Samara opened a container of dip and set it on the plate beside the vegetables. "And what else?"

"Well, it was just so good to have the old Terry back . . . only better. It's like he was catching up. Anyway, we kept walking and then we—well, Terry held my hand." Jackie rolled her eyes. "And we kept on walking . . ."

"And talking." Samara nodded.

"And then we came back here." Jackie smiled, then she shook her head. "And then Terry's sister barged in and ruined what could have been a beautiful moment."

Samara stared, then she began to laugh. "No! Did I really? I'm so sorry."

"That's okay." Jackie leaned forward and picked up the plate. "But now you need to tell me how it went with the two men in your life."

Samara wiped up the food scraps and pushed them down the disposal before she answered.

"They were both delightful. Rick was the perfect guide and child minder while I was taking pictures. Adam was the perfect tutor and made sure I got all the best shots, and they both got on . . . perfectly."

"And what about you?" Jackie dipped a slice of cucumber.

"Me . . . ?" Samara sighed as she walked toward the door. "I'm exactly where I was this morning, but with a whole lot more pictures."

Terry was still sitting on the couch and Adam was in the chair opposite when the girls walked in from the kitchen. Terry moved slightly to indicate that Jackie should sit beside him. For the first time in months Samara noticed that the slow grin and deepening dimple she had always loved were evident on his face. Even his eyes seemed clearer as he watched the two girls.

"Adam's been telling me about some of your sanctuary adventures today." He frowned. "I can't remember the last time I went down to Currumbin. It must be over five years ago."

"Well, you should go." Adam slid his hands into his pockets as he stretched his legs out in front of him. "It'd make a great place to go on a date."

Jackie smiled shyly as Terry grinned.

"I'll mention that to Mum and Dad." He glanced at Samara as she suddenly looked around. "They've gone out . . . on a date."

"A date?" She stared at her brother. "A date? Mum and Dad?"

"I know. Hard to believe. But when we got home there was a note from them on the table and that relief lady on reception." Terry shook his head. "They just said they'll be back late."

* * *

"Hi . . . Are you there?" Samara poked her head in through the kitchen doorway at Sister Patterson's house. After spending some time with Terry and Jackie, she and Adam had decided to do some film processing that evening. A quick phone call had shown Sister Patterson to be true to her word about Samara being able to come over anytime. It was nearly eight thirty when she knocked on the door.

"Hello, dear. Come on in." Sister Patterson put down a bowl of cookie dough she was mixing and wiped her hands on a towel. "I've been expecting you."

Samara walked in with Adam close behind, and as he closed the door Sister Patterson held her hand out toward him.

"And you must be Brother Russell. Tracey has been telling me all about you."

Adam looked surprised as he shook her hand, but Sister Patterson didn't seem to notice.

"Have you come to help Samara with her photos?" she gestured behind her in the direction of the darkroom. "I guess you have, so I'll have to surrender my seat in the darkroom for this session, but that's all right. I'll have a nice batch of cookies ready for you when you've finished."

"You didn't tell me your darkroom came with cookies." Samara smiled. "You may have to come and knock on the door to remind us to eat." She lifted her camera. "We have a heap of work to do."

"Well, you just tell me when you want them and I'll come knocking," Sister Patterson said as she led the way down the hallway and stopped by the garage door. "I'll leave you two to find your way out there."

Samara led the way through the garage and found the light switch, and Adam whistled quietly as he looked around the small room when the light came on.

"Brother Patterson was a very keen amateur." He walked to the bench and gently touched some of the equipment. "This is good stuff."

"I know." Samara nodded as she put her bag down and began to pull some trays out from under the bench. "I studied all about setting up a darkroom, and all the time I was wondering how I could ever get all my own equipment. And suddenly . . . here it was." She smiled. "A testimony to visiting teaching and the power of prayer."

Adam nodded as he sat down on the stool and watched her get the equipment ready. As she set some trays on the bench she stopped and tapped the black plastic with her fingers. It was unnerving to think that he would simply sit and watch her, especially in a small, dark room. She took a deep breath and turned to him.

"You know, I'm trying to look all efficient here and I do think I know what I'm doing but do you think you could . . . advise me as I go—like describe the routine so I know that I'm doing the right thing."

"Sure." Adam leaned forward and rested his hands on his thighs. "You're doing just fine so far."

Samara looked down at the two plastic trays and began to laugh. She'd felt such a mixture of emotions as they'd driven over to Sister Patterson's . . . anticipation at working professionally with Adam and complete nervousness at the thought of being in a confined space with him. She shook her head and put her hand to her cheek.

"Now I feel like an idiot."

"Don't . . . that can come later when I tell you off for doing something wrong." Adam stood up and lifted some bottles down from the shelf where she'd stored them. He studied the labels and set them on the bench as he turned toward her, but a fit of coughing suddenly stopped him. As the coughing finally eased, he shook his head and cleared his throat. "We don't have much time and there's so much I want to show you."

There was something so serious in the tone of his voice that Samara felt her breathing become unsteady as he leaned toward her. She lowered her eyelids to stare at the floor as he brushed against her shoulder.

"Let's start with getting the film ready." He picked up her bag and pulled out the camera. "I'm looking forward to seeing these shots."

It took several minutes for Samara to fight the desire to laugh as Adam busied himself with organizing the developer and a tray with a siphon. She had been expecting some sort of physical contact, but he was all business as he kept up a running commentary on what he was doing. "Did you get that part?"

She could barely make out the shape of his head in the darkness but she knew he was looking at her. "I'm sorry . . . yes." She repeated the quantities he had just listed as she prepared some sheets for printing.

"So how long should you process it for the best effect?" Adam leaned back against the bench.

"I watch for the tonal qualities. If the tones of gray are too close there's not enough contrast." She tried to keep the questioning sound out of her voice. "I want more contrast, although shades of gray can heighten the intensity if they're used well," she finished more definitely and confidently. "I think I got some really good pictures with Toby in his dark shirt against the dark background of the building with his blond hair and the really pale koala."

"And the afternoon light was good then as well." She could see Adam nod. "Let's start with those ones."

They continued to work, and as the professional influence of Adam's advice began to become apparent in the trial prints, Samara began to feel a growing awareness of the nature of tuition she was receiving.

"I feel like I've stepped up to a whole new level of awareness." She carefully studied a print with a magnifier. "I never noticed things like this at school."

"I said you had good perception." Adam washed another print in the tray until the image began to appear. "Not just with taking the photos but also in developing them. I really think your exhibition will be a winner. You have a definite gift for this."

Samara swallowed hard as she listened to his comments, and as she stared hard at the bench, the outline began to blur. Suddenly she was a fourteen-year-old girl again, standing on a beach with a total stranger, asking him to teach her how to take photographs. She thought about the journey from that point, fighting against her family's negative response to her dream, the hours of work saving for her camera and equipment—all the time hearing Adam's voice in the back of her mind, patiently explaining what would make the finest picture. And now he was standing beside her, still patiently explaining . . . but she wasn't fourteen any longer.

She smiled to herself in the darkness and quickly wiped the moisture from her eyes.

"Sam?" His voice was very quiet in the darkness. "Are you all right?"

"I'm fine." She sniffed slightly. "These chemicals work havoc with my sinuses at times."

There was a long silence, and she fought to keep her lips from quivering.

"Where were you just now?"

Samara pressed her fingers to her eyebrows and took a deep breath before she answered.

"Just now?" She smiled and looked directly at him. "Just now I was back on a beach in New Zealand with a kind stranger, asking him to show me how to take photographs."

"That's funny." He almost chuckled. "The way I remember it—I asked you to pose for a picture and you demanded photography lessons in return."

"It was lots of pictures." She responded immediately and felt a smile forming. "And I'm sure I didn't demand. I was a polite child."

"You were . . . very polite." He nodded. "But you were also very determined. I think you would have kept me there forever asking questions."

Samara shook her head slowly. "I wanted it to last forever." She rolled her tongue over her bottom lip. "You made me feel so . . . special. I'd never been treated like that before."

There was another silence, and she heard the swift intake of breath as Adam turned to the bench. "Neither had I." She heard his voice break slightly and he coughed. "You gave me so much more than I gave you, young Samara. You hung on every word I said and made me feel important, and nobody had ever done that for me. Then you shared your testimony, and it was so sweet and simple that I wanted to feel the same way." He hesitated. "You gave me an image that has kept me going for years . . . through lots of hard times."

"About three thousand days of hard times." She murmured quietly.

"Three thou . . . ?" She heard the question in his voice, and then he gave a short laugh. "I get it. Has it only been that long?"

She took courage from his tone.

"Probably three thousand and three, but the last three have been about dreams coming true."

She could almost feel the silence.

"I take it you mean that your father is recognizing your dream."

Samara stared into the darkness beyond his shoulder.

"Actually, I meant the dream of you seeing you again."

There was a longer silence and she felt her throat begin to dry.

"Then let's hope the dream doesn't become a nightmare." Adam's voice was gentle in the darkness.

* * *

Somehow she managed to act normally as they tidied up the darkroom and put the prints out to dry. She stood and studied the prints one more time as Adam put the last of the trays under the bench.

"You've done well." He spoke behind her and she tried not to react as her heart beat faster. "You can see a real difference from those first shots to these last ones."

"I think I was enjoying myself as much as the children by then." Samara folded her arms and hunched her shoulders. "And I wasn't so scared of doing the wrong thing."

"You mean you were more confident of doing the right thing." Adam pointed to the picture of Emily kissing the wombat. "I really like this one. You've captured the wonder in her face."

"She thinks all of the animals love her now." Samara smiled as she mimicked the little girl. "They really, really love me."

"That's a good way to be. Imagine how much happier we'd all be if we thought everybody loved us." Adam bent to pick up his bag.

"Perhaps." Samara didn't look at him as she opened the door and blinked at the sudden light hitting her eyes.

"Well, hello . . . isn't that perfect timing!" Sister Patterson stood on the other side of the door holding a plate of cookies. "I was just going to knock and leave these outside for you. Peter used to get so upset if I didn't knock first, but he'd forget to eat as well once he got inside that room."

"Photography has a habit of doing that to people." Adam responded easily as he walked out behind Samara and helped himself to a cookie. "That's why people like us rely on people like you to keep us grounded." He chewed and nodded. "And well fed. These are really good."

"Oh, well . . . anytime." Sister Patterson waved a hand but Samara could tell she was delighted with the compliment.

"We've finished the first round, but I'll need to come back tomorrow, if that's all right." Samara took a cookie. "It shouldn't take as long."

"You take as long as you like, dear." Sister Patterson turned to lead the way upstairs. "It feels good to have someone else around, even if you're locked away downstairs in a little room." She hesitated. "It's funny . . . I never thought about being lonely when Peter was alive. It just . . . sneaks up on you. That's why I think you should fill your lives with people and things you love." She turned and reached out to pat Samara's hand. "And that's why I enjoy you being here."

She gave them both a warm hug as they left, handing Adam a plastic bag filled with more cookies and waving at the kitchen door until they reached the end of the driveway.

"She's a delightful lady." Adam murmured as he stopped waving. "I like her philosophy."

"Fill your life with people and things that you love." Samara clasped her hands behind her back as they walked. "I see a future filled with cameras and photos."

"No people?" Adam stared straight ahead.

She lifted her face to the sky, then shook her head. "Not many. Cameras and photos don't hurt you."

"Samara . . ." Adam stopped and briefly touched her arm. "Don't make the mistake of blocking people out . . . no matter what they've done to you." He started walking again with his hands in his pockets. "Photographs make cold companions."

Chapter Twelve

The hands on the classroom's clock seemed to take forever to reach two, and what was usually her favorite class seemed interminable. Even her favorite lecturer failed to say anything enlightening, and Samara was the first out of the door whereas she usually lingered to help tidy up while she waited for Jackie. She checked her watch as she ran for the bus, knowing this earlier ride would get her home nearly an hour sooner than going in the car.

"Please, please, still be there." She talked out loud to the bus as she ran down the pathway and made a final burst of effort as she saw the bus signaling to pull out.

"You just made it." The bus driver grinned as Samara panted, climbed the steps, and made her way to the back of the bus. She chose a seat where she could sit next to the window and where she knew she wouldn't have to talk to anyone else.

It took a minute before her breathing calmed. Then she sat back and rested her arms on her bag and let the rocking motion of the bus soothe her as it traveled down the highway.

Although her body felt tired, her mind was still racing as it had all through the night and through her classes. Samara smiled slightly as she tried to remember anything that she'd been taught this morning, but there seemed to be a void. She leaned her head against the window and the motion of the bus seemed to intensify, the noises sounding more strongly in her head so that it was peacefully numbing. She felt herself drifting and it was pleasant, like riding on a cloud.

Anytime sleep had tried to sneak up on her during the night, a sudden vision of Adam and of being close to him would waken her and start her thinking again. As she relaxed now, the same image suddenly filled her mind and pulled her back from the haven of sleep.

"Don't even try and sleep." Samara muttered to herself as she shifted on the seat and stared out of the window at the endless gray and yellowish orange of the highway scenery, a perfect backdrop to her thoughts.

They had walked the rest of the way home in silence last night, going past the reception area to the back kitchen door before he stopped and stood staring at the ground. It was Samara who had spoken first.

"Thank you for helping me, Adam." She had felt a surprising surge of emotion as he'd looked at her. "For helping me discover a new world."

He'd stood a long time, then with his hands in his pockets he'd leaned forward and kissed her very gently on the forehead.

"Thanks for being part of my journey, Sam. Thanks for making it worthwhile."

Then he'd walked to his motel unit, turning at the door and raising a hand in a brief salute. She hadn't seen him again before Jackie picked her up for school in the morning.

* * *

"What do you mean, 'they've gone'?" Samara stared at her mother in disbelief. "How can they just be gone?"

"They've gone . . . on an urgent trip up to Cairns." Tracey tapped a single key on the computer. "The trucking company called your father this morning, just after you left. One of the drivers came down sick and they had to get a load up there quickly."

"And Adam went too?" Samara tried to keep the disappointment out of her voice.

"He seemed eager to go." Tracey glanced at her daughter. "In fact, he suggested it." She shrugged. "I guess he's used to being on the move. He was ready to go with your father in less than twenty minutes."

"So . . . how long are they going for?" Samara looked across at the large desk calendar in front of her mother.

"About four or five days." Tracey pointed at a date, then she pointed at another earlier date. "But something else has cropped up in the meantime. I got an e-mail this morning from your Auntie Nan in New Zealand."

Samara stared at the calendar while her mother talked, then she slowly looked up at her.

"Pardon?"

"Your Auntie Nan . . . my big sister." Tracey put her hand to her chest. "She's coming over for a visit in a few days."

"Why?" Samara frowned. "I thought you two didn't get along that well."

She watched her mother's cheeks color slightly.

"It's not that we don't get on . . . we just haven't seen a lot of each other . . . for many years."

"About twenty years." Samara put in quickly.

"But we've always kept in touch." Tracey started to draw the tiny boxes on the desk pad. "And we've had the children come and stay. You loved it when Meredith came over a couple of years ago."

"*You* loved it." Samara knew she sounded irritable. "You had her cleaning the motel units after the second day."

She ignored the hurt look on her mother's face.

"I couldn't help the cleaner getting ill and Meredith being happy to help. She said it made a good change after all the university studies."

"What else could she say, Mum?" Samara sighed as she picked up her bag, but she stopped as the tears began to flow down her mother's cheeks. For a second she battled with her own feelings, then she put down the bag and walked behind the desk to her mother's side. "I'm sorry, Mum. I guess I'm in a bit of a mood. I'm really happy that Auntie Nan is coming over."

She tentatively put her arm around her mother's shoulders and immediately felt her relax, although the tears flowed more freely. After several minutes, her mother drew back and wiped her eyes.

"My goodness . . . I'm sorry I'm such a cry baby." She dabbed at the corners of her eyes. "I'm trying to cut down on my tablets and I think it's taking its toll."

"Or maybe you are just pleased that Auntie Nan is coming." Samara tried to be comforting, but her mother shook her head as she put her face between her hands.

"A little bit pleased . . ." She shivered. "But mainly terrified."

"Terrified?" Samara stared at her mother. "Why would you be terrified of Auntie Nan?"

"Oh, I don't know. I mean, she's lovely . . . and kind and clever and spiritual." Tracey ran her finger over the pen imprints on the desk pad. "And she's married to a wonderful man who's a bishop and they have four lovely children and two of them are on their missions . . ." She looked up. "Shall I go on?"

Samara shook her head slowly. "I think I'm getting the picture, but . . ." She frowned. "I had no idea you felt like that. You always like to hear from her, and her Christmas card always goes up first."

"That's because she always sends one first." Tracey smiled weakly. "I forgot to mention organized, didn't I." She turned and pointed to the lounge. "Can we talk for a bit? I think there's some things I need to tell you."

Samara had to fight the immediate desire to refuse her mother and go straight to her room. There were too many other thoughts crowding her mind, not the least of which was the fact that she had been anticipating seeing Adam all day and now he was gone, without a word, and she had no idea when she would see him again.

"Mum, I . . ."

"Please, Samara." Tracey's voice had a quietly urgent edge to it, making Samara look more closely at the expression on her mother's face. She hesitated briefly before she nodded and led the way into the lounge, she was about to sit down at the table, but her mother stopped her and pointed at the couch.

"Come and sit with me."

They sat silently on the couch and Samara waited for her mother to say something, but it was several minutes before Tracey finally spoke, her hands clasped tightly in front of her.

"Nan is eight years older than me and I always looked up to her so much. She practically was my mother when I was growing up . . . not that Mum wasn't there, but Nan simply took over looking after me. We shared a room and she was the first person I saw in the morning and the last person before I went to sleep at night."

She leaned forward and took a deep breath.

"I always wanted to do the right thing because Nan always did . . . it just seemed the natural thing to do." She bit her lip. "I loved going to church because Nan loved going to church. I had a testimony because Nan had a testimony."

Samara watched her mother's hands clench and unclench, and she felt her own stomach tightening into a knot as Tracey kept talking.

"When Nan got married, I was her only bridesmaid, and when we went up to stay at the temple motel the night before the wedding, we went for a walk and she asked me to promise that I would marry there as well." Her voice caught. "And I did promise . . . her and myself."

A large tear slid down her cheek and she slowly shook her head.

"When I was nineteen I decided to come to Australia and have my big overseas experience. I came with a friend from university and we had a great time, but . . . she wasn't a member of the Church, and we started going places that weren't quite where I knew I should be."

"And you met Dad?" Samara could barely move as she watched her mother nod her head.

"We went to a rugby game with some boys we'd met and . . ." Her lips twitched in a smile. "It was very romantic . . . your father ran up to the sideline to throw in the ball from the lineout, and I was standing there . . . and he looked straight at me." She stared straight ahead. "It seemed like for the longest time he just looked, and then he winked . . . right at me."

"I presume he threw the ball." Samara tried to make the comment light but she felt her voice tremble.

"Oh, yes . . . and they won . . . and he invited me to the party afterwards . . . and a barbecue the next day . . . which just happened to be Sunday."

"And you didn't go to church." It was more of a statement than a question and Tracey nodded.

"That week . . . or the next. He just made everything so much fun and nobody knew that I wasn't going to church." She spread her hands out. "My friend had hooked up with another couple of guys and headed up north, and so I stayed near your father . . ." She hesitated and took a deep breath, but Samara spoke first.

"Because he was Terry's father by then."

She watched her mother's eyes close as she nodded.

"When I knew I was pregnant I knew I couldn't go home. Your father was good in that he said we would get married. It wasn't that he didn't love me and wouldn't support me . . . so I simply wrote to my family and said I was getting married. We got married in a registry office in Sydney and moved to Alice Springs because your dad could drive the trucks and earn more money. He was determined to look after us."

"That was nice of him." Samara commented dryly as she studied the pattern on the carpet. "And he came back every now and then to check on you . . . and have me."

"Samara . . . we loved each other . . . and we still do." Tracey turned to her daughter. "It's just a . . ."

"Different sort of love." Samara interrupted as she sat back and rested her head against the back of the couch. "So that's why you've never gone back to New Zealand or gone to see your parents or your sister. You were too ashamed."

Tracey clenched her jaw. "Once I separated myself from them it was easier to keep it that way . . . and I was busy looking after you children and then the motel." She ran her hand through her hair. "And it's not like I've broken all ties. Your grandparents have come over a few times. They were here when you were baptized."

"But my father wasn't," Samara murmured as she sighed. "We're not exactly a regular family, are we? I can see why you wouldn't feel good about seeing Auntie Nan again."

"It's not that I don't feel good anymore." Tracey frowned. "It's just knowing how to . . . break the silence. I've been trying to think of a way since I started going back to church . . . even praying."

Samara was silent as Tracey began to nervously pleat the material of her skirt, then she leaned forward and rested her head in her hands.

"You've never lost your testimony have you, Mum . . . of the gospel?"

"No, never." Tracey's answer was quiet but quick. "All these years . . . I've worshipped in my own way and with you children . . . I was determined that you would at least have the gospel like I had when I was a child. You have to give your father credit that he has supported me in that." She reached out and put her hand over Samara's. "You have no idea how wonderful it's been to see you grow up and develop your own testimony. You've been my example." Her voice trembled as she squeezed Samara's hand. "You're a lot like your Auntie Nan."

"And Sister Patterson said I was a lot like you." Samara smiled as she linked her fingers through her mother's. "And Adam said I got my creativity from Dad. It's no wonder I get confused . . . I'm a strange mix."

Tracey tightened her grip on Samara's hand.

"I think you got the best genes from all of us . . . the little we had to offer." She swallowed with difficulty. "That's why it's so important that you don't waste it . . . like I did."

"Waste it?" Samara looked puzzled. "What do you mean?"

"I mean . . . the way things are . . . with Adam." Tracey pursed her lips together. "I don't want you to get hurt."

"With Adam?" Samara moved her hand away. "I don't know what you mean."

"Yes, you do, Sam." Tracey sighed quietly. "You're in love with him."

Samara stared at her mother briefly and lifted her chin.

"Mum, everybody's in love with Adam. He's made everyone feel better since he's been here." She put out one hand. "Look at how Dad has opened up, and Terry . . . he's looked after him and helped him talk. None of us has managed to do that and you . . . you act differently when he's around."

"I admit that." Tracey nodded. "He's very charming and he does have a unique way of seeing into your soul."

"But . . ." Samara interpreted the tone of her mother's voice.

"But . . . I know he's a member of the Church, but I've just noticed that he doesn't talk about it much." Tracey shrugged her shoulders. "He has a lot of wisdom but . . . it seems like it's more from his experiences."

"Well, that's mainly what we've talked about." Samara protested. "You and Dad have been hanging off everything he's said about his traveling and everything."

"I know and it has been exciting having him here. I'm not denying that." Tracey held up her hand. "I just noticed that you . . . light up when he's around." She gave a small shrug again. "I recognize that look . . . and I just want you to be careful."

Samara stared at her mother, then she slowly stood up and folded her arms.

"I appreciate what you're saying, Mum, but I'm fine. I'm making the most of Adam being here and helping me with my work, and I do enjoy being with him but I'm not about to make any mistakes and besides . . ." She pointed at a small photo of her father on top of the television. "Adam is a lot different from Dad."

She began to turn away but suddenly stopped and bent to give her mother a tight hug and a kiss on the cheek.

"Mum, I'm glad Auntie Nan is coming, and I'm sure everything will work out fine between you. You're doing all the right things now." She looked at her watch. "Now I'd better go to Sister Patterson's and get some more work done."

Tracey watched silently as her daughter left the room. Then she stood and walked to the television. She stared at the photo of her husband for a long time before she touched it gently with one finger.

"Don't be so sure, Samara. Adam is a lot more like your father than you think." She whispered as a door shut somewhere upstairs. "A lot more."

* * *

There was no response when Samara knocked on the door at Sister Patterson's, and she waited for awhile before searching for the spare key that she'd been shown. It felt strange to let herself in and walk through the house, but once inside the darkroom she closed the door and it was as if she'd stepped into her own private world.

She found herself concentrating more intently and giving herself the instructions out loud, because when she only thought herself through the processes, it was Adam's voice that she kept hearing in her mind.

"But he's gone." She murmured at the blank piece of paper floating in the tray. "Gone without a word." She gently stirred the paper with some tongs. "Arrived one day without warning and gone another . . . just like my father."

She put the tongs down on the bench and sat down on the stool. For some reason it made her think immediately of his being there, and she stood up again just as the small timer on the bench suddenly buzzed. She quickly flipped the print over and lifted it with the tongs. The photo appeared as miraculously as it always did, and she caught her breath as it gained definition.

Toby had been determined to visit the emus before they'd left Currumbin, and he'd taken some food to give to them. While he had been tentatively holding out food for one of the tall, skinny birds, another one had reached its long neck out and pecked at the back of his trousers. Samara had caught the moment exactly as Toby had grabbed his bottom and dropped the bird food. His mouth gaped open in surprise, and his eyes were completely round, dramatically exposing the whites, while the naturally wide mouth of the emu made it look as if it were laughing. Toby's carefully spiked blond hair was also reflected in the sparse, spiky eyebrows of the emu as they faced each other.

The picture was comical but it was the background that caught Samara's attention. Rick was standing to the right of the emu, his face crinkled with laughter as he watched his little brother. It was a totally spontaneous shot but it caught the way his eyes creased at the sides when he laughed and the generous grin that was never far from the surface.

Samara remembered the sound of his laugh at the time, but she also remembered the way he'd quickly stepped in and helped Toby when the emu became more determined in its bid for food.

"Rick to the rescue." She lifted the picture and placed it out to dry, staring at Rick's image until it blurred in front of her. "Why can't I be happy with that?"

CHAPTER THIRTEEN

She woke to the sound of a door slamming and raised voices coming from down the hall. Without opening her eyes, she rolled over onto her stomach and pulled the pillow over her head to block out the familiar noise. Something else banged and she flinched slightly. Then directly outside her door she heard her mother's voice reach a desperate pitch.

"Terry! No!"

Samara's eyes flew open as she realized what was happening and she sat up quickly. Terry had been so good over the last few days. Why was her mother yelling at him now?

"Terry . . . for Pete's sake!"

She heard the deeper tone of her brother's voice further down the hall and then the kitchen door shutting a few seconds later. She moved quickly to the window and watched as her brother walked across the parking area, pulling a jacket on and hunching his shoulders as he zipped it up. At the edge of the road he stopped and looked around as if undecided where to go, then he lunged out onto the street. Samara caught her breath as a car appeared suddenly around the corner, narrowly missing Terry and blaring its horn as it braked. She watched as Terry brought his fist down on the bonnet with a sharp smack then stepped aside and ran down the path to the beach.

"Oh, Terry . . . what are you doing?" Samara whispered as she heard a tap on her door. She turned as her mother opened the door, but as soon as she saw Samara looking out the window, she rested her head against the door and closed her eyes.

"What happened?" Samara stayed where she was.

"I think he's going through some sort of withdrawl." Tracey shook her head. "He's been so good, and then he woke up this morning and it was like . . . he was so aggressive. I heard things thumping in his room, and when I went in he was throwing his trophies across the room." She stared at the door. "I have no idea what to do."

"Will he be all right now?" Samara pointed out the window. "He just about got hit by a car because he wasn't looking." She frowned. "He's gone down to the beach."

"Then let's just hope he doesn't catch up with some of his druggie friends down there." Tracey sighed. "I think I have to talk to the bishop about this. Eddy didn't want me to, but . . . I'm so scared that Terry will do something stupid."

Samara nodded as she finally walked toward her mother. "I think you're right and it's not like Dad is here to help." She stopped and rested her hand on her mother's shoulder. "I'll do whatever I can, Mum, but you have to make the decision."

It seemed as if her words sparked something in her mother because Tracey suddenly drew herself up and pressed a clenched fist against the door. "You're right. I need to do this." She nodded as if to convince herself and pointed at the phone. "Why don't you call Jackie just in case he goes over there? It'll be better to let her know what to expect."

"I think she might be getting used to it." Samara turned to pick up the phone. "And she seems to be able to handle it."

"But she shouldn't have to." Tracey's voice was surprisingly firm as she closed the door behind her.

* * *

Samara didn't really expect to find Rick at home, so it was almost a surprise when he opened the door.

"Oh, you are here!" Samara pushed her hair back off her face. "I wasn't expecting you."

"Then I'm sorry." He looked puzzled. "Did you come to see Mum?"

"Umm . . . no." She looked away.

"Toby?" Rick leaned against the doorway.

"No . . . I came to see you." Samara finished with a rush. "I just didn't think you'd be here."

"Now I'm confused." He stood aside and held out his hand to invite her inside. "Why don't you come in and see if I can get a better grip on this?"

She was still frowning when she sat down at the kitchen table.

"Why are you here?" She sat with her hands in her lap.

"I was waiting for you to call," Rick answered easily as he opened the fridge door and held up a jug of juice. When she shook her head, he still brought it to the bench and poured two glasses. "Now, am I allowed to ask why you're here?"

Samara buried her face in her hands as he put the glass in front of her, but there was a trace of a smile on her lips.

"Now I feel really stupid." She took a deep breath and spoke down to the table. "Terry threw a real fit this morning and ran away, and Mum and I didn't know what to do. She was going to call the bishop and I only had one tutorial this morning, so I skipped it and went looking for Terry down at the beach." Her voice trembled. "I looked for ages and couldn't see him. I didn't know what to do . . . so I came here."

"Even though I wasn't here." Rick sat down on a chair facing her.

"But you are here." She still couldn't look at him. "I kept hoping you would be."

"Well, I nearly wasn't but the doctor's office called and asked me to come in this morning to change the dressing." He held up his bandaged arm. "I just got back before you arrived."

"Perfect timing." She forced a smile. "Except that now I'm here I'm not sure for what. I don't really know what I expected you to do."

Rick slowly sipped his drink before he leaned forward and rested his elbows on the table.

"Why don't we drive around for a bit and see if we can find him. It probably wouldn't hurt to stop in at Jackie's place. Does she know?"

"I've called her . . . as soon as he ran off." Samara ran her finger over the tiny droplets of water on the outside of her glass. "She was going to stay home as well, but she had a big test this morning. She said she'd come home straight after it."

"So we're covering a few of the bases." Rick stood up and put his glass in the sink. "Can I ask just one question?"

She somehow knew what he was going to ask and she shrugged her shoulders.

"Adam's gone up north."

"When?" He sounded surprised.

"Yesterday . . . with my father. On an urgent trip." She attempted a smile. "It seems like birds of a feather . . ."

"Usually fly back to the nest sometime." He picked his car keys up off the table, threw them up in the air, and caught them again in a tight fist. "Let's go find Terry."

They cruised up and down the main highway through Broadbeach, and Rick drove in and out of the smaller tributary streets where they knew some of Terry's acquaintances lived. They saw a few of them hanging out at some of the park areas, but Terry was nowhere to be seen.

"At least he's not with them." Samara looked back over her shoulder at a couple of boys who were sitting on a bench near the beach. They were throwing stones at a bent can and missing. "You know, I look at those boys and I can't comprehend how they can get so . . . lost."

"They probably never intended to." Rick pulled into a parking space facing the beach and turned off the engine. "You know for sure that Terry never planned to get into this stuff."

"He's the last person that I ever thought would." Samara nodded. "A couple of silly mistakes and now he's paying the price."

"But he is trying to stop." Rick rested his arm along the window. "Mum gave me a book to read about drugs and things—from an LDS perspective—and it said that things usually get really tough when people try to stop."

Samara stared at him.

"Why would your mother have a book about that?" She tried to smile. "Have you been hiding something from me?"

"Nah . . ." Rick smiled as he leaned his head against his hand. "You know my mum . . . she's big on prevention, whether it's for her own kids or someone else's. She figures it's better to be informed than get a big shock and wonder what happened."

Samara nodded. "You just summed up my family very well."

"Hey, it's not just your family." Rick stared straight at her. "You know, I may be overstepping the mark by saying this, but it seems to me that you've got to stop being so paranoid about your family, Samara. It's eating you up."

She opened her mouth to protest, but she nodded instead.

"You're probably right . . . that's pretty much how I feel at the moment . . . like I'm being eaten up from the inside out." She put her hand over her face. "My mother just shared the sordid details of her past, my brother is going crazy, my father is away somewhere being . . . unaccountable." She waved her hand in the air and looked out of the window. "Do you think we should try Jackie's place now?"

"Maybe . . . I'm not sure." Rick turned to face the front, drummed his fingers on the top of the steering wheel, then started the engine and glanced in the rearview mirror. He was about to put the car into gear when he hesitated. "Then again, you know the story of the butterfly coming to rest on your shoulder . . ."

"What?" Samara stared at him as if he wasn't making sense.

"You know . . . if you chase a butterfly it'll always fly away but if you sit still long enough it'll come and rest on your shoulder." Rick gestured with his thumb back over his shoulder as he switched off the engine again. "I think our butterfly has come to rest."

Samara turned quickly in her seat to see Terry walking slowly over a grassy area not far from the car. He didn't appear to have recognized the car or to have seen them as he walked slowly with his hands deep in his trouser pockets.

She took a deep breath. "Do you think I should go and get him?"

Rick watched Terry for a second then pulled the door handle.

"He might be more approachable if I go. You wait here." He got out but leaned back down into the car. "I might just walk with him for a bit. I'll wave if I need you."

She watched as Rick sauntered over the grass, but he didn't attempt to catch up with Terry until their backs were toward her in the car. Then he caught up and she saw Terry turn his head slightly in Rick's direction. They kept walking toward the beach without looking back.

Samara waited for but when they didn't reappear, she turned and curled up on the seat, facing the steering wheel with her back resting against the door. In that position she began to take note of all the things in the car that were so typical of Rick. Two empty wrappers from his favorite chocolate bars were screwed up inside a small plastic bag that hung on the cigarette lighter, along with some old receipts and some apple cores and orange peels. The pocket on the inside of the door held a slim road map and another thicker notebook that she knew even without reading the title was a guide to identifying Australian birds and animals and their habitats.

In the backseat was a pile of books and manuals which she knew were from the Institute course he'd been studying and from the Young Men program where he was deacons quorum adviser. Sitting on top of the books were a well-used Bible and Book of Mormon. Each had several pieces of writing paper sticking out of them, all with notes scribbled on them in Rick's large, rounded handwriting.

The thing that drew her attention, though, was the small photo of his family tucked inside the corner of the glass on the dashboard. It was one of the cheaper studio shots that were usually offered at the shopping centers, and the whole family was smiling happily, even though she remembered Rick complaining about his mother's insistence that they have the annual photo done.

"You moan about the photo but you wouldn't be without it." She half smiled as she turned to check out the window in time to see Terry and Rick walking toward the car. Rick laughed and lifted his hand to rest it briefly on Terry's shoulder. Then he looked directly at the car and waved it higher. Samara recognized it as a signal and she quickly turned to open her door.

She almost expected Terry to look surprised when he saw her but he didn't even lift his head as she began to walk toward him. He didn't acknowledge her until she was standing right in front of him, and she felt her heart begin to beat more quickly. She glanced at Rick and he made a slight movement with his arms to indicate a hug, so she took a step toward her brother and held her arms out to him. He still didn't look as he took the other step and wrapped his arms around her, burying his face against her shoulder. There were no tears or words, but she felt the tension begin to leave his body as she held him closely.

After a minute or so, he lifted his head and looked sideways, still unable to meet her eyes.

"Can I get a lift with you guys?" He nodded toward the car. "It might be better if you drive me past temptation."

"That sounds like a good idea." Rick moved immediately to the car and Samara followed, closing the door behind Terry as he settled into the backseat. They didn't speak for some time as they drove back along the highway. Samara noticed that Rick was driving the long way rather than going directly to the motel. He also kept glancing at Terry in the rearview mirror. Once she turned to see Terry looking at the notes in the scriptures. Even from the front seat she could see the words quite clearly, so she knew he would be able to read what Rick had written.

"What's all the scripture study for?" Terry finally spoke.

"I've got to talk in sacrament meeting on Sunday," Rick acknowledged briefly. "I'm actually enjoying the study . . . pity I have to spoil it by talking about it."

Terry almost smiled, then he nodded.

"I remember a talk you gave before your mission. It was about the Holy Ghost."

Samara glanced back quickly. She remembered the talk but it surprised her that Terry had. It also appeared to take Rick by surprise.

"You remember that?" Rick raised one eyebrow.

"Yeah . . . you talked about how you first recognized feeling the Spirit and how you wanted that feeling all the time." Terry picked up the Book of Mormon. "Do you mind if I take a look at these notes?"

"Go ahead." Rick glanced at Samara. "They're just my first thoughts but sometimes they're the best." He grinned. "I'm hoping anyway."

They rode on in silence while Terry read over the notes and Rick turned on some mellow music on the car stereo. Samara sat still, not wanting to spoil the peaceful feeling in the car, especially the sound of pages being turned in the backseat. As the car kept traveling she glanced up at Rick to find him watching her. She felt her throat constrict at the tenderness of the look and responded by holding her hand close to her leg and crossing two fingers. As she put her hand back down Rick reached over and briefly squeezed her hand. It was the smallest gesture but she felt a renewed strength from it.

"So what have you learned?" Rick glanced in the rearview mirror as he finally turned down the street to the motel. "You might be able to give me some insight."

"You've got it pretty well covered." Terry spread his hand over the open scriptures. "It's funny how when you can see lots of verses all together on one subject, it has so much more impact . . . like you realize that Heavenly Father really means what He's saying."

Rick nodded. "That's exactly how I felt when I saw all those references. When I decided to write them all down, I think I actually started to get the message a whole lot better."

"Like how many times he says "How long . . ."" Terry's voice broke and Rick finished the sentence for him.

"How long will ye choose darkness rather than light?"

"Umm . . . I was thinking more of the other bits . . . how long will ye suffer yourselves to be led by blind and foolish guides." Terry coughed as he read the scripture out loud. "And how long will ye suppose that the Lord will suffer you." He coughed again. "I think He must be about through suffering with me."

He sounded so dejected that Samara had to look at him.

"Every one has difficult times, Terry." She bit her lip.

"That's what I liked about this talk." Rick added easily. "You realize that Heavenly Father doesn't want you to be lukewarm about things that matter because He wants you to get the full benefit of His blessings. If you choose darkness, that's what you get, but if you choose light . . . the world is open to you."

"And isn't that why the Savior died?" Samara offered tentatively as she looked at Rick for reassurance. "So that even if you do go down the wrong path, there's always a chance for you to get back—"

"To the light at the end of the tunnel." Terry finished for her but it was almost a grunt. "I just hate the way the light keeps coming and going right now. One minute it seems really bright and then it seems to fade away so fast."

"It doesn't mean the light isn't still there, Terry." Rick pulled into the driveway and turned off the motor. "It just means there's a bit of a bend in the tunnel." His voice softened. "You've got to work your way around the bend until you see the light again."

"Yeah . . . I guess." Terry sat silently for a minute, then he leaned forward and held out his hand through the gap in the front seats. "Thanks, Rick."

Rick reached around and shook his hand, then Terry quickly squeezed Samara's shoulder before he got out of the car. As he got out he leaned back inside the door.

"I might even come and listen to you give that talk on Sunday."

"I'd like that." Rick nodded, then he held up his hand. "Hey . . . let me know if you think of anything else I could use . . . any scriptures or anything."

Terry stared at him, and then he stood up. Samara could barely hear his voice as he closed the door.

"I'll see what I can find."

They watched as he walked around the back of the house. When he was gone, Samara dropped her head onto her chest and closed her eyes.

"Thank you so much." Her words came out in a whisper. "I actually think he might go and look up those scriptures."

"That would be great." Rick leaned both arms across the steering wheel and faced her. "I'm beginning to think that maybe this sacrament talk was for him rather than me."

"Possibly . . . but he needed you to get him started on it." Samara folded her arms and shivered. "I feel like something really happened for him just now . . . something really positive."

"Mmm . . . I was worried that he was taking it all negatively for a bit, there." Rick frowned. "When he started talking about the Lord only suffering about him, I thought he might have got the wrong end of the stick."

"Yes, but he also talked about the foolish guides, which shows that he knows what is happening to him." Samara shook her head. "And somehow we have to keep him away from those foolish guides."

"Which is why we should probably go over to Jackie's right now and fill her in on what's happened. She's the ultimate good guide for him right now." Rick leaned back and stretched his arms. "That's if you want to."

Samara considered for a moment then shook her head.

"I think I'd better go in and explain everything to Mum right now." She let her hand rest on the door handle. "I'll tell her how much you helped."

"She doesn't need to know anything except that Terry is all right." Rick shrugged. "I'll go over to Jackie's and let her know."

"Okay." Samara began to open the door, then she quickly turned and leaned over to Rick and kissed him on the cheek. "Thank you . . . for everything."

She went to leave but he suddenly covered her hand and pulled her back toward him. For a second he stared straight at her, then he lifted her hand to his lips and gave her knuckles a swift kiss before releasing it.

"You're welcome, Samara."

She was barely out of the car before he started the engine and backed out of the drive, but there was a tiny smile playing on her lips as she walked inside.

* * *

"You look pleased with yourself." Tracey looked up from her perpetual seat behind the reception desk. "Did you find Terry?"

"Yes, he went around to the back door." Samara pointed to the rear of the house. "We drove around looking for him for ages then parked down at the beach and he happened to walk by. Rick got out and talked to him, and he came back with us."

"And he's . . ." Her mother stopped and put her hand to her throat. "Is he . . . ?"

"He's okay. He hadn't taken anything and he actually read some scriptures and stuff that Rick had in the backseat of his car." Samara leaned against the desk. "Did you call the bishop about him?"

"I tried but he wasn't home. His wife said he'll call back later tonight." Tracey drummed her fingers on the counter. "I wish your father would call so I could talk to him about it."

As soon as her mother mentioned her father, something seemed to break inside Samara's chest. All the anticipation and the peace she had just experienced with Rick as they'd looked for Terry seemed to dissipate as the old frustration with her parents bubbled to the surface.

"Why do you need him to call? So he can say 'no, we can handle this on our own and don't talk to the bishop.'" Samara felt the peaceful feeling slip away as she shook her head. "We need to get some proper advice and not be stopped by pride anymore."

"I'm sure it's not pride . . ." Tracey started, but Samara waved her hand.

"Okay, it's not pride then, but there's something that stops Dad from facing reality about some things, and he's away so much he can't see what's really happening."

"He sees, but . . ." Tracey faltered.

"But he doesn't do anything except get angry." Samara interrupted again as she walked around the desk to the door. "Well, that's just great too. We could wait forever and lose Terry in the process."

"Samara . . . that's enough!" Her mother suddenly spoke sharply. "I won't have you speak like that!"

"Then do something about it, Mum!" Samara turned back. "Stand up for yourself and for Terry and maybe . . ." She looked at the floor.

"Maybe what?" Tracey stood still as her daughter slowly raised her eyes to meet hers.

"I was going to say maybe stand up for me, but I don't think I need you to anymore." Samara shrugged her shoulders wearily. "I don't even think I want you to."

Tracey stood helplessly as Samara weakly said, "Having Adam here had made me think that, somehow, we could all just change and everything would be better."

"But it can be." Tracey went to put her hand on Samara's shoulder, but she turned away again.

"Even being with Rick made me feel like we could make our way through this, but as soon as you mention Dad, it makes me want to scream." She brushed the tears from her eyes. "Adam has done more to help us in three days than Dad has done in three decades but now they're together wandering around the continent, and I don't know who to trust anymore." She leaned over and picked up the keys to her mother's car. "I'm sorry, Mum, but I'm going over to Jackie's and maybe to Rick's. At least I know where I stand with them."

* * *

Jackie was getting a pile of books out of the back of her car when Rick drove up to her house. She waited for him as he got out of the car.

"Hey, what are you up to?" She rested her hand on the books before they slipped off the car.

"I've been with Samara . . . looking for Terry." Rick nodded at her questioning look. "We found him down at the beach."

"And?" Jackie screwed up her face. "Is he all right?"

"He's fine." Rick stood with his hands in his pockets. "He hasn't done anything except walk for a few hours."

"So how did you get involved?" Jackie pointed over at the two wooden chairs on their front veranda and they walked over to them.

"I'd just gotten back from the doctor's and Samara turned up at the door a few minutes later." Rick set the pile of books he was carrying down on the small table between the chairs.

"How did she know you were home?" Jackie looked puzzled. "She didn't say anything about seeing you when I talked to her earlier."

Rick smiled as he settled back in the chair and stretched his long legs out in front of him. "She didn't know what else to do."

"So she turned to good old Rick." Jackie shook her head.

"Just like Terry turns to good old Jackie." Rick pointed at her and she laughed ruefully.

"Okay, so I'm as much of a sucker as you are." She folded her arms. "What else happened?"

"We drove around for a bit and then we stopped down at the beach. Next thing, Terry walks past, so I got out and walked with him for a bit." Rick pressed his fingertips together. "He's confused and he's gotten to the point where he knows what not to do, but it's almost like he needs the stuff to get up the courage to not use it."

Jackie nodded thoughtfully. "I know what you mean. It's not like he's heavily into it but he's become dependent enough that he doubts himself more now. Like he can't be happy or enjoy himself without it."

They sat in silence, then Rick leaned forward. "Do you think he would go into rehab?"

"I don't know." Jackie shook her head. "I did suggest it the other day but he said he didn't need to . . . that he could kick it on his own."

"Do you think he can?"

"I have no idea," Jackie responded immediately. "I don't know enough about this sort of stuff." She shrugged. "I feel really naive about it all, actually."

"Same." Rick nodded. "Samara did say her mum was going to talk to the bishop about it. He'll probably refer him."

After they sat in silence for awhile, Jackie kicked Rick's foot.

"So how are things between you and Sam?"

Rick kicked her foot back.

"How are things with you and Terry?"

"I asked first."

Rick shrugged then frowned slightly. "Maybe we should be asking how things are between Samara and Adam." He stared at his feet. "She lights up when he's around, and she hung on his every word when we were at the sanctuary the other day." His brow furrowed. "The trouble is that he seems to have made a real difference to her parents accepting her photography, and I know I shouldn't say that there's anything wrong with that . . . in fact, it's great, but . . ."

"But there's something else?"

Rick nodded. "I want to dislike him but I can't. I mean, he's easy to talk to and he's interested in whatever you're saying, and he's interesting as well."

"And he's old." Jackie put in quietly.

"Well, he's definitely more mature." Rick agreed quietly as he rested one foot on top of the other and swung it back and forth. "The thing is . . . he seems to be all the things that Samara has ever wanted. He's the great photographer, he's traveled everywhere on the planet . . ."

"And he's even a member of the Church." Jackie interrupted. "Did you know that he joined the Church because she shared her testimony when they met?"

"No, I didn't." Rick looked despondent. "So is there anything else in his favor or shall we just notch him up as perfect?"

"Maybe you should think of him as worthy competition." Jackie smiled.

"Ah, but the question is whether he's the competition or whether I am." Rick blew his hair up off his forehead. "The fact is . . . I'm glad he wasn't here this morning and that Sam came to me for help. Would she have done that if he had been here?"

Jackie sat silently, then she shrugged.

"Are we sad people that we seem to be hanging in there, waiting for the Danes children to need us?"

"Yes," Rick responded, chuckling. "We could just forget the Daneses and you and I could hang out again."

"It would probably be a lot easier." She nodded then looked serious. "Rick, I really, really want to help Terry get through this. He's such an amazing person . . ." Her voice broke and she struggled to keep her composure.

"And you love him." Rick finished quietly while she nodded.

"I've tried not to. I've told myself over and over that there are plenty of others with . . ."

"With divine potential." He smiled as she tried to.

"But he's got the most. Stupid, eh?"

Rick leaned forward and took hold of her hand to pull her up. "Then I guess I'm stupid, too, because that's how I feel about Samara."

Jackie nodded, then she grinned and wiped her eyes. "Do you realize that if both our dreams came true we'd be related?"

Rick thought about it for a second. Then he put his arm across her shoulders and gave her a tight hug so that she leaned her head against his chest.

"Then I guess we're both in this for the long haul, eh, sis?"

Jackie laughed and hugged him back before she gathered up her books.

"Let's get an apple juice and drink to our shared mission. Then I'll go over to see Terry."

Neither of them saw Samara's car as it turned the corner into the street. She had slowed to take the corner and now she drew the car up to the curb, watching as Jackie laughed and hugged Rick and they both walked inside. After the turmoil of the day, the sight of them laughing together left Samara feeling deflated. She rested both hands on the top of the steering wheel and rested her forehead on them. It took a few moments to gather her thoughts, and she felt the physical sensation of emotion emptying from her. It felt cold but safely distant from everything and everyone.

"Everyone can be happy if they don't have to think about us." She pressed her head harder against her hands as tears welled. "Maybe it is time to go away and let Rick get on with his life and I can get on with mine." She turned the car away from the curb in the direction of the beach, driving straight past Jackie's house.

CHAPTER FOURTEEN

At the end of a third day of sharing the cabin of a truck, Eddy and Adam had still only scratched the surface of their combined travel experiences. The miles had been eaten up by story after story of mishaps and adventures. Eddy had a captive audience and he was loving it.

"Oh, man." He patted his chest after laughing hard at a story Adam had just recounted. "I haven't laughed this much in years. I can't believe you've gotten away with things like that."

Adam smiled as he shook his head.

"Sometimes I think I've had a pretty charmed life. I probably should have met my Maker a few times, but I got through."

"Same here." Eddy took a deep breath. "I'd be out in the middle of the desert with no one around and a breakdown could mean the end, but someone always happens along, or else I'm the one there to help somebody else. It's a bit freaky sometimes how it all works out."

"The Lord works in mysterious ways." Adam quoted calmly as he rested one foot up against the dashboard.

"Do you actually believe that?" Eddy concentrated on the road ahead.

"What?" Adam looked puzzled.

"That the Lord . . . that God does things . . . to help us?" Eddy lifted one eyebrow skyward.

"Don't you?" Adam matched the eyebrow movement. "It seems like you've had enough experiences to prove it."

"Yeah . . . but those can be put down to coincidence or . . . fate."

"I guess they could." Adam responded mildly. "I guess it depends what you want to believe."

"So tell me what you believe." Eddy pointed at Adam. "Tell me what Adam Russell really believes."

They both sat without talking for a couple of miles, then Adam leaned forward to look out at the sky.

"Ten years ago I'd say I believed in anything that sounded appealing and could make me feel good about what I was doing."

"Which was?" Eddy glanced at him.

"Having a good time, traveling, drugs, alcohol, you name it."

"Serious?" Eddy looked surprised.

"Absolutely." Adam nodded. "Then I got really ill while I was in South America and I thought I'd had it, so I decided to change my ways . . . but I didn't know what to do." He clasped his hands together. "I decided to clear my head in New Zealand, and while I was at a pretty deserted beach, I met a young girl."

He watched for Eddy's response but he was staring straight ahead.

"She looked like a sea urchin—her long, dark hair all wind-swept—so I asked her to pose for me in some pictures. She refused and when I persisted she agreed on the condition I show her how to use the camera."

"And the rest is history." Eddy grunted. "So her obsession with photography really is all your fault?"

Adam nodded with a smile. "I take full responsibility for uncovering the amazing talent that your daughter has, and I make no apology for it." He glanced sideways at Eddy. "In fact, I think it would have been a crime for it not to have been brought to the surface."

"Which would have been the case if it had been left to me." Eddy tightened his grip on the steering wheel.

"Possibly . . . although Samara is a very determined person. She probably would have found a way in spite of both of us." Adam pointed at the small family photo that Eddy had tacked to the dashboard. "Who would you say she was most like?"

Eddy took his time between negotiating the truck around some bends and looking at the photo. Then he pointed at the picture of Terry.

"My boy is more like his mother . . . very methodical, organized . . . sensitive . . ."

"And kind and caring."

"Yeah, that too." Eddy shrugged.

"And Samara?" Adam folded his arms.

"Samara." Eddy exhaled a long breath. "I think Samara skipped a couple of generations. She's named after two of her great grandmothers . . . Samantha and Lara . . . makes Samara." He used two fingers to show a connection. "They were both feisty women who were real tough stock . . . take on anyone and anything from what I've heard."

"And so you see Samara as taking after them?" Adam looked puzzled. "What about you . . . don't you think she's a lot like you?"

"Me?" Eddy grunted again and shook his head. "Doubt it . . . we don't get on at all."

"I didn't ask whether you got along, I said I thought you were alike." Adam pointed back in a general southerly direction. "That daughter of yours has a lot of Eddy characteristics from what I can see . . . including that strong creative streak."

"Now you're talking through a hole in your head!" Eddy almost laughed. "Samara can't give me the time of day without challenging me on it."

"But she's also fiercely independent, loves to travel, hates injustice, and speaks out when she feels strongly about things." Adam shrugged. "And I've only really known her for a few days. Both of you, for that matter, but the similarities are pretty clear to me." His voice lowered. "And possibly why you don't agree on things."

Eddy took awhile to answer. Then he spoke very quietly.

"I loved that little girl of mine. I brought her on a couple of trips when she was really little, and she sat there in your seat and chattered the whole time about everything she was seeing." He shook his head. "She'd make up stories on the spot about all the animals and people and so I'd tell the next part of the story and then she'd keep going."

"So what happened?" Adam asked quietly.

He watched Eddy's jaw muscle work up and down as the man fought for control and rubbed his large hand over his face.

"I was driving road trains back then . . . huge trucks with multiple trailers, and sometimes I'd be away for weeks. I only took Sam on the short trips." He took a deep breath. "Anyway, as the kids got older, things weren't that good between Trace and I for awhile. She was always angry or oversensitive or something. I felt like I couldn't do a thing right, so I took on more long-hauls . . ." He bit at his lip. "I met a woman up north, and for awhile . . . I preferred it there to being at home."

Adam waited as Eddy hit his fist against the steering wheel.

"Tracey found out and she confronted me about it the next time I was at home. We argued . . . really bad . . . but we didn't know that Samara was listening to it all in the next room." He tilted his chin. "I'll never forget the look on her face when she came into the room. Then she ran out . . . and we've hardly spoken a civil word to each other since."

"She seemed all right the other night when we were talking about your trips."

Eddy lifted one hand off the wheel and shrugged his shoulders. "I don't know if she was behaving like that because you were there, but it was certainly different." He nodded. "It was nice."

They drove on in silence, the truck consuming the miles of highway that stretched ahead. Adam stared out at the seemingly endless shades of blue that were ocean and sky. An occasional wisp of white cloud seemed to float in among the peaceful palette of cobalt and turquoise, brightened in its intensity by the light of the sun.

Adam pointed out at the horizon. "You know, when I look out at a scene like this I begin to think more about eternity."

"It does look like it goes forever." Eddy nodded. "I tried to paint it once . . . watercolors."

"Ah . . . the creative streak." Adam caught up on it immediately but Eddy only chuckled.

"I said once." He shrugged. "Though I guess Sam does have a bit more of the Danes blood than I care to admit."

"Which takes me back to the whole eternity thing." Adam responded easily. "What do you think is going to happen to you after this, Eddy?"

"After this?" Eddy looked sideways. "I've got another load to haul as soon as I get back, then it's pretty full on for another month."

Adam grinned as he sat back against the seat and stretched out.

"I wasn't really talking about right now . . . I was thinking more about after this life." He waved his finger in a circle. "After you die."

"Oh, deep stuff." Eddy gave a short laugh. "Quite frankly, I don't think about it much. Why . . . have you got some ideas?" He stopped and held up his hand. "Hang on . . . you're just going to give me the Mormon stuff, aren't you?"

"Possibly." Adam nodded. "I was actually asking the same question your daughter asked me when she was fourteen."

"My Sam . . . talked to you about eternity?" He looked doubtful.

"She did." Adam nodded. "And I think that's why I listened. She was so young and yet so sure about everything she was saying, and whatever I asked her. She had an answer that seemed to work for me."

"Sam had answers about eternity?" Eddy still looked dubious.

"She bore her testimony to me—right there on the beach—that she knew her family could be together forever. That we could all be forgiven of our sins and that Heavenly Father wanted us to be happy." Adam gently smacked his fist against the palm of his other hand. "The contrast between her and what I'd just come from was huge . . . and I knew I'd been to hell and back."

"So you wanted a bit of heaven?" Eddy looked skeptical. "And my daughter actually told you all those things?" He shook his head and rubbed one hand over his eyes. "That would've been just before she found out about me . . . before Trace and I had our argument. Sam had just come back from New Zealand." He sat for a moment, then he hit the steering wheel hard with his fist.

"Well, she did tell me those things and she was so serious and determined about it . . . like, why didn't I know these things?" Adam kept talking as he watched Eddy's face twist with emotion. "Do you wonder why I showed her how to do the photography?"

"To shut her up?" Eddy tried to laugh, but Adam could hear a different tone in his voice.

"Partly." He pointed a finger on both hands toward the sky. "But mainly because I felt she had insight about the big picture that I didn't have. In just a few minutes she began to observe things that I hadn't seen before, and it all seemed so simple and logical to her."

"She can be pretty intense about things." Eddy nodded in agreement as he wiped the corner of his eye. "I can imagine her, actually, telling you about everything."

"About things she cares about." Adam corrected him quietly. "And she cares about you and your family."

Once again, Eddy drove on in silence, deeply occupied with his own thoughts. Occasionally he opened his mouth as if to speak, but he lapsed into silence again. Adam sat quietly, absorbed with the ocean scenery.

"We should stop for lunch." Eddy finally spoke as he nodded toward a roadside café. As he hauled on the huge steering wheel he looked straight ahead. "How about we eat and you tell me what else that daughter of mine was shooting her mouth off about."

* * *

Samara ran along the beach at first, jogging so fast she had to breathe deeply and concentrate on the movement. Somehow it felt as if the energy she expended might reduce the torment she was feeling. When her lungs felt as if they would burst, she slowed to a fast-paced walk, deliberately treading in the softer, wetter sand so that it took more effort to move her feet up and down. Eventually she slowed to walk in the foamy remains of the incoming waves, letting the ebbing water drain away around her ankles.

As she slowed, she began to notice the other people on the beach around her. Some individuals were running or walking, some were in family groups, tidying up after their day at the beach, while other couples walked hand in hand in the gathering dusk. She found herself studying the expressions on their faces and noticing that most were laughing or seemed at least serene.

She felt her heart give a small flip in her chest when a man with a sandy-colored beard walked down to the water in front of her.

"He doesn't even look like Adam." She muttered to herself as the man gave her a polite smile before he stopped at the edge of the oncoming waves. "And Adam is miles away with your father, anyway."

She hooked her thumbs through the belt loops on her shorts as she kept walking, staring at the ground as she went. She started as a couple ran past, kicking water at each other in the shallow waves. They were both in their twenties, and the girl was short and blonde while the man was tall and dark-haired.

Again, Samara felt her breath come in a quick gasp as the man laughed out loud and caught the girl against him. Instinctively, she turned away from their happiness and began to walk up the beach until she reached the soft, dry sand. The evening air was beginning to cool around her, and she shivered slightly as she sat down and crossed her legs, leaning on them with her arms folded.

"It's just like when you get a new car . . . you suddenly see all the same models that you've never noticed before." She talked to herself quietly with lips barely moving. "Adam . . . Rick . . . there are plenty of other models just like them that you could choose from."

She spread her hands out to the side and began to drag them in semicircles through the warm sand, enjoying the soft grittiness rubbing against her skin. On one sweep, her fingers hit against a single shell buried beneath the surface. She picked it up and shook it clean, then she turned it backward and forward between her fingers.

"I wonder how you ended up here." She made a small mound of sand and set the shell on top. "Sitting on a beach talking to some lonely woman." Samara smiled in spite of herself and glanced around. "Some lonely, weird woman who talks to shells."

There was nobody even close by, so she began to relax in her solitude.

"Seeing we're alone, maybe you could listen to my problem . . . you see, there are two men . . ."

She walked two fingers up to the mound and moved them as if to bow to the shell.

"This is Rick . . . he spends a lot of time with a girl called Samara. He'd like to spend more time with her but she won't let him. She says she doesn't know if she wants a steady relationship because she wants to travel the world and take photographs. Rick gets confused as to how he should act around her, so he tries to be a good friend and have an occasional little kiss. He knows she likes that because she smiles . . . sometimes."

Samara frowned as she moved the other hand forward toward the other side of the mound.

"Then this is Adam and he's come from a far place in distance and in time. He knew Samara when she was younger and he came to see if she's become a good photographer like she promised she would when they first met. He wants to help her become a better photographer, but . . ."

Samara choked as the words caught in her throat.

"But now she thinks she loves him." She whispered the words as if she didn't want to hear or say them, but it almost came as a relief to hear them out loud and it gave her courage to go on. "At least, she thinks she loves him, but then he went away with her father on a trip without saying anything and she felt really disappointed in him. Then Samara had a problem with her brother and Rick was lovely and helped her, and now she's really confused because she felt like she loves Rick as well . . . but it's a different feeling from being with Adam." She gulped hard as the words stuck, and she seemed to watch from a distance as her tears began to fall on the dry sand, leaving miniature craters that were dark against the lighter background. One ran down her nose and she sat still, unable to decide which hand to use to wipe it away. Then she suddenly pulled both hands from the sand and picked up the shell. She stared at it for a moment and then looked along the beach. There was nobody around so she stood up and threw the shell down toward the outgoing tide as hard as she could.

"Then one day she decided that it might be better to go away . . . from Rick and from Adam and from her family . . . and start all over again on her own."

She pressed the palms of both hands against her face and whispered into them.

"But she doesn't know if she has the courage."

* * *

Samara sat at her desk, staring at one pile of photos. Since her walk along the beach, the idea of actually leaving her family and going away had been playing over and over in her mind. She only had to finish her exhibition for school and her studies, then she would be free to do whatever she wanted . . . anywhere in the world if she chose to. She tapped the photo against the desk and stared out the open window. She wanted to love her family but they made it so hard. Maybe she would love them more from a distance.

"So get the studies finished and you can go." She muttered at the pile of photos and pulled her chair closer to the desk. "Go wherever you want to."

"Sammy . . . are you in there?" She heard the soft tap on the door as Terry opened it slightly and leaned his head around. "I need to talk to you."

"What about?" Samara turned in her chair as he walked in and sat down on the edge of her bed. He had showered and shaved and was wearing a pale blue polo shirt and jeans. Even his hair had been trimmed and styled with some gel. It was the first time she'd seen him neatly dressed for a long time.

"This looks serious." She attempted a smile. "Where's the party?"

"No party." He shook his head. "Did you forget that all of the young adults are going bowling?"

"Actually, I did." Samara pointed at a pile of papers and photos on her desk. "But I really can't go. I absolutely have to get this part of the assignment done by tomorrow."

"But it's only for a couple of hours." Terry frowned. "I was really hoping that you'd be there . . . with me."

"So you're going?" Samara looked surprised as Terry nodded and dug both hands into his pockets.

"Jackie convinced me. She said the best way to stop doing something bad is to fill the time doing something else that's good." He shrugged. "So I'm going to give it a try."

"Oh, Terry." Samara stood up slowly and walked toward him. He met her halfway, and she was surprised at the tightness of the hug he gave her. It was almost as if he were drawing strength from her, and she felt her resolve weakening. She'd promised she would help him as much as she could and here he was, pleading with her.

Terry spoke in her ear. "I'd really like you to come, Sammy. I haven't been to one of these things for such a long time." He hesitated. "And Rick asked if you were coming and I said you would be."

At the mention of Rick's name, Samara drew away. Did she want to spend the evening with Rick?

"Hey, I'll tell you what." Samara took a deep breath and pointed an accusing finger at the stack of photos. "I truly have to get this done, but I promise that I'll work really fast and if I get finished by eight, I'll come on down. Mum shouldn't be using the car."

Terry sat still for a moment, then he stood up and ran his hand through his hair. "Are you quite sure?"

"Absolutely." Samara tapped the pen on the papers again. "As soon as this is finished with."

Terry nodded slowly as he put his hands in his pockets.

"Maybe I won't go . . . I don't really feel like bowling and all that noise and everyone talking." He frowned. "It's probably better that I stay at home."

"No, you should go." Samara stood up as well and she rested her hand on his shoulder. "I know it's been awhile, but you just stay close to Jackie and you'll be fine."

"I'd be finer if you come." Terry looked sheepish. "Although I can't believe I'm saying that to my little sister."

"Well, your little sister can't come right now and so you'll have to make it on your own for a couple of hours." Samara leaned forward and kissed him on the cheek.

Terry immediately put his hand up to his face. "It's been awhile since you did that, too." His voice broke, and she quickly did it again and again until he held up his hand to stop her. "Okay, enough . . . I'll go, but if you don't get down there I'm going to wake you up when I get home to tell you about it."

Samara smiled as she looped her hand through his arm and walked him to the door.

"Don't worry about waking me up . . . I'll be there." She squeezed his arm. "And you will be fine . . . you're going bowling, and there's not a whole lot that can go wrong between here and the bowling alley."

CHAPTER FIFTEEN

Samara found it difficult to concentrate for some time after Terry left. She wandered back to the desk and absently picked up some of the photos, but she was looking without seeing anything. A car engine started down in the parking area but she knew straightaway that it wasn't Terry's car. As she sat down in her chair she found herself waiting for his car's distinctive motor but after several minutes, there was still no sound.

"You're going to be late, Terry." She glanced at the small alarm clock beside her bed and back out the window. "You'll lose some points with Jackie for not being punctual."

Even the mention of Jackie's name made her take a quick breath and shake her head.

"Then again, maybe Jackie's too occupied to notice whether you're late or not."

She finally heard Terry's car start just as the phone rang. She picked it up to hear Jackie's voice on the other end as the engine revved loudly.

"Hi, it's Jackie . . . are you guys coming? We're all ready and waiting." Her voice was bright and cheerful and Samara frowned.

"Terry's just on his way, but I've got a pile of work that I have to get organized for tomorrow. Even the best bowling score won't cut it with my professors." She studied a framed black-and-white photo of Toby and the thistle. "Terry should be there any minute and I'll try and get down later."

"Okay." She heard the question in Jackie's voice. "Should I get Rick to come back and get you?"

"No. I'll get Mum's car if I need to." Samara closed her eyes. "You guys just enjoy yourselves."

She hung up before Jackie responded and quickly set the phone back on its stand. The movement felt decisive and she abruptly pulled her chair up even closer to the desk so that she was tight against the wood.

"So, get to work if that's all you have to talk about." She muttered to herself as she leaned over to the small stereo beside the desk. The music was very slow, quiet, and mellow, so she quickly turned the knob until bright music with a distinctive beat crackled into clarity. She then cranked the volume, and as the music filled the room, she accompanied the rhythm with her fist on the table.

"Now, get on with your future, Samara Danes."

* * *

For the next half hour she did her work in time to the music, deliberately swaying her body to the beat as she made decisions about photographs to include in her exhibition. The constant movement seemed to help, and she actually found herself becoming absorbed in the work. So much so that when the phone rang beside her she jumped and dropped the picture she was holding. It fluttered down onto the table as she picked up the phone.

"Hello . . . Samara?" Adam's voice was distinctive though a bit distant. "Or is it Tracey? Are you there?"

"Umm . . . yes." Samara felt her throat go dry.

"Samara?" The connection crackled so that his voice sounded disjointed.

"Yes." She held the phone with both hands.

"I can hardly hear you." His voice was faint. "Hang on . . . I'll go outside."

The few seconds of silence gave her a chance to take a deep breath. What was she going to say to him? Did she have anything to say?

"Is that better?" His voice came through clearly and she nodded. "Samara?"

"I'm sorry." She grinned at her own foolishness at merely nodding, and it seemed to help her relax. "I was nodding. Couldn't you hear?"

She heard Adam chuckle.

"I thought I heard something. I didn't realize it was your brain."

"That's what happens when it gets overloaded." She smiled. "It can't handle the workload."

"So how is the preparation going?" He sounded genuinely interested. "Have you selected all your photos?"

"Pretty much." She looked down at the table. She had dreaded talking to him, but it was easier to discuss her work. "I've got to have eighteen prints and I've settled on twelve so far. But I'll have the rest done by tonight."

"What . . . Friday night and you're not out on the town?" he teased.

Samara changed the phone to the other ear and stared out the window. The sky was a darkening blue and the streetlights were just turning on.

"The others went bowling, but I've got too much to do." She shrugged. "And I didn't really want to go anyway."

"Why not?"

"I just didn't feel like throwing a ball at a bunch of wooden pegs." She began to feel impatient as she flicked her hair behind her shoulder. "So what have you been up to?"

"Oh, driving . . . sharing stories . . . driving . . . and more driving."

"That must be fascinating." Suddenly the memory of returning home and discovering that he and her father had left on their trip began to surface, and Samara felt the emotion bubble in her throat. She had difficulty swallowing as Adam spoke again.

"I'm sorry we had to leave so quickly." He seemed to sense what she was thinking. "Your father had to leave straightaway, and it seemed like too good an opportunity to miss. I've never been up this way before."

"Well, I hope the trip's been worth it." She made a conscious effort to control her voice.

"I think it has." Adam's voice was noticeably quieter. "I've talked with your father a lot."

"That must be nice for you." She couldn't stop the derisive response.

"It has been. We've talked about a lot of different things." Adam kept his tone constant. "About traveling adventures . . . more of them. About you . . . about religion."

Samara didn't try to stop the sharp snort of laughter.

"About me and religion! Has he been drinking?"

"No . . . in fact, he has been extremely sober." Adam paused. "I think you'd be surprised by what we've talked about."

"On those topics, I'm sure I would be." Samara leaned back in her chair and rested her leg against the table. The worn patch on the knee of her jeans had some strands of white cotton fraying and she absently twisted them. "My father doesn't discuss religion and we don't talk to him about it. That's a long-standing arrangement in this house."

"Then it's surprising what he's learned without talking or discussing it. You must have been a powerful example while he's been around."

Samara took her time in responding, and she frowned as she twisted the cotton into a tight cord.

"So what exactly has he been talking about?"

She heard Adam cough and clear his throat.

"Well . . ." He coughed again. "I told him how you bore your testimony to me when you were fourteen and how much it impressed me."

Samara was silent so he kept talking.

"I told him how it led to me investigating the Church and how I'd found answers to questions that I hadn't found in all my travels."

"And he believed you?" Again, she heard the skepticism in her own voice.

"I don't know that he believed me, but he certainly has asked a lot of questions." Adam chuckled. "He kept me talking till the early hours of the morning. I even had to ask if we could talk the next day."

Samara shook her head as she tried to visualize her father involved in that type of discussion.

"You know, I really can't imagine him doing that. It just doesn't fit, somehow."

"Are you calling me a liar?" Adam's voice still had a hint of laughter to it, but she knew he wasn't laughing at her.

"No . . . maybe a bit of creative talking involved or maybe you've been closed up in the cab of a truck too long." Samara felt herself smiling. "Cabin fever does strange things to people."

"Well, if this is cabin fever, I hope it lingers." He hesitated. "Samara, we talked about some other things, as well."

She sensed the change in his voice and she bit her bottom lip.

"Like what?"

"Like forgiveness." Adam answered promptly and clearly. He kept talking before she could respond. "Your father really feels bad about the things he's done in the past, Sam. He knows he's hurt you but he wants to put things right."

"Then why hasn't he told me?" She tightened her grip on the phone. "Why does he have to get someone else to speak for him?"

"He didn't ask me to speak for him." Adam's voice was mild and controlled. "In fact, he would probably be very upset if he knew I was telling you this."

"Then why are you?" Her knuckles whitened with tension.

"Because I think you need to know, and because he doesn't know how to tell you, and because I think you have what it takes to reach out to him."

"That's a lot of reasons." She felt suddenly deflated and her shoulders slumped. "And I honestly don't know that they're right. I wouldn't have a clue how to talk about . . . those sorts of things to my father." Her throat constricted with unshed tears.

There was a long silence, then Adam spoke very quietly.

"Samara, nine years ago you bore a beautiful testimony to me about families being eternal."

"And that was when I was naive enough to think it could happen and about one month before my father ruined any chance of it ever happening," Samara interrupted.

"But has that testimony changed? Do you still believe it?" Adam persisted.

"I believe it can happen . . . for other people." Her voice trembled. "Adam, I don't see any point in continuing this conversation."

"But I do." His voice was firm and it compelled her to keep the phone to her ear. "I've made mistakes in the past, Sam . . . just like your father . . . and after talking to him I realize how much I would love to be forgiven. Through talking to him I know that I've behaved like him in lots of ways . . ."

"But you didn't have a wife that you cheated on!" Samara interrupted fiercely as she sat up to the table. "You didn't have children who knew what you were doing and who had to put up with listening to their mother cry night after night while you were away."

"No, I didn't have children." Adam's response was short and barely audible, but it seemed to ring out loudly in Samara's head as she took in what he was saying. She began to shake her head as the tears flowed down her cheeks.

"I got married seven years ago, Sam." The words seemed to drop like pebbles in a pool. "But I had an affair . . ."

Samara never heard the rest of his sentence as she slowly lowered the phone and held it tightly against her stomach, trying to quell the silent wrenching. She held it there for several minutes as she fought for control of her thoughts.

"I got married . . . but I had an affair." She whispered the words over again as she laid the phone on its cradle.

Adam was married and Adam had had an affair.

She stared at the arrangement of black-and-white photos spread out on the table then slowly reached out and picked one up. Emily's puckered lips as she kissed the wombat blurred into shades of gray as Samara gripped each side of the picture and slowly ripped it down the middle. Then she took the two pieces and laid them on top of each other and methodically ripped again and again until the photo was a pile of tiny, misshapen pieces lying on the table.

The phone rang again, but she only picked it up to reset it in the cradle. As she walked to the door it rang again, but she ignored it as she reached for her jacket. The ringing continued as she walked down the hallway and then down the stairs. At the back door it finally stopped, and she stood still, leaning her forehead against the cool wood of the door frame. She really didn't know where she was intending to go, only to get away.

"Samara! Samara, where are you?" She suddenly heard her mother's voice in the lounge, urgent and shrill. "Samara!" The urgency increased as the door to the kitchen swung open and her mother stood staring at her, her face devoid of color as she held out the phone.

"There's been an accident!" Her hand began to shake uncontrollably. "It's Terry . . . and Jackie. They think she's dead!"

* * *

The ride to the hospital seemed to take forever, and as Samara drove, she fretted at the evening traffic, but she was more frustrated by her mother's helpless sobbing.

"Stop it, Mum! Crying isn't going to help them!" She spoke sharply as much to quell her mother's tears as to give vent to her own fears. "We don't know that it's that bad."

"But Rick said that Terry was bad, and Jackie . . ." She stopped and pressed a tissue against her face. "Jackie is in intensive care."

"Which means that she's getting the best care possible." Samara gripped the steering wheel tightly and braked as another car suddenly pulled out in front. "At least she's not sitting for hours in a waiting room."

Her mother didn't seem to have an answer to that logic, and so she sat quietly, twisting a tissue between her fingers and sniffing. Samara breathed deeply as the hospital entrance appeared ahead of them.

Rick was waiting in the reception area when they arrived, and he came to them as they walked through the door. His face was a picture of concern, and Samara's first impulse was to run straight to him but instead, she gripped her mother's elbow more tightly and guided her inside.

"Where's Terry?" Tracey took hold of Rick's hand as he walked on her other side. "And how's Jackie?"

"Terry's in having X-rays and tests. They seem to think that it's mainly his leg and arm. They thought there were internal injuries but it's probably more like deep bruising." He gestured toward another door and they followed.

"And Jackie?" Samara finally spoke.

"Jackie's not good." Rick glanced at her. "She took most of the impact and her head bore the brunt of it."

Samara had an instant vision of Jackie, laughing out loud with her head thrown back and her long, blonde curls swinging in the sunshine.

"Her head . . . or her face?" She pressed her hand to her stomach as nausea washed over her.

"It's more the side of her head." Rick answered quietly. "When I got to her there was so much blood . . ." He stopped for a second.

"There was so much we couldn't really see what was hurt but the doctor said it's mainly the side and the pressure has crushed the forehead."

"Oh, the poor girl. She's so beautiful." Tracey almost whimpered the words as they entered a waiting area.

Several other people, including Jackie's parents, stood up as they entered, and Samara went straight into the outstretched arms of Jackie's mother. They held each other closely as Samara finally cried. Jackie's mother had been a solid foundation for her for so many years, and the sight of her and the pain on her face made all Samara's thoughts about her own situation disappear as they shared their fear for their daughter and friend.

"Thank you for coming up, Sam." Sister Novelli finally stepped back. "The doctor just came out and said that she's in stable condition."

"Which could mean absolutely anything." Jackie's father stood beside his wife with his arm around her waist. "But he did smile as he was saying it." His attempt at joviality failed as his face puckered slightly and he ran his hand over his face. "They're taking her straight into surgery."

"What . . . what will they have to do?" Samara was almost afraid to ask.

Brother Novelli touched the front of his head. "They're going to have to reconstruct her forehead with plates or something. Her skull has been crushed . . ." He stopped talking and merely nodded at the wall.

Samara glanced at her mother, who watched Brother Novelli with tears streaming down her face.

"Um . . . do we know how it actually happened?" She made an attempt to change the subject but it only created an instant change in the atmosphere in the room. The Novellis looked at each other and then they both looked at Rick. He stared at them. Then he folded his arms and cleared his throat.

"I guess Terry was trying not to be late. They were going pretty fast on the road down to the bowling alley and . . ." He stopped and described an arc with his hand. "They crossed and another car had pulled out and it couldn't stop."

"So, it was Terry's fault?" Samara tried to swallow. "There's no doubt about it?"

"I'm afraid so." Rick barely nodded. "The ambulance guys seem to think he wasn't really . . . in control of things."

"In control?" Tracey gave a low moan. "You mean he was high?"

"The police seem to think so." Rick looked away. "He didn't seem to register what had happened after the accident."

"So, does he know how Jackie is?" Samara asked quietly without looking at Jackie's parents. She kept her gaze fixed on Rick.

"I think he realizes that she's hurt, but not much beyond that," Rick answered quietly.

They all stood in silence, then Brother Novelli led his wife and Tracey to sit down. Rick put his hands in his pockets and rocked on his heels while Samara again tried to fight the feeling of nausea that washed over her. She finally shook her head and walked over to her mother with her cell phone in her hand.

"You'd better call Dad and let him know what's happened." She handed the phone to Tracey, who took it hesitantly.

"Can you do it?" She looked up at her daughter, her eyes pleading. "I don't know that I can."

Samara fought back a response and nodded.

"Just dial the number, then." She tried to keep her voice controlled as she waited for her mother to dial. Then she took the phone back. The phone rang several times before she heard Adam's voice.

"Hello . . . Adam?" She saw Rick's quick look and turned away with her finger to her other ear. "It's Samara . . . I need to talk to Dad. Terry's had an accident."

She waited a few seconds; then she heard her father's deep voice.

"What is it? What's happened?" He made no attempt to say hello and she breathed deeply to get composure. "Who's hurt?"

"Terry's had a car accident. He's not seriously hurt, but Jackie was in the passenger seat and she's badly hurt." Samara heard her voice, level and clear, as if it were making a news release. "It seems that Terry had taken something but they're not sure of the extent of it."

"So it was his stupid fault?" Her father seemed to spit the words into the phone. "Where's your mother?"

"She's not quite up to talking right now." Samara answered calmly. "She's pretty upset."

"She would be." Again his tone was brisk, and it seemed to make Samara feel even more distant. "I'll get back as soon as I can."

"Oh, don't hurry." Samara responded coolly. "I don't think he'll be going anywhere fast, so there'll be plenty of time to tell him what a fool he is." She held the phone away and firmly pressed the off button. Her mother had been watching and she half stood.

"What did he say?"

"Nothing worth repeating and he'll get here as soon as he can." She shrugged as she began to walk away up the hallway toward the water cooler. "Probably after he's loaded another shipment."

The water from the cooler was icy cold and she drank two glasses, letting the iciness work from the inside out, soothing the heat of her face and her feelings. As she crumpled the plastic cup in her hand and threw it into the bin, she became aware of Rick standing behind her. He didn't speak but she knew exactly what his expression would be like if she turned around. She pretended to hunt in her bag for something but there was nothing to pretend with so she finally zipped the bag and hung it over her shoulder.

"Don't you hate it when you think you have something and then it's gone?" She tried to talk brightly as she turned, patting the handbag.

"Yes . . . I do hate it," Rick responded quietly.

There was a brief silence and she couldn't help looking up at him. Rick's brow was creased with a frown, and he was staring straight at her with a questioning look.

"She'll be all right, won't she?" Samara gulped. "She always bounces back."

"Yes . . . she does." He nodded. "She's an amazing person."

Suddenly the blank, pale-colored wall opposite seemed to become a silent movie screen as images of Jackie and herself began to flash in front of her. The very first time she had seen young Jackie sitting in church, her blonde, curly hair bobbing as she talked busily with her sister and mother and how Samara had experienced a curious mixture of dislike and envy. The first time she had plucked up the courage to answer an invitation to Jackie's birthday party and found herself enjoying the experience. Sleepovers at the Novellis', where she'd listened to Jackie's very accurate mimicking of people they both knew . . . especially boys. Doing things she never would have done on her own, but with Jackie beside her it had been fun.

"Samara?" Rick spoke quietly beside her and she slowly turned to look at him.

"Why do bad things happen to good people, Rick?" She swallowed hard. "Why can some people keep hurting others and they just sail on through life without getting hurt themselves?"

He didn't try to answer because she was already shaking her head, and he knew her mind was somewhere in the cabin of a truck, a long way away.

Chapter Sixteen

They were allowed to see Terry first. He was propped up in the bed, staring out the window, when Samara and her mother walked into the room. His left leg was lying outside of the covers with a heavy cast on it and his left arm was also in a cast and encased in a sling. When they walked in, he kept his face turned away from them.

"Terry?" Tracey crossed to his bedside while Samara stood beside a chair at the end of the bed. "How are you feeling, love?"

He didn't answer straightaway but Samara watched the muscle in his jaw working hard as he finally shook his head against the pillow. When he still didn't speak, Tracey gently put her hand over the top of his and leaned forward to kiss him on the forehead. He still didn't look at her but his eyes squeezed tightly shut and he took a deep, quivering breath.

"The nurse said Jackie's out of surgery." His voice was so low Samara had to strain to hear it.

"She is." Tracey nodded and patted his hand. "And they said the surgery was successful."

Terry barely nodded.

"What did I do to her?"

Samara caught her breath at the agony in his voice, and as the tears began to flow down her mother's cheeks, she stepped forward slightly.

"She hurt her head badly." Samara gripped the rail at the end of the bed. "They had to reconstruct parts of her skull . . ."

"Her head?" Terry actually turned to face her, and she saw the look of horror on his face. "Her skull?" It was barely a whisper.

"She's in intensive care, Terry." Samara felt her own voice quiver and she swallowed hard. "But the surgeons think she'll be all right. They're almost certain there's no brain damage."

"Brain . . ." He pressed his head back against the pillow with his eyes shut again. "What have I done to her?"

They were saved from giving him an answer when a nurse stepped briskly into the room and lifted the clipboard at the end of the bed. She glanced briefly at his face and then at Tracey, and Samara could see her professionally weighing the situation.

"Time to get a few vital statistics, Terry." She smiled brightly and looked meaningfully at Samara and Tracey. "Can you pop back in a few minutes?"

Samara could see the relief on her mother's face as they quickly left the room, but right outside the door, Tracey leaned up against the wall and exhaled deeply.

"I have no idea what to say to him." She shook her head. "Now that I can see the agony he's in about Jackie, I just want to comfort him and say everything's all right, but I know he has to come to terms with so much more than that."

"But maybe not just yet." Samara responded quietly. "I think he's going to have to deal with a few more issues of his own, first."

"The drugs?" Tracey began to rub her forearms as Samara nodded.

"Maybe being in here is a blessing in disguise." She glanced around at the walls. "The doctors might be able to help him a whole lot more than we ever could."

Her mother was silent as she pondered Samara's words, then she nodded. "I hope you're right . . . although he's still going to have to deal with everything about Jackie."

"And again, maybe this will frighten him into doing something positive."

"But he *was* doing something positive." Tracey's voice was almost a moan. "He was trying to go to the young adult activity, and he told me he was going to come to church on Sunday."

"But then he obviously felt the need to have something in order to get through the activity." Samara folded her arms. "You remember saying once how Dad always needs to have a drink before he goes out so that he can enjoy himself better."

"But he doesn't have a lot." Tracey reacted immediately, then was silenced by the look on Samara's face. "But I see what you mean."

"We could say a lot more 'buts,' Mum, but the main thing is that Terry has to be accountable for this, and that could be a good thing . . . in the long run," she added quietly.

"Well, I hope so." Tracey straightened up. "At least when Jackie comes around we can encourage him to be there for her. I think he really likes her."

Samara was silent as she stared at her mother. Her mother really did seem to exist in another world at times, apparently only able to deal with what mattered to her immediately.

"Yes, Mum. I think you might be right." She pulled her hair back with both hands and let it swing down around her shoulders. "Let's just focus on getting Terry better."

"Yes, that's what we have to concentrate on." Tracey murmured as she stared at her daughter and she nodded. "And your father and Adam will be here soon as well."

The nurse suddenly walked out of Terry's room, so they stopped talking. She smiled again and nodded for them to go back in, but as Tracey walked past her, the nurse gently touched Samara's arm.

"The doctor will be up to see him later. Terry's going to have to go through a bit of withdrawal, so we'll need to talk to your mother about it when she's not so upset."

"I see." Samara nodded. "We'll do whatever it takes."

"I'm sure you will." The nurse smiled kindly and nodded back toward the room. "Sometimes things like this are a blessing."

Samara smiled weakly. "I did just say that to Mum." She took a quick breath. "I surely hope it is."

* * *

Jackie's parents were still in the waiting room when Samara and Tracey returned. Sister Novelli was sitting on a chair with her face buried in her hands while her husband sat beside her with his arm around her shoulders. Rick stood staring at the floor.

"What's happened?" Samara went straight to him. "I thought Jackie was all right."

"She just took a turn for the worse . . . internal hemorrhaging." Rick shook his head. "The operation on her head went well, but this is completely unexpected. They've taken her back into surgery."

"Oh, my goodness." Tracey's face drained of color. "The poor child." She turned to Jackie's parents. "I am so sorry. I do hope everything goes all right."

Brother Novelli slowly lifted his head and stared at her through tear-dimmed eyes. "I'm sorry too, Sister Danes." His shoulders slumped. "And I only hope I can forgive your son if anything happens to our Jackie."

Tracey's hand went to her mouth as she realized what he was saying. Then she turned to Samara. "I . . . I think we should go."

"Are you sure?" Samara glanced at her mother and then back to Rick. "Should we?"

"Perhaps," Rick answered quietly and gestured with his head down the hallway. Samara and her mother followed immediately, and when they were just out of earshot, he stopped and ran his hand through his hair.

"I think I'd better just prepare you . . . the police came up before and with these complications with Jackie . . ." He hesitated and folded his arms. "It appears that Terry may face charges anyway for driving under the influence of whatever—but if anything happens to Jackie—it could be a lot worse."

"Worse?" Samara felt her throat go dry.

Rick nodded. "If she dies he'll face manslaughter charges."

Samara heard her mother's groan and it seemed to coincide exactly with the rolling, sinking feeling in her own stomach. She wasn't sure if it was the actual thought of Jackie not making it through or the fact that Terry might end up in prison that hit hardest. Both thoughts were fighting inside her head as she stared at Rick. In that split second he seemed to be representing everything that could possibly hurt her and she directed her resentment straight at him.

"You're saying my brother will be a murderer?" She kept her voice low and quiet as her fingernails dug into the palms of her hands.

"No, I'm not saying that, Sam," Rick answered quietly.

"Yes, you are. You've already condemned him." Samara felt all her fear feeding her resentment, and his voice seemed to echo hollowly in her ears.

"I'm saying that the police may press charges if there are any complications and that you should be prepared."

"Oh, that makes it better. Thank you for the glad tidings." Samara nodded grimly and took her mother's arm. Tracey offered no resistance as Samara began to lead her down the hall, only pausing briefly to look back at Rick.

"We'll just go and make sure we're well prepared for the trial."

* * *

The tiny pieces of black-and-white photograph were still spread over the desk where she'd left them. Some had fluttered to the floor from the breeze through the open window. A draft of the cool evening air wafted through the window as she bent to pick up the pieces and some others drifted down beside her. She gathered them up and walked over to the window.

Down below, several new cars were parked in the parking area and lights were showing in the motel units that had been empty earlier that morning. Samara looked at her watch as she closed the window and drew the curtain.

"And life goes on," she murmured as the curtains blocked out the scene below. "Or sometimes it does."

As the words left her lips, Samara felt tears forming and she gripped the curtains tightly. As control came back she turned and contemplated her bed. Thoughts of sleep were still far away, but she found herself mentally negotiating the distance to the side of her bed . . . the side where she usually knelt to pray but where she'd been an infrequent visitor for some time. She stood still as if a hand were holding onto her shoulder, pulling her back.

"Don't be stupid, Samara. Jackie needs all the help she can get." The words were like a starting gun being fired and she physically pulled herself away from the spot. But she passed the bed and went on toward the set of drawers by the bed. The top of the dresser held some boxes with jewelry in and several framed photographs. Her hand trembled as she picked up a shiny ebony frame.

The frame contained a white mat with three long rectangular spaces cut to accommodate three black-and-white images. On one side, her own image laughed back at her, a wide smile still showing behind a large ice cream. Her eyes were huge and sparkling. On the other side, the image was of Jackie, again smiling broadly, her hair tumbling around her face and an ice cream held in her hand.

Samara smiled reluctantly as she took the frame in both hands.

The center picture was of both her and Jackie. It was taken the same day as the others, but they were sitting on a fence, laughing at something in the distance. The wind was blowing their hair back from their faces and they looked completely happy. Rick had taken the photos, insisting they remember the day.

"We were happy." Samara whispered as she set the frame upright. "First year at university, out in the world but with no complications and no relationships to worry about . . . except wondering who we'd go to the next dance with." She lightly drummed her fingertips on the edge of the dresser. "Friends forever." She read the flowing silver script that she'd scrawled in the corner of the photo mat, and suddenly the years began to flash by in her mind—years filled with activities, spiritual experiences, and confidences—all shared with her best friend.

"Oh, Jackie . . . I'm so sorry." The tears began to flow down her cheeks as she slowly backed down to the side of her bed and knelt on the small braided mat on the floor. She didn't even try to wipe the tears away as she leaned against the bed and felt the familiar embrace of the mattress and quilt against her arms. With her heart hammering, she closed her eyes and clenched her hands together. "I've been so selfish. Please forgive me."

Tears mingled with her prayers as she began to share her feelings with the only One she knew would understand . . . One who loved her unconditionally.

* * *

Samara went up to the hospital by herself the next day. Her mother had managed to get up in the morning, but a severe migraine had rendered her unable to move, so Samara had called on Sister Patterson to look after her and the motel reception while she went out.

A phone call to her tutor at school earlier in the morning had reassured her that she was free to work on her project on her own time, and a brief message on the answering machine from Sister Novelli indicated that Jackie's condition was not only stable but improving. It seemed as if the things she had petitioned Heavenly Father about the night before were coming to fruition, and she felt a renewed strength of conviction. There was a different feeling as she drove to the hospital, and she began to hum a simple Primary tune as she approached the gates.

She parked the car on the far side of the parking lot and took her time walking to the main entrance, but her steps faltered slightly as she walked through the foyer and saw Rick coming out of the small gift shop. He was carrying a paper bag that he tucked under his arm as he pushed his wallet into his back pocket. He might have walked straight in front of her, but he seemed to hesitate as if he'd forgotten something, and then he turned toward her.

Samara fought to quell the disappointment that rose as he nodded politely. A sudden recollection of the way she had treated him the day before made her cheeks drain of color.

"Hello, Rick."

He only nodded again, but he did wait and fall into step beside her. She took a deep breath and attempted a smile, focusing on the positive feelings she'd been having since her prayers the night before.

"I got the message that Jackie is improving." Samara held the bag of things she had brought for Terry close against her chest. "Isn't that wonderful?"

"It is." Rick walked with one hand in his pocket and the paper bag in the other hand. "Her parents are very relieved."

"We all are." Samara noticed that he kept looking straight ahead. "Do you know when we'll be able to see her?"

"Brother and Sister Novelli are with her now."

"So are you going up?" Samara felt her breath catch as she asked, but she had a sudden image of Jackie and Rick laughing together at Jackie's house. Somehow it seemed right that Rick should be the next one to see Jackie.

"No . . . I'm actually going to see Terry." Rick swung the bag by his side. "I thought I'd take him some stuff."

"You're going to see Terry?" She didn't do anything to disguise her surprise, but she was startled by his reaction. He stopped in his tracks, stared at the wall ahead, and shrugged his shoulders.

"I was but I'll just wait here if you find the prospect too unpleasant or potentially incriminating." He extended one hand forward to indicate for her to keep going. "You obviously think I'm the one who's going to put him into prison."

Samara stopped as well and was immediately hit from behind as a woman failed to see her from behind a large bouquet of flowers. She fell forward slightly and Rick caught her by the arm, but he released it as soon as she regained her balance.

"Thank you," she mumbled as she tucked her hair behind her ears. "I didn't mean that I didn't want you to see Terry . . ." She hesitated, but he didn't respond. "I just thought you would be going to see Jackie."

"I might, later on." Rick barely nodded. "Her family is most important for her right now."

"But you've been here since it happened." She licked her lips as she stared at his lowered eyelids. "You're always there for people."

She didn't see Rick frown again but she heard his quick intake of breath.

"Well, I imagine she would want to see you more than me . . . seeing you're her best friend." He hesitated. "Unless that's changed as well."

"Um . . . I hope she wants to see me." Samara gripped the bag. "I was praying so hard last night—" She stopped as her voice caught and she turned her head away. "I haven't prayed like that for a long time."

She didn't notice Rick's silence as she struggled for control. Then she felt herself being pulled to the edge of the hallway. A large family moved past them with the mother calling to several young children who were running ahead. The temporary commotion gave her the chance to get her composure, and it seemed to help Rick as well. He leaned against the wall and studied her in his familiar way.

"I feel like you know every thought in my head when you watch me like that." She maintained a careful study of his shirt pocket.

"I used to think I did, as well. I used to think that I was getting to know you better than you knew yourself." He didn't smile and his tone was quiet. "Now I'm thinking that I never did know you."

Samara glanced up quickly and her heart did an unusual flutter as she looked straight into his eyes.

"What's happened, Samara?" He sounded genuine but remote, as if he were searching for a solution to a mystery. "Fill me in on where Samara Danes is at the moment because I really can't figure it out."

"I . . . I, um . . ." she stammered as she thought about the prayers she had offered last night—for things to get back to normal, to be able to restore old friendships and happiness. She took a deep breath. "I guess I'm trying to figure that out, too." She hesitated. "But things keep happening that make me get upset with the situation."

"And none of it's your fault," Rick stated quietly. "But you seem to have to deal with it all and everyone anyway."

"That's what it feels like." She nodded, appreciating his understanding.

"And sometimes it feels like they're blaming you and you don't even get to defend yourself."

Samara glanced up, impressed with how well he was reading the situation. Then she saw the look on his face and the way he folded his arms almost defensively. In a second she knew he wasn't really referring to her, and she remembered the look on his face yesterday when she had swept past him and left the hospital.

"And that's exactly how I've been treating you." She looked straight at the top button on his shirt.

"Pretty much." His answer was casual but instant, and she watched the frown on his face deepen with a sense of foreboding.

"Samara . . ." He raised one hand as if to try and get a point across. "I do want to help you and your family, and Jackie . . . and her family, but there's a limit to the way you can treat people. I won't just be there whenever you feel like you need someone to be nice to you."

The corridor seemed unnaturally quiet as no other people came by, and Rick's words seemed to hang in the air between them. Was that how he saw their relationship? Was that how she saw it? She stared hard at his shirt.

"I'm sorry," she quietly responded. "I didn't mean to."

"I know you didn't," Rick added. "But someone's got to tell you that you do it."

"Jackie does as well," Samara whispered as she tried to smile. "Even Adam. I must not be a very good listener."

The mention of Adam's name seemed to bring an instant change to the atmosphere. Rick straightened abruptly and gestured up the hallway.

"Well then, I think you listen, but you forget too easily." Rick's voice was gentle but quietly decisive. "Let's go and see Terry."

They began to walk in silence, Rick matching his stride with hers, but outside the door to Terry's room, Samara hesitated.

"I really am sorry, Rick."

She watched as his familiar smile half tilted the side of his mouth, and he shook his head as he pushed her gently toward the door.

"Samara Danes . . . life would be so much easier without you."

Chapter Seventeen

Terry was moving slowly around on crutches within two days, and his main motivation was to see Jackie. She had regained consciousness and her father had brought the good news when Samara had been visiting Terry.

"So is she all right?" Samara watched Brother Novelli's face carefully. "Really all right?"

He chose his words carefully but there was a smile on his face.

"She's heavily sedated, and her face and head—" He swallowed hard. "Well, you can come and see for yourselves."

"We can come now?" Terry's voice broke and he raised his good hand to cover his face. It took him awhile to regain his composure, then he smiled weakly. "That's all I've been thinking about and now that you say I can . . . I'm too scared."

"I'm scared too, Terry." Brother Novelli ran a finger down a line on the bedcover. "But yours was the first name she said when she regained consciousness so I think you should go to her, pronto."

"She . . . she said my name?" Terry stammered as he looked over at Samara. "But I was the one who hurt her."

"I think it would pay you not to remind me of that, son." Brother Novelli deepened the impression on the blanket. "I'm still working on the whole forgiveness thing with you, but my daughter has always been the one to teach me things, and she's leading by example now."

Terry stared as he spoke and then he shook his head.

"I don't think I'll ever forgive myself, even if you do. I've had time to do a lot of thinking just lying here and . . . I really want to get my act together." He hesitated. "Before the accident I knew that I should change but now . . ." He looked right at Jackie's father. "I've been praying so hard for Jackie, and I've realized that I have to pray for myself, and now I really want to get better . . . and it's different, somehow."

Brother Novelli nodded silently and held out his hand to Terry. Very solemnly, Terry held out his hand as well and the two men shook hands . . . only one firm shake, but it seemed to seal an unspoken agreement.

"Right, then . . ." Brother Novelli was immediately brisk. "Do we need to get you a wheelchair or are you already racing on crutches?"

"I'll do crutches." Terry spoke firmly as he gently lowered his leg to the ground. "I want to be standing when I face Jackie."

Sister Novelli met them outside Jackie's room. She was leaning against the wall in the hallway and using a tissue to wipe her eyes. As they approached she held up the tissue and smiled weakly.

"I have to come outside and do my crying every now and then so Jackie doesn't hear me."

"Then it's probably a good thing she can't see or those bloodshot eyes would be a dead giveaway." Brother Novelli tried to sound jovial as he put his arm around his wife's shoulders and kissed her quickly on the forehead. "Is she still awake?"

"She comes and goes but she's responding at the moment."

Samara watched Terry's face as he listened to their conversation, and the color seemed to drain out of his face with every word.

"Is Jackie . . . blind?" His voice quivered.

"No, not blind. The doctors have checked and she does respond to light, but there's so much swelling around her eyes that they've got them bandaged." Sister Novelli put her hand on Terry's arm. "Just remember that it is our Jackie in there—even if it doesn't look like her."

Terry nodded and glanced at Samara as if for reinforcement, and she quietly stepped up beside him as Brother Novelli opened the door.

The first impression was of the number of tubes that were connected to Jackie and then the whiteness of the bandages that encased the upper part of her head. Only her lips and nose were visible, and those were badly swollen and bruised. From what Samara could see, there was nothing about the person in the bed that resembled her friend except the two beautifully manicured hands that lay limply on the bedcovers.

Samara heard Terry's gasp and she quickly put her arm around him as he swayed. Brother Novelli was watching as well, and he moved a chair in behind him close to the bed. Terry never moved his eyes from Jackie's face as he awkwardly sat down.

"Jackie, love . . ." Sister Novelli leaned close to her daughter to speak quietly but clearly. "You have a visitor."

There was the slightest hand movement to indicate that Jackie had heard, so her mother leaned over again.

"Terry's here, dear. Terry's come to see you." She watched Jackie's hand but the movement came from her daughter's lips this time.

The sound was barely audible and her lips hardly moved, but Samara knew Jackie was saying her brother's name, and the way the single word came out held a world of meaning. Terry seemed to have frozen in his seat as he watched her closely, but then Brother Novelli put his hand on his shoulder and pointed to Jackie's hand lying closest to him. The fingers were raising slightly off the bedsheet, and he indicated for Terry to touch them.

As Terry laid his hand under Jackie's, her fingers softly tightened around it, and he moaned slightly as he laid his other hand on top of hers and bowed his head onto them. Samara watched in awe as her brother's shoulders heaved as Jackie's whole body seemed to relax.

Samara looked at Jackie's parents and she could see that they were as overwhelmed as she was at the connection they were witnessing. Brother Novelli silently nodded his head toward the door, and she quietly followed them both outside. Terry was oblivious to them leaving.

"I had no idea." Sister Novelli wiped the tears from her eyes again as they stood outside the door. "I had no idea that they felt like that about each other." Her face puckered again and she pulled out another tissue. "You could feel it."

Her husband was nodding, but he seemed incapable of speaking.

"Jackie told me recently that it's always been Terry." Samara took a tissue as Sister Novelli held it out to her, and then she couldn't speak for awhile either.

"It's amazing what a crisis like this can do." Brother Novelli shook his head. "It makes us all realize how we truly feel."

"And there's no time to pretend or be deceitful." His wife nodded. "I have told Jackie so many times how much I love her over the last few days, and yet I don't really say it very much usually." Her voice broke again and her husband hugged her.

"You say it in so many other ways, love. Jackie knows you love her."

"Yes, but I realized how much I needed her to hear me this time. I needed her to hear me say that I loved her," she repeated quietly, but the words seemed to ring loudly in Samara's ears.

"Well, I get the feeling she's probably hearing it a whole lot more right now." Brother Novelli stared at the door to his daughter's room, then he turned to Samara. "And Samara, thank you for being here for Jackie. Your friendship is priceless to her and we really appreciate that."

His quiet words settled on Samara.

"I . . . I really don't know what I'd do without Jackie, either." Actually saying the words made them a reality, and Samara turned her head away as the tears fell. In a second, she felt herself cradled against Brother Novelli's chest, his wife's arms around them both.

* * *

There was the usual lull at the motel reception in the early afternoon, so Samara used the time to evaluate some of the final photos for her exhibition. She lifted two prints out of a folder and laid them on the reception desk side by side, then she stood back to study both photos carefully. They were similar in composition, with Toby wearing the large snake around his neck, but she had used a different exposure for each photo. She tried squinting her eyes to discern the variations in shading, but the choice seemed too difficult to make.

"Are you in pain?" The doorbell hadn't rung so the voice was unexpected.

Samara jumped as she looked up. The blood rushed to her cheeks.

"Adam . . . what are you doing here?" Her tone was so accusing that he glanced behind him then looked back.

"Um . . . I'm staying here?" He stepped through the doorway and the bell sounded so that she jumped again. "Are you all right?"

"Yes, yes, I'm fine." She answered almost too quickly and he nodded as he set his bag down on the ground.

"And Terry?"

"Terry's all right. Mum has gone up to the hospital to pick him up. He's even moving around on crutches."

"And Jackie?" He was standing with his hands in the front pockets of a well-worn, khaki fishing vest and it somehow began to stir memories for Samara so that she answered automatically.

"Jackie's fine, too." She frowned as the images became clearer in her mind. "She's going to be in the hospital for awhile, but they're happy with her progress." She put her head to one side. "How old is that jacket?"

"This?" Adam moved one hand to the left pocket so that it swung open. "Probably twelve years old . . . maybe fifteen."

Samara nodded thoughtfully. "You were wearing that the day I met you at the beach." Her voice softened. "It fascinated me how you had rolls of film in the little pockets and lenses in the big pockets."

"You remember that?" Adam looked taken aback, then he smiled. "I probably shouldn't be surprised because I always wear it. It makes me feel professional."

She laughed as he did and it seemed to break the ice between them.

She pointed down at the desk. "I wasn't in pain before. I was squinting to see which of these pictures has the best contrasts." She held one up. "I'm leaning toward this one."

Adam walked closer to the desk to look at the photo, and she felt her heart immediately begin to beat faster.

"It's good." His summary was characteristically brief but she knew that he meant what he said and she nodded, trying to quell the tremble in her stomach as he came closer.

"Then I'll use it."

"What if I'd said the other one was better?" He rested one elbow on the desk and looked straight at her.

"I . . . then I'd probably use that one." She frowned. "I trust your judgment."

"But that doesn't teach you to trust yours." His voice suddenly became raspy and he turned aside to cough heavily. She noticed that there were darker shadows under his eyes and that his cheekbones seemed more pronounced. He and her father must have done more talking than eating.

"Trust my judgment?" Samara laid the photo back down carefully. "I'm not very good in that department. I'd rather leave it to the experts."

"You'll have to take responsibility someday." He cleared his throat and rested his hand against the doorjamb as he bent down to pick up his bag. His voice was unexpectedly gruff as he pointed at the desk. "Your mother said she'd put me back in the same unit when we got back. Is it still free?"

Samara stared at him for the briefest moment, then she ran her finger down the page of the bookings.

"She's put a cross through that unit for three days." She nodded. "I guess she wasn't sure when you'd be here."

"Mmm . . ." He smiled as he turned toward the door. "Your father said she always expects three days leeway when he's traveling."

"Yes . . . apparently they have an understanding." Samara quickly wrote his surname onto the register, then she frowned. "Where is my father, by the way?"

Adam gestured out of the door. "He dropped me off on the way to the hospital. He called your mum and she was on her way up there, so they'll come home together."

"With Terry." Samara nodded as she underlined his name and set the pen down. "That'll be interesting. It'll either be a very silent ride home or they'll be arguing the whole way."

"I think they'll be fine," Adam responded quietly. Then he hesitated. "You know, Sam, I think your parents really do have an understanding that suits them."

"Well, it suits me too." She frowned slightly. "It always suits me if my father is away. I just wish my mother would stand up to him sometimes."

"Maybe she doesn't want to . . . or need to." Adam leaned against the door.

"Well, I think she does. She lives on drugs to help her cope with life." Samara placed the pen down carefully. "That is not a life . . . at least not the life I feel like she should have, and it's my father that's done it to her."

"Is it your father?" Adam raised one eyebrow. "Or could it be that you've done it to her?"

"Me?" Samara looked up quickly. "That's ridiculous!"

Adam shrugged. "I talked to your dad about his affair. He admits that he reacted badly to a bad situation, but he and your mother have resolved things."

"You mean she forgave him?" Samara shook her head. "She shouldn't have."

"But that's just it, Sam." Adam spoke quietly but firmly. "She feels she did, and your father feels she did, but you were there and you've never forgiven either of them . . . your father for doing it or your mother for taking him back."

"Because it's always miserable when he does come back," Samara said.

Adam was silent for a long time. He walked over to the desk and leaned against it. Samara could feel the warmth of his body emanating across the counter.

"Have you ever thought what it must be like to live with your own child judging you day after day?"

Samara stared at him. "You mean . . . me?"

Adam nodded. "Like it or not, Sam, your mother loves your father, and he feels the same way, but they both know how you've felt all these years, so he has stayed away and they've both lived with the guilt of letting you down."

"But what about Terry?" Samara was immediately defensive. "He's had to put up with it as well."

"Terry has had to put up with the consequences." Adam gave a half smile. "I don't think Terry feels quite as strongly as you do about many things."

Samara stood silently, letting the full impact of his words sink in. There was no doubt that her mother was often happier when her father was coming home, but it never seemed to stay that way.

"But they argue so much when Dad is home. I hate it." She knew she was sounding defensive.

"And he knows that," Adam responded immediately. "But think how he feels. He knows how things should be, but your mother is out of it a lot of the time, and so he feels like he has to make her realize while he's here what she should be doing to help herself." He began to cough as if the long explanation had taken his breath away. Samara opened her mouth then shut it again until he'd finished and taken a deep breath. His voice was very low and quiet when he finally spoke.

"He really does love all of you, Sam, but he's had a rough life and he doesn't know how to express it very well. You could help him." He turned toward the door then hesitated. "I've been thinking a lot about that day we met . . . remembering in a lot more detail, and it seems to me that you loved your father then."

He didn't wait for a response as he walked through the doorway and slid the door to a close behind him.

* * *

No other guests arrived at the motel before her parents arrived home two hours later, and Samara was grateful for the time to think. She never moved from the desk after Adam left, and the time was spent reliving an endless stream of events from the last nine years. Her brain sifted through all of the negative incidents that she had experienced with her parents, especially with her father. For a long time she felt herself mentally defending her actions to Adam. Then there seemed to be a period when she felt nothing.

"Have you ever thought what it must be like to live with your own child judging you day after day?" she whispered as she added another line of drawing to the complex pattern she'd already made on the desk pad. "Your parents have resolved it, but you've never forgiven either of them."

Samara laid both arms on the desk and rested her head on them. Then a chain of images ran through her mind. She could see herself as the tight-lipped spectator to the interactions between her parents over the years. Had she really been the cause of some of their problems?

The sound of car doors closing outside made her sit up quickly and rub her hand over her face. She picked up a pen and pretended to look busy as the door opened and Terry eased his way over the low step on his crutches. His mother walked behind, prepared to help him if he needed it. Samara looked up slowly and was surprised to see both of them smiling.

"Hey, Sammy." Terry swung forward awkwardly as he tried to steady the crutch with his bandaged arm.

"Take it easy, Terry." Tracey immediately supported her son's elbow. "You can only go slowly."

"I know, Mum." Terry winked at Samara, but she was still frowning slightly. "What's been happening here, sis? You look dark."

"Who, me?" Samara shook her head and faked a smile. "You took awhile. Mum left ages ago."

"Your father met us at the hospital, and then we met up with the Novellis, and then . . ." Tracey hesitated and glanced at Terry.

"And then we had to talk to the police." Terry looked suddenly serious and Samara swallowed hard.

"What did they say?"

"What didn't they say?" Terry rolled his eyes and leaned heavily on his crutches. "They went through the whole accident in detail and then into all Jackie's injuries until I was a mess." He shook his head and his eyes glistened. "I may not have had a lot of recall of what happened before, but I sure do now."

"But what did they say about . . ." Samara hesitated. "About convicting you or anything?"

Tracey put her hand on Terry's arm.

"The Novellis aren't going to press charges. Jackie's adamant about that." Tracey's lips began trembling and she fought to gain control. "But the police say he's still got to face charges for irresponsible driving and being under the influence . . ."

"Which probably means community service, a fine, and losing his license." Eddy had walked in behind his wife, carrying a bag in each hand. He set them down on the floor and rested his hand on his wife's shoulder. "Which means he got off lightly." His voice was gruff, but there was a different sound to it, and Samara stared at him.

"I have to go to court and the police said I'll probably be ordered into rehab as well." Terry glanced at his father. "I never thought I'd be glad to hear something like that."

Samara stared as her father merely nodded, but she could see his eyes glisten as he bent to pick up the bags.

"Serves you right, but you'd better learn your lesson properly." He sounded brusque as usual as he nudged Tracey's arm and gestured with his head toward the desk. "Anyway . . . enough mucking around. Samara should be working on her stuff . . . not doing your job."

Chapter Eighteen

Samara had already taken Terry some breakfast the next morning and was having her own breakfast in the kitchen when her mother suggested that Adam travel in to town with her for the day.

"I was talking to him late last night and he said he'd like to have a look around Brisbane." Tracey stirred some scrambled eggs in a pan. "I knew you were going in to school so I suggested you give him a ride. You can take my car instead of using the bus."

"Thanks, Mum." Samara bit into her toast. "But I may not finish until really late. I have to set up the exhibit today."

Somehow the thought of spending time with Adam caused a tight knot in the pit of her stomach.

"Maybe he could help you." Tracey persisted. "I'm sure he's done things like that before."

"He can't help, Mum." Samara shook her head. "I have to do it all myself."

She stopped talking as the back door opened and Adam walked in behind her father. The size of the two men suddenly made the kitchen seem very small, and Samara studied the piece of toast in her hand so that she didn't have to look at them. She almost didn't suppress her moan when her mother immediately turned to Adam.

"Sam says she'll need to work late at the university. Will that be a problem for you?"

Samara refused to look up as there was a slight pause while Adam pulled out a chair and sat down across the table from her.

"No problem for me." His voice was quiet but clear and she looked up. His face was a better color than the day before, and the dark shadows were a lot less pronounced. She could even see a suggestion of a smile playing at the corners of his mouth, and she found herself responding.

"I haven't got time to play the tour guide." She put the last piece of toast in her mouth and stood up. "But if you want a ride, I'll be leaving in half an hour."

"How gracious of you." Eddy spoke for the first time and she saw him raise one eyebrow as he nodded toward Adam. "I could run you in later if you want."

Adam didn't hesitate as he glanced at Samara.

"Half an hour will be fine."

* * *

"Do you ever wear that little gold ring your father gave you?" The question was completely unexpected, and Samara swerved slightly across the lane as she looked at Adam quickly. Somebody tooted their car horn behind and she forced herself to concentrate on the road.

"Um . . . I still have it somewhere." She shrugged. "But I don't wear it."

"Why not?" He looked straight ahead at the highway and the endless line of cars in front of them. It was early in the morning and they were right in the middle of rush hour traffic into Brisbane.

"I . . . stopped wearing it when he had the affair." She gripped the steering wheel. "There wasn't any point wearing it after that." She finished abruptly.

"So you stopped loving him right then?" Adam looked curious as he stroked his beard.

"Pretty much." Samara glanced at him. "You don't give up, do you? I thought you were coming for the ride, not to interrogate me."

"I'm not interrogating, I'm just interested." He shrugged. "But I'll stop if it makes you feel uncomfortable."

Something about the gentle tone of his voice made her instantly more aware of the smallness of the car interior and the distance between them, and she shifted in her seat.

"Actually, I was going to tell you that I kept dreaming last night . . . well, not actually dreaming . . ." She frowned. "You know you said that you'd been remembering when we met at the beach?"

Adam nodded and she held up four fingers.

"I must have gone over it at least four times last night during the night. I don't remember sleeping, but I didn't feel tired this morning so I don't know if I was actually dreaming, but I knew what I was remembering." She sighed. "It was just so vivid."

"So tell me how you remember it." Adam turned slightly to face her.

It took the rest of the journey in to town to recount the things she'd been thinking about, and Adam nodded and smiled, interrupting only occasionally.

"Well, that's pretty much how I remember it too." He finally nodded as she parked the car. "Except that I recall you were far more outspoken with your testimony of the Church. That was what really impressed me."

"You mean it wasn't my stunning, young model looks?" She forced a smile then frowned when he didn't respond. "Maybe I was just younger and more uninhibited then. My mother used to say that I had no shame about things I cared about."

"Possibly." Adam reached for the door handle. "Or maybe you cared more then."

Samara took her time getting out of the car, and she frowned as she locked the door. Adam was already standing outside as she opened the trunk of the car and pulled out her folder of photos. He held out his hands to take them, but she shook her head and slammed down the lid to the trunk.

"Have I hit a touchy spot?" He began to walk beside her with his hands in his pockets and the camera bag slung over his shoulder. "Because I'm trying to."

She stopped in her tracks and stared at him but he kept walking,

"I really don't know what you're trying to do or what you're talking about." She began to walk ahead of him. "But I do think that you've spent too much time with my father."

She felt his hand on her arm again but she shrugged it away. There was no tingling sensation this time, only a sense of irritation, and she walked faster, glancing at her watch.

"We'd better hurry or I'll miss the tutor."

Neither spoke until they reached her building and Adam was a model of courtesy as she primly introduced him to a couple of her tutors. Within minutes he was engaged in a technical conversation with one of the older female tutors, and then they excused themselves as she took him to view the rest of the exhibits from the other students.

Samara forced herself to concentrate as she mounted her selected photos onto thick sheets of polystyrene and began to fix them onto large sheets of board that she'd covered in a deep red Hessian fabric. Soon the process became almost automated as she repeated it and her mind began to wander.

"Maybe you cared more then," she muttered under her breath as she fixed an excessive amount of double-sided tape to the back of a print. "Maybe you don't know how much I care now, Adam Russell."

She fixed the photo in position and turned to the next.

"Maybe you think you know me, and you don't."

The phrase made her instantly aware of the conversation she'd had with Rick just a few days before.

"I used to think I knew you better than you knew yourself." She surprised herself by remembering his words, and she stepped back, frowning. "But now I'm thinking that I never did know," she repeated quietly as she bent back down to her work.

"Maybe I don't know myself."

Samara stopped and stared at the photo of Toby with the snake wrapped around his neck, and her gaze blurred as she looked at the wide grin that was so much like Rick's. Without thinking she ran her finger around the outline, then quickly pulled it away.

"Maybe I really don't know myself."

She didn't realize how long Adam had been away until he wandered back into her area and began to study the photos she'd hung up. He didn't acknowledge her, and she kept her head bent over her work until the soft tuneless whistle he was breathing out began to irritate her.

"Don't you know a hymn or something?" She didn't look up.

"Sorry?" He turned and looked mildly puzzled.

"You were whistling . . . I suggested a tune." She glanced at him quickly then back to the last photo she was backing. Suddenly she felt ridiculous for being so annoyed, and she began to laugh quietly.

"Are you finding a happy place?" He asked quietly so that she immediately recalled the conversation they'd had all those years before about laughing with Terry.

"Not really." She shook her head and sighed. "I just realized that I was annoyed with you and there probably wasn't any need to be, and I was laughing at how stupid I was being."

"I agree." Adam smiled. "So if you're through being annoyed with me, is there anything I can do to help, or should I disappear again?"

"No . . . you should stay," she answered softly as she sat back on her stool and stared at him. "So where have you been all this time?"

"Oh, all around." He waved a hand in the air. "That tutor remembered some work I'd done, and she knew she had the magazine somewhere, so she was determined to find it to show me what I'd done, and along the way she introduced me to some others. I got taken to lunch and . . ." He grinned. "I even got offered a job."

She tried not to smile.

"And are you going to take it?"

"Goodness me, no." He shook his head as he turned to another photo. "It's for the end of next year and I never think that far ahead."

Somehow it was the answer she would have expected. Samara nodded as she finished the last application of photo to polystyrene and held it up.

"Done! I'll finish hanging this and we're through."

Adam watched as she fixed it to the board, then they stood side by side to survey the finished display. She had arranged the prints at different heights so that the entire arrangement of black-and-white prints seemed to flow in a wavy line around the cubicle.

"Very good." Adam nodded as he pivoted slowly on the spot. "Very, very good. You've done well, Sam. I think we really are through."

She took a long, deep breath as she stood with her hands on her hips, and then she ran her hands through her hair.

"Thank you." She rolled her shoulders to relax the tension. "And whether you admit to it or not, you have been a major inspiration."

"Ah, now inspiration I don't mind being." He pointed one finger in the air. "It's when you rely on me that I object."

"Well, I was going to rely on you right now to decide what we could do because I don't feel like sitting in the car for another hour.

But then I realize that you don't know your way around, so we could find somewhere to eat because that's something else I haven't done all day." She knew she was talking fast but it seemed to sum up the way she was feeling. She liked him being there but at the same time she was still annoyed by him, and that felt frustrating.

Adam smiled as he extended one hand for her to lead the way. "I think that's a great idea and I know what else I'd like to do."

Samara hesitated. "Oh, have you discovered something else in your travels today?"

"Well, I haven't been off the campus but I mentioned to that very enthusiastic woman that I was a member of the Church, and she said that the Mormon temple was close by and that you can walk there, so I thought we could do that."

"That sounds fine." Samara walked ahead of him. "What else did you mention to my tutor?"

"Oh, not much." He pushed the door open. "But she was surprised to learn that you were a member of the Church. She said you've never mentioned it in the three years she's known you."

Samara was silent as they left the building, and when Adam stood aside to let her go through the last door ahead of him, she kept her arms around her bag.

"You know, the subject of religion has never really come up." She walked slowly and he fell into step beside her. "But I get the feeling you were telling me off just then."

"No, not at all." He breathed in the cool evening air. "It was just an observation."

"An observation that I don't bear my testimony anymore . . . like you said before."

"Perhaps . . . or maybe it's being in this environment. Sometimes university types don't appreciate religion." He stopped and pointed ahead. "Is this the path to the temple?"

When she nodded he kept walking.

"Actually, I haven't borne my testimony for a long time." She spoke into the silence. "I usually leave it up to Jackie. She always has something she's grateful for."

"So you don't have anything to be grateful about?"

Samara took her time answering.

"It's not exactly that." She struggled to explain, but the growing darkness seemed to make it easier to share her thoughts. "It just seems that the answers I've been wanting haven't been that obvious . . . especially at church."

"What about in the scriptures? I remember the young Samara telling me very confidently that the answers to every problem you could possibly have are in the scriptures. Don't you believe that anymore?"

He was walking more briskly and she took longer strides to keep up. "Yes, I do believe it . . . but . . ." She frowned.

"But you haven't tried it for awhile." He didn't wait for an answer as he suddenly pointed ahead. "Now that is really beautiful."

The Brisbane Temple sat high on the cliff overlooking the river, the clean lines of gray marble and tall spire lit by spotlights illuminating the whole area so that it looked ethereal against the darkness of the river and cliffs.

"It is." Samara stopped beside him as he began to rummage in his camera bag. Within seconds he was taking a series of photos. She noticed again how intense his concentration became when he took pictures.

"I haven't been up here for a long time."

Adam stopped to put the lens cap back on the camera. "You should come often, Sam." He glanced at her before he put it back into the bag. Then he hesitated and undid it again. "Actually, I'd like to get some shots of you in these pictures." He motioned for her to stand in front of him then changed his mind as he lined up some of the tall palm trees that surrounded the temple.

"Let's go for silhouettes." He gently guided her to one side.

She could tell by the tone of his voice that it was useless to argue so she moved at his bidding, letting his hand guide her so that she held her head high and looked toward the temple. As he stepped back to take the pictures, a light breeze blew, and her silky hair lifted off her shoulders.

"Perfect."

She heard the camera whir rapidly, and she smiled wistfully as the memories came flooding back again. She stared at the temple.

"Don't you wish you could go back in time and start over?"

"Always," Adam answered straightaway as he came to stand behind her. "Especially after my wife and I split up."

His words seemed to echo in her head, and she forced herself to breathe slowly. How could she enjoy his company so much and delight in being with him, basking in precious memories, and then suddenly feel anger at his deception? She was as fickle as he was.

"You split up?" She stared at the temple. "Was that after you had your affair?"

She knew he was staring at her but she refused to turn her head.

"My affair?" She could hear the question in his voice.

Samara nodded. "You said over the phone the other night that you were married but that you had an affair." Adam was silent for a long time. She felt her skin beginning to prickle and she rubbed her arms. "I guess that's why you get on so well with my father. You have so many things in common." There was no bitterness in her tone, only a sense of dull acceptance.

"I actually wondered if you'd heard what I said the other night." Adam spoke very quietly. "You hung up so suddenly."

"Only because I didn't want to hear any more." Samara rubbed her arms.

"But if you had listened, you would have heard me say that I had an affair . . . with my work." He emphasized the last word and she felt it sink into her consciousness.

"Your work?" She could barely say the word.

"About two years after I joined the Church I got married in the temple to a lady named Helen." Adam still stood behind her so she didn't have to look at him. "But my career was taking off and I was traveling so much that we started having . . . differences."

"Differences?" She only seemed capable of one-word questions.

"Helen wanted me home more and . . ." He hesitated. "She wanted a family and I didn't."

"Family?" She finally turned around. "You didn't want a family?"

He shook his head. "I guess I might have, eventually, but the prospect didn't really appeal because my own family had been a disaster."

Samara nodded. She could relate to that.

"Anyway, we split up after a year and a half and I went crazy running around the world, taking on all sorts of assignments, especially dangerous ones. It was like I had to prove that the decision had been the right one." He bowed his head. "Helen sort of did the same with her work, and she's now a highly successful banker. We're still friends." He finished simply.

His words seemed to mix with the breeze that had suddenly sprung up and swirled gently all around her while her mind absorbed what he was saying. Adam had been married, but he hadn't had an affair. He wasn't exactly like her father but he understood her feelings about her own family. He was still the Adam that she had felt so comfortable with all those years ago. The relief seemed to settle over her like a warm blanket that she wanted to keep wrapped tightly around her.

"Thank you for telling me all that." She finally turned around and looked straight into his eyes. "I had been having a lot of conflicting feelings, but that makes a lot of things clearer."

"I figured you were struggling." He smiled. "You're not very good at hiding your emotions."

"No." Samara nodded. Then she tentatively put her hand up to pick a small, white thread off his jacket. "And that's why I don't see any point in trying to hide that . . . . I have fallen in love with you."

The only sounds then were the far distant noises of the city at night. Samara held her breath so that not even her breathing disturbed the silence. She slowly dropped her hand from his jacket as his face gave nothing away, but then he took ahold of it and wrapped his fingers around hers. For a second he stared up at the sky. Then he gathered her tightly against his chest.

"Oh, Sam . . . my little Sam." His words were buried in her hair as he held her close.

* * *

Samara had to be at school from early in the morning until late at night for the next two days. All sorts of interested people were visiting the students' photography exhibition, and she had to be on hand to answer questions and to field inquiries about her work. The response was constant and the reviews were positive, so that she began to feel as though her chosen field finally had career prospects. An offer from one advertising company even promised work in Sydney if she chose to make the move.

As she sat on the last bus back home on the second evening, she opened her bag and pulled out the brochures and business cards that the men from the advertising agency had left with her. As she flipped through the colorful, glossy pages, she felt the same excitement she'd felt when the men had met with her earlier in the day.

"You're good. You're very good," one of the men had commented, and she'd had an instant flashback of Adam standing in front of the pictures saying the very same words.

"I am good," she murmured, and she smiled as she stared out the window. And with the night's darkness causing a reflection on the glass, she saw herself smiling back. "I am very, very good."

She had barely seen any of her family over the last two days and had actually preferred it that way. The thought of seeing Adam had caused a fluttering feeling in her stomach, and so she had left him a note each day. Both evenings, though, the lights had been off in his motel unit when she arrived home, so she had stayed in her own room. Sleep had come easily despite the occasional fleeting recurrence of her childhood memories.

It was with some surprise that she walked down the driveway late in the evening after getting off the bus and saw lights shining from all the downstairs windows in their house. There was even the sound of music playing, and it got louder as she walked through into the lounge. As she opened the door, she heard the popping of corks and clapping.

Terry was standing at the table balancing on his crutches and pouring sparkling grape juice into a glass. Tracey and Eddy were filling other glasses, and Adam was standing across the room beside Brother and Sister Novelli. Sister Patterson and another older woman stood beside the couch as they all clapped in her direction.

"What's going on?" Samara looked around with a frown on her face. "Do you realize what time it is?"

"We do, and we thought you were never going to get home." Her mother held out a glass of juice and turned to her husband. "You tell her."

Eddy took his time clearing his throat and Samara stared as she watched her father—in a freshly ironed, pale blue shirt and navy trousers—raise his glass in the air.

"Everybody . . . let's toast Miss Samara Danes, university graduate and budding photographic journalist on the world scene."

Samara watched in amazement as everybody in the room raised their glasses and repeated her name. The whole thing seemed surreal and she unconsciously looked back toward the door.

"There's no need to run away." Tracey came forward and patted her on the arm. "This really is for you." She turned and pointed across the room. "To celebrate your graduating. And Adam has a special surprise for you."

"You don't think this is enough of a surprise?" Samara found it difficult to look straight at Adam. He was pulling a folded piece of paper out of his jacket pocket so he didn't make eye contact. When he did look at her his eyes were completely crossed so that she laughed out loud. None of the others noticed, but they all joined in the laughter. He also pretended to clear his throat. Then he took a few steps forward and held out the paper.

"I thought this might get your career off to a good start."

It seemed as if everybody was holding their breath as Samara unfolded the paper and read the business address at the top. The frown on her face became more quizzical as she mouthed the words, then saw who it was addressed to.

"Read it, for Pete's sake." Terry gently stomped his crutch on the ground. "We've been waiting for hours."

Samara looked down at the main part of the letter.

"We already know what it says, seeing it was addressed to me," Adam commented quietly. "But it is for you."

She read it slowly and again her brow furrowed. She read it again and looked up at Adam.

"Are . . . are they serious?" She found it difficult to speak.

"Absolutely." He nodded and raised his glass. "That's why we're toasting you. Your first international photographic submission is successful, and I'm sure it's only the first of many."

"But I never submitted . . ." she stammered, and Adam simply shrugged.

"I thought you might need a little encouragement, so I went ahead and sent the images to my friend, Dave, in New York."

"So, it's because of you . . ." Samara looked down at the letter.

"Only the sending of the pictures." Adam interrupted. "Dave would never print something just because I saved his life." She looked up quickly but he was smiling. "I'm just kidding. Dave knows talent when he sees it and he thinks you're really good."

"Isn't it amazing?" Tracey couldn't keep quiet any longer as she walked across the room and took the arm of the older woman beside Naomi Patterson. "Adam got the letter this morning and told us about it and your Auntie Nan got here in time for the celebration. It's all so exciting!"

Samara looked up dreamily as she registered what her mother was saying. She blinked as she suddenly noticed the similarity between the two sisters as they walked toward her. Nan Harvey was slightly taller and thinner than her younger sister, but they both had the same distinctively high cheekbones and wide smile. Her aunt held out her arms and even though she had only met her once before, Samara walked straight into the embrace as if it was the most natural thing in the world.

After that it was a round of constant talking and congratulations. Eddy whistled as he handed around food and replenished glasses, and Tracey seemed to have had a butterfly-like transformation as she brought out Samara's folder and began to show off her work to their visitors.

In a quieter moment, Samara felt a light touch on her elbow and turned to find Brother and Sister Novelli standing close beside each other.

"It's getting late, dear, and so we need to get away, but we're so proud of you and we wanted you to know that we told Jackie the good news." Sister Novelli glanced at her husband and her lip trembled. "She began to cry when we told her but it was a happy cry. She said to tell you that it's only what she expected of you."

Samara felt the tears rush to the back of her eyes and she pressed her fingers to her lips to stop them from trembling. "She could tell you that?"

"Oh, yes. Very slowly, but she can be understood." Brother Novelli nodded. "We know you've been busy the last few days, but so has Jackie. She's improved so much the doctors can hardly believe it. The swelling on her face has gone right down, and she can say a few words at a time."

"We know it's the blessings she's had but it's still a miracle to watch." Sister Novelli pointed at Terry, who was busy entertaining his aunt. "And Terry has made a huge difference to her. Your father has brought him up every day and he sits with her, sings to her, and tells stories about when they were little."

"My father takes him up to the hospital?" Samara almost didn't hear the rest of what they were saying.

"And picks him up again." Brother Novelli smiled. "I had no idea they were so much alike because I've never really seen them together."

Samara looked across at her brother and then back to her father.

"I guess they are." She nodded slowly and looked back to the Novellis. "I don't have to go into school tomorrow so I'll be sure to get up to see Jackie."

"She'll be delighted." Sister Novelli bent to pick up her handbag. Then she snapped her fingers as if remembering something. "My goodness, I nearly forgot to tell you . . . about Rick."

"Rick? Is anything wrong?" Samara felt her heart leap and an instant tightening in her chest. "Is he all right?"

"Oh yes, he's fine . . . everything is fine." Sister Novelli shook her head. "Your parents invited him over tonight, but he had to leave urgently this morning and he couldn't get in touch with them so he sent his apologies through us." She smiled. "He said to say he was thrilled for you and he knew you could do it."

"But where has he gone?" Samara looked puzzled as she fought a feeling of disappointment. "He never mentioned that he was going anywhere."

"Oh, he had to leave immediately, but he did say he'd try to call later." Sister Novelli clasped her hands together. "It's such a great opportunity for him."

"But where has he gone?" Samara tried not to sound too impatient.

"Northern Territory." Brother Novelli interrupted his wife as he beckoned to Sister Patterson and began to guide them both out the door. "He's had a job offer up on the Kakadu wildlife reserve, and they wanted him to go up immediately to see if he wanted to take it on."

"Kakadu." She repeatedly quietly as she waved good-bye. "I didn't even know he'd applied."

Samara was thoughtful for several minutes after they left until Terry swung past on his crutches, and she put out her hand to stop him. "Terry, did you know about Rick going away?"

"Only from the Novellis." Terry jerked his thumb back over his shoulder to indicate north. "Apparently he's not sure how long he'll be away and he may even stay up there permanently if it works out."

"Who's going where permanently?" Adam came to stand behind Samara and she jumped slightly.

"Rick has gone up north to see about a job. He went this morning."

"To Kakadu," Terry added for emphasis. "To the land of crocodiles, goannas, and dingoes."

"Sounds impressive." Adam nodded and stifled a sudden yawn. "Maybe I'll look him up."

Samara glanced up at him but she didn't say anything. Something in that simple sentence seemed to personify Adam's approach to life.

"Mate, you look tired." Terry studied Adam's face, and then he looked at his watch. "Then again it is nearly one o'clock—although to look at the present company you'd think they could go all night."

They all looked over to the couch where Tracey and Nan sat side by side, facing Eddy in the chair. He was describing something with both hands, and the sisters were laughing and leaning against each other.

"Dad's got a captive audience." Terry grinned. "Auntie Nan is catching up on twenty-five years of stories, and Mum just can't believe they're all in the same room and laughing together."

"Well, I can't believe what I'm seeing." Samara shook her head. "I feel like I'm in a completely different place."

"I think you are," Adam observed quietly and stifled another yawn. "I also think I really must turn in. It's been a long day." He looked down at Samara and his voice dropped. "How do you feel about an early walk along the beach?"

Samara ignored the look that Terry gave her as she nodded.

"I'd love to."

"Sunrise?" He raised one eyebrow. "Down at the beach?"

"That sounds perfect." She held up the paper that she still held in her hand. "And thank you so much . . . for everything."

His only response was the slightest nod of his head as he touched his finger to his forehead in a quick salute, and then he was gone.

"Fancy your finding him on a beach." Terry spoke behind her. "He's an awesome guy."

Samara tapped her mouth with the folded paper and stared at the door. Then she turned to Terry and gave him a quick hug. "You're absolutely right."

* * *

"Do you think Adam's like our family's guardian angel?" Terry balanced on his crutches while he tried to load some glasses in the dishwasher a little while later. "Sent here to save us from ourselves."

He was smiling but Samara could also see a slight frown on his face.

"I don't think one would be enough," she answered shortly.

"Well, he's certainly helped a lot." Terry closed the door to the dishwasher. "I was terrified to see Dad the other day, but apparently Adam had been talking to him while they were traveling."

"Yes, I hear they did a heap of talking." Samara frowned. "Adam had some interesting insights."

"Well, whatever they talked about, it worked. Dad came in and I saw Mum's face, and it was like this mix of terror and pleasure . . . like we were both waiting for the explosion." He hesitated. "But it never came."

"So Dad didn't get angry . . . at all?"

Terry shook his head. "It may have helped that the Novellis came in—and then the police—but there was still something different about the way he behaved. It was a bit freaky, really."

Samara nodded and then stared up at the ceiling. "Terry . . . did you know that Dad cheated on Mum?"

She waited as her brother looked at her. He settled himself back against the kitchen table. It was as if the movement gave them both time to consider her question.

"I didn't . . . at the time."

"So when . . . ?" She looked puzzled.

"When did I find out?" He shrugged. "About four years ago."

"How?" Samara began to rub her forearms.

Terry played with a small piece of rubber on his crutches and took his time answering. "I came home late one night and Mum and Dad were talking, or at least Mum was sobbing."

"He hadn't done it again, had he?" Samara felt her stomach churn.

"No . . . Mum was saying something about never being forgiven and that she couldn't see the point in living sometimes." He pursed his lips. "It was pretty intense and I probably shouldn't have listened but then Dad said something about how he'd messed up and that it was his fault and she couldn't keep blaming herself . . ." He stopped.

"And . . ." A sudden shiver ran down Samara's spine.

"And then Mum said she'd never forget the look on your face when you found out and that it haunted her every day."

It seemed as if the ticking of the kitchen clock was right inside Samara's head as she stood silently. Terry never moved but she could feel him watching her.

"Adam said that I was the one making things difficult for them . . . that they'd forgiven one another." Samara swallowed hard. "I never realized . . ."

"Me neither." Terry held out one hand and she moved to stand beside him. As he rested his arm across her shoulders she leaned her head against his shoulder. "Can you forgive *me*, Sammy?"

Samara didn't move.

"It's funny, but now that you're getting better I can hardly remember that I was angry at you." She tilted her head slightly to look up at him. "I'm just so happy to have my big brother back."

Terry squeezed her shoulder, then he cleared his throat.

"Sam, don't you think you'd be happy to have our parents back?" He took a deep breath. "They would try if you'd let them."

She took her time answering, but it was more because she was analyzing her own feelings than her parents' actions. She finally nodded.

"Rick told me the other day that there was a limit to the way I could treat people. I never realized that I was the one who was being . . . conditional."

"I'll love you if you love me." Terry pointed to her and then to himself. "It's so much harder to love unconditionally. It's a good thing we've got Rick and Jackie."

Samara folded her arms as he said Rick's name and she felt the tears begin to build up.

"He said he wouldn't be there just whenever I felt like I needed someone to be nice to me . . . and now he's not."

"No, he's not." Terry hugged her. "But I am, Sammy. I promise."

CHAPTER NINETEEN

Samara was surprised how easily she awoke the next morning. Even with only a few hours of sleep she still felt bright and energetic as she dressed and went downstairs, picking up two apples on her way through the kitchen and slipping them into the front pocket of her sleeveless jacket.

She glanced at Adam's motel unit but the curtains were open with the door shut so she knew he must already be down at the beach. She quickened her steps as she walked down the pathway.

The sun was beginning to send a bright gold light across the water as she walked onto the beach. It hadn't quite reached the stage of being a glaring light off the water but she still had to shield her eyes as she searched both ways along the beach. She spotted him quickly, a tall silhouette against the shimmering sea, a camera up to his face.

She was smiling as she walked down to where he stood nearly at the water's edge, but as she approached he turned quickly and held his finger to his lips to tell her to be quiet. Samara held up both hands and automatically began to tiptoe as he pointed toward a small seagull standing in the tide several yards to his left.

Adam took another photo as the bird suddenly lifted out of the water and flapped its wings until it met with a larger seagull that appeared overhead. The birds then began a silent dance in the air, the small bird following the movements of the larger bird in a synchronized dipping and wheeling that looked perfectly orchestrated.

After several wide sweeps over the water's edge the larger bird then lifted far higher up in the sky than before and the small bird began to drop away as if the move was beyond its strength. It dived down to the water and settled on the surface, dipping its beak and ruffling its feathers. After several seconds it began to move quickly backward and forward, apparently in search of the larger bird.

"Where did it go?" Samara shaded her eyes to look high in the sky, but Adam pointed over to their left with his free hand.

"It's watching from over there." He answered quietly. "It's keeping an eye out from a distance."

Sure enough, the larger bird was perched on the end of a long boat pulled up on the beach. It was very still, but it was definitely watching the smaller bird.

"Do you think it's the mother?" Samara whispered as the bird suddenly lifted off the boat and began to soar up into the sky again.

"Probably." Adam pointed down where the small bird had been. "But it looks like junior is moving on."

The small seagull had flown back along the beach where several other birds were perched on a lifeguard tower. It fluffed its wings once and settled onto the rail beside them.

Adam looked up in the sky where the large bird was making a wide sweep. Then it suddenly lifted and headed off into the bright gold sunrise until it was barely a dark dot.

Samara blinked as she watched the bird until it couldn't be seen anymore.

"That was beautiful." She fell into step beside Adam as he began to walk. "I've never seen birds do that before."

"I haven't either." Adam put the camera back into its case. "It was inspiring to watch. They'd already done the whole process twice before you got here."

"Then I'm glad I saw some of it." Samara put her hands into her pockets and felt the two apples she'd brought with her. She pulled them out and offered one to Adam.

He gave a short laugh as he took it.

"Are you tempting me?"

She didn't bother to respond as she bit into her apple. They walked in silence for some time.

"I woke up this morning and that letter was on my desk, so I knew last night wasn't a dream."

"No, it's definitely not a dream." Adam walked with his hands in his trouser pockets. "You've worked hard and you deserve the recognition."

Samara clasped her hands behind her back and raised her shoulders.

"I was offered a job yesterday, as well." She glanced at him. "Two men offered me work at an advertising agency . . . in the heart of Sydney."

Adam kept walking without looking at her.

"Sydney's a big, busy place. Are you ready for that?"

She put her hands back in her jacket pockets.

"Actually, I was wondering what you thought of it. Whether it was worth following up?"

"And if I said it was?" She saw the ghost of a smile at the side of his mouth.

"I'd probably take it." She began to smile.

"And if I said you shouldn't?"

"I probably wouldn't." She was openly smiling now as she lifted her face to the sun's radiant warmth. It seemed to enter her whole body and fill it with light.

"I'm leaving, Sam."

Adam had stopped and turned to face her and the water. She stopped but kept looking straight ahead with the smile fixed to her face.

"I knew you would." She tried to control it but her voice began to quiver as he took a step closer.

"You're going to be fine, Sam. You're very good." His voice broke and she felt the tears begin to flow down her cheeks.

"I am good." She tried to smile through the tears. "I'm darned good and I know how to make the right decisions." Her voice faltered. "I've had the best teacher in the world."

She felt the warmth of his arm across her shoulders and then the briefest pressure of his lips on her forehead.

Samara shook her head. "I don't want you to say good-bye. *I* never will. I'll always imagine you just like this."

She felt the pressure of his arm tighten and then relax around her as she found herself continuing to hold on to him in her heart.

"Or watching me through the lens of a camera." She felt the sun begin to warm her body as he left her. "Or turning up on a beach somewhere."

She began to walk, sinking her feet into the soft, damp sand as waves moved up with the tide. "Or teaching me how to hold the camera."

The tears flowed as she walked and a sudden wind whipped them off her face. "Or sitting behind me in church when I least expect it."

A large group of children raced noisily past her into the water and she stopped and slowly turned around. "Or telling me things I need to hear when I don't want to hear them."

Her own footprints showed clearly in the damp sand, but she had to strain to see where Adam's had been. "Or watching over me."

* * *

She walked the beach for a long time, and then as shops began opening, she made her way over to the Pacific Fair shopping mall and spent several hours looking at all the shops and seeing nothing. For awhile she sat on a bench and simply watched the people passing by, but when a girl swung by on a pair of crutches her thoughts turned to Terry and to Jackie and she decided to catch a bus to the hospital.

At the door to Jackie's room she hesitated before knocking. It had been a terrible shock to see Jackie the first time, and although her parents and Terry had been positive about her progress over the last few days, Samara still felt cautious.

"You're fine to go in." A nurse spoke cheerfully behind her as she passed by wheeling a stainless steel trolley. "She was awake a few minutes ago."

"Okay." Samara knocked gently and pushed the door open. A curtain was still drawn around the end of the bed, so she tiptoed in and whispered Jackie's name.

"Sam?" she heard her name immediately, although it sounded slurred, so she carefully drew back the curtain and poked her head around. Jackie was partially propped up in the bed and her head was flat on the pillow, but whereas the bandage had covered her eyes before, her face was now uncovered. Dark blue and purple bruising extended over her entire eye area so that her eyes were mere slits, her nose barely discernible from the swelling across her cheeks. Her lips and chin were more like their normal proportions but still swollen.

"Oh, double ouch." Samara automatically coined the phrase she and Jackie had always used when either was hurt.

"Mmm . . ." Jackie's head and eyes didn't move but her lips parted in a half smile and she waved her fingers to point at the chair beside her. Samara quickly sat down and leaned forward.

"The swelling's gone down a whole lot since the other day." She tried to sound positive. "How are you feeling?"

"Very . . . brainy." Jackie motioned toward her head. "Big head."

"Well, you've always had a big head . . . now you're going to be impossible." Samara tried to joke and was rewarded with a smile.

"Thanks, friend." The words were slurred and it was obviously difficult for Jackie to move her lips properly, but Samara could understand her clearly.

"You're welcome." She realized that she was going to have to do most of the talking, so she put her elbows on the bed and rested her chin in her hands. "You know, you're not only a brainy big-head, I hear you're a bit of a miracle worker as well. Your parents told me last night that my father has been bringing Terry up to visit, and that has to rank as a miracle. I can't remember the last time they were in a car together . . . or spoke civilly for that matter."

"Terry's happy," Jackie responded slowly. "Makes me happy."

"And that's pretty obvious." Samara grinned. It felt good to stretch the muscles on her face, which seemed to have dried up with her morning tears. "Terry is like a different person . . . in fact, I think someone switched my brother."

"Someone loves your brother." Jackie's words were soft and deliberate, and she reached out to touch Samara's hand. Samara met her halfway and held her hand gently but tightly.

"Thank you for being that someone." She could barely whisper the words as Jackie's eyes closed shut. They sat in silence for awhile, then Jackie's hand moved and she patted Samara's fingers.

"Congrats." She struggled with the word. "Your photos . . . winning."

"Well, not actually winning, but they'll be in a pretty important magazine." Samara nodded. "It's very exciting."

"You'll be famous." Jackie squeezed her fingers.

"I doubt it." Samara squeezed them back. "But I'd settle for rich."

"Rich to travel." Jackie took her time to swallow. "You'll forget . . . us."

"Oh, no, that's not possible." Samara shook her head. "I need you to be my business manager and keep me organized."

"No . . . Adam is."

Samara took a deep breath and exhaled very slowly.

"Adam's gone." She stared out the window. "He left this morning."

"Gone?" Jackie's voice sounded surprised. Then she tapped two fingers on the bedcovers. "Adam gone . . . Rick gone."

"Well, thank you for reminding me." Samara tried to put a smile into her voice as she closed up Jackie's hand into a fist. "And that makes . . . none." She patted the fist. "So you and Terry better get used to a threesome."

"No." Jackie's response was immediate and Samara smiled.

"Shutting me out already, eh?" She shrugged. "In that case, I'll just have to go away . . . far away and seek my fortune on my own. I'll send postcards occasionally from distant countries and you can show my numerous nieces and nephews where their maiden aunt is traveling to around the world. Then I'll pop back every year to take the official Danes family photo and then head out again."

"No." The response came slowly again but it was quieter. "Only . . . little while."

Samara felt Jackie's hand beginning to relax in hers, and she realized her friend was falling asleep so she gently slipped her own hand out and laid Jackie's on the cover. She watched her silently for a little while until her breathing was deep and regular. Then she stood up.

"Maybe for a little while then, Jackie. Just to see what I can do on my own."

* * *

Her parents were sitting together on the couch when Samara arrived home, and they both looked up in surprise as she walked into the lounge.

"Where have you been, Samara?' Tracey stood up. "We've been so worried about you. You left early this morning and you've been out all day."

"I've been leaving early every morning this week and getting home late, Mum. Today's no different." Her brain seemed to ring out an instant objection to her mother's words, but she ignored it and tried to speak calmly.

"Today was very different." Tracey clasped her hands in front of her. "Adam left."

"I know." Samara nodded.

"But you didn't say good-bye." Her mother persisted until Eddy stood up and rested his hand on his wife's shoulder.

"Maybe Samara said good-bye down at the beach." He looked directly at Samara, and she nodded silently.

"Oh, well that's all right then." Tracey rubbed her forehead. "I was so sad to see him go. I didn't realize how much he's become part of the family. It's as if he knew us all before he even met us. He was so good to Terry and he's helped your father and I so much. It was almost like getting professional help and yet it didn't feel like it because he was so kind . . ." She finally ran out of words and sniffed loudly. "Oh, dear, I am going to miss having him around. He was like a ray of sunshine."

"He said he'd miss us all." Eddy coughed and Samara stared. Her father never showed emotion but she could see him fighting to control himself. "He said that we'd become like the family he never had."

"He surely picked a crazy family then." Samara tried to smile but her voice broke slightly. "But I'm sure we'll see him again. He has a habit of turning up when you least expect it."

"I don't know that we will. I got the feeling that this good-bye is pretty final." Eddy's voice was gravelly. "It's a darn shame because I've never had a mate that I could talk to like that. Mind you, I reckon we would've got up to some pretty hairy adventures if we had known each other when we were young." His voice broke and he shook his head. "But Trace is right. He helped me to see where I was going wrong. He's been good for us all."

Samara could see her father struggling, but she still hesitated before walking over to him. It was as if the width of the room represented a lifetime and she didn't know how to cross the distance. Then she heard Adam's voice in her head. *"I think you have what it takes to reach out to him."*

When Eddy didn't look up she walked over and put her arms around him and for the first time that she could remember, she cried with her father instead of because of him.

* * *

"Mum, have you seen Terry?" Samara paused only to put her head around the door to the reception area where her mother sat at the desk. "He was going to go with me to visit Jackie."

"Um . . . I'm not sure where he is." Tracey's voice was quiet and she didn't look up.

Samara hesitated then walked up to the desk. She bent forward slightly to see her mother's face more clearly and was surprised at the red-rimmed eyes that Tracey tried to hide.

"Mum, what's been happening?" She put out a hand to touch her mother's shoulder. "Why are you crying?"

"I'm not crying now." Tracey tried to smile but her face crumpled and she shook her head. "I thought everything was going perfectly. Terry's been fine and your father has been an angel but . . . I blew it."

"You?' Samara looked puzzled. "I thought you were doing really well."

"I was." Tracey nodded and rested her head on her hand. "But last night Terry didn't come home until late and I was really tired and I immediately suspected the worst so I challenged him when he did get in because his clothes smelled . . . like when he'd go partying." She stopped and her shoulders heaved.

"Had he been out?" Samara asked quietly, not really wanting to hear her mother's response. When Tracey nodded, she took a deep breath.

"Was he high?"

Her mother sat back against the chair and stared up at the ceiling.

"He tried to tell me that he'd given himself a test . . . to see if he could go to the party and not have anything."

"And did he?"

"I don't know." Tracey shook her head. "I was so upset that I just got angry with him and told him off for being so stupid; that he should avoid temptation and not put himself right in it."

"And what did he do?" Samara swallowed hard. Terry had been doing so well since Adam had left that she really couldn't imagine he would go back to using drugs or alcohol.

"He just walked back out and slammed the door. I haven't seen him since." Tracey began to cry silently. "Then your father called and I told him what had happened, and he told me I should have had more control, so I hung up and promptly went and took my own pills . . ." She buried her face in both hands. "I'm worse than Terry. I'm totally to blame."

Samara stood helplessly for a second because she'd been having similar thoughts as she'd listened to her mother, but she moved behind the desk and held her tightly. Neither moved for some time until Tracey stopped crying. Then she leaned weakly against Samara's shoulder and tried to laugh.

"Funny how we go to pieces after Adam leaves. It's like we need him to be normal."

"We don't need him, Mum." Samara gave her mother a squeeze. "We need each other, but we need to be more rational." She hesitated. "I'll find Terry and see what the story is, but I think you both need to take this whole addiction rehab a step further. It's like the crisis thing has worn off and now we have to learn to really live with it and deal with it." She squeezed harder. "I know I can't help you enough, but you have to decide to let somebody else help you . . . professionally." She hesitated. "I think that's what Dad wants to see you do as well."

Tracey nodded. "He did mention something before he left on his trip, but I wanted to show him I could do it on my own."

"Getting help *is* doing it on your own, Mum." Samara stood back. "But you'll be doing it with the right sort of direction instead of guessing and hoping the whole time."

Her mother stared at the desk pad for a long time. Then she gave a tiny laugh. "Maybe Terry and I could make it a mother-and-son date each week . . . going to rehab together."

"Whatever it takes, Mum." Samara leaned forward and gave her a quick kiss on the cheek. "Would you like me to ask Terry what he thinks about it?"

"If you can find him." Tracey nodded. "And if he still wants to talk to me."

* * *

Samara took her time going down to the beach. After leaving her mother she went to her room and spent a long time on her knees, asking for help.

The initial feeling of loss at Adam leaving had been followed by an almost surreal atmosphere in their home for several days. Terry was at the hospital with Jackie most of the day and had even been back to the university to organize his studies for the following year.

Eddy had agreed to do two more long-haul trips before finishing, and Samara had noticed that upon actually committing to finishing the driving he had become very quiet and introspective. Tracey had been in a permanently good mood, smiling brightly and chattering almost nonstop. No one had mentioned Adam again.

At the end of the pathway to the beach, Samara stopped and shielded her eyes against the sun as she tried to make out Terry's figure among the other people walking near the wave line on the sand. She couldn't see him, so she began to walk along the beach to the place where she knew he usually went if he needed to think.

A lone seagull dipped and wheeled over her head, and she glanced up and smiled as she lengthened her stride. Fifty yards away she spotted Terry sitting on the white sand.

"I thought I might find you here." She sat down beside him and crossed her legs. Terry didn't respond, so she leaned forward and pressed her hands into the sand and then dusted them off. A shallow imprint remained in the sand. "Do you remember when we were little how you used to walk along the beach and I would try to walk in your footprints?"

Terry nodded his head but he didn't speak.

"You used to take extra long strides until I'd fall over, and then you'd do little ones so I could manage."

"I wanted to make sure you were trying hard," he murmured and traced a question mark into the sand. "What are you doing here?"

She copied him and drew another question mark.

"I want to know what happened."

Terry glanced sideways. "You've been talking to mum."

"Mmm." Samara nodded. "She thinks you're doing drugs again."

"Do you think I am?"

"I hope you aren't," Samara answered immediately. "But I realize people sometimes make mistakes."

She waited as Terry retraced the question mark.

"Do you think people will always look at me with a big question mark over my head?" He shrugged. "Will Jackie be like Mum and always wonder if she can trust me or doubt me if I'm not home on time?"

Samara took her time answering. She rested her elbows on her knees and stared out at the ocean. "I think Mum doubts you because she doubts herself. I don't think Jackie would feel that way." She hesitated. "Where did you go the other night? Mum says you smelled like you'd been to a party."

Terry picked up a fistful of sand and let it run through his fingers.

"I did go to a party. I went to the university to check out my classes, and who is the first person I see?"

Samara felt a knot form in her stomach. "Doug?"

Terry nodded. "None other than the man himself, and the first question he asked was when I was going to a party."

"So you went?" Samara frowned. "The first time he asked?"

"Hey, it wasn't like that." Terry held up his hand in protest. "I'd spent the last evening wondering if I was really and truly off the stuff because it seemed to have been too easy, almost. I mean, I've been at the hospital and with Jackie and everything, but I kept wondering if I'd really be able to resist it . . . if the occasion arose."

"Which it did," Samara filled in briefly.

"Which it did." Terry nodded. "And so I decided to see if I could resist it, so I went."

"And did you . . . resist?" She almost didn't want an answer, and when Terry slowly shook his head, she stifled a small groan.

"I was fine to begin with and I was feeling pretty pleased with myself . . ." He hesitated.

"But?" Samara took a deep breath. "What happened?"

"I was going to leave when Doug suggested I have one for the road, and I remember thinking, why not . . . it's the last one ever." Terry put his hands over his face. "I enjoyed it, Sammy. It felt great . . . and now I'm back to square one. Jackie won't be able to trust me."

"Not square one, Terry." Samara rested her hand on her brother's shoulder. "You've gone back a bit but I think you've only managed to prove to yourself that you need some help."

"I really didn't think I needed anyone else." Terry shook his head. "I thought loving Jackie would be enough motivation."

"Loving somebody doesn't necessarily make everything right," Samara said quietly. "I think I'm becoming an expert on that principle."

Terry rested back on his hands and screwed up his face against the brightness of the sun.

"Don't you sometimes wish we had a gene pool that learned from other people's mistakes?"

"Sometimes." Samara almost snorted, then she smiled grimly. "I guess our challenge is to actually learn and not to ignore our mistakes . . . which means that you need to get some help, big brother."

Terry nodded slowly with his eyes shut.

"Will you help me, Sammy? I don't want to put Jackie through this . . . I want to get better for her."

Samara nodded. "I'll be here, Terry, and Mum will too. In fact, she's just decided she needs help as well." She smiled. "She suggested that the two of you have a mother-and-son date at rehab each week."

They both sat quietly, then Terry gave a low chuckle, and soon Samara was laughing with him. He stood up and helped her to her feet, and they began to walk back toward home.

* * *

"Oh my goodness, you are looking so much better!" Samara stood in the doorway of Jackie's room and watched as her friend poured herself a glass of water from a jug. Her blonde hair was newly washed and blow-dried, and it billowed around her shoulders like a cloud, partially obscuring her face. As Samara spoke, Jackie turned to reveal the full extent of the injuries, especially where the hair had been shaved at the front. The swelling was almost completely gone, but the bruising was still a fierce blend of purple and yellow.

"Do you like my face paint?" Jackie smiled, and her speech was quite clear. "I had one of the nurses do it specially."

"It looks perfect for Halloween." Samara walked in and gave Jackie a hug, careful not to get too close to her face. "We'll have to take photos so we can copy it for next year."

"Oh, no we won't." Jackie barely shook her head. "Once this disappears I don't want to go there again."

She picked up the glass before walking over to the bed and climbing back onto it. Her movements were quite slow and measured, and she held her head straight, but there was a vast difference from her condition of even a few days before.

"I had some good news this morning." She eased herself back against the pillows. "The surgeon says I can go home tomorrow."

"Tomorrow?" Samara frowned. "But it's only been . . . ten days and you've still got all those things in your head."

Jackie touched her forehead gently.

"Five plates and forty-something screws and a wee bit of wire, and they're going to stay in there for quite some time." She wrinkled up her nose. "I'm already tired of all the jokes about having a screw loose and being bionic."

"Then I promise not to mention it again." Samara smiled and pointed back over her shoulder. "Does Terry know you're coming home tomorrow?"

"Not yet. I thought I'd wait till he came up this evening. He said he'd be late because he had a meeting to go to." Jackie frowned. "He didn't say what meeting, though. Do you know where he's going?"

Samara hesitated, then she walked over to the window.

"He and Mum have signed themselves in to a rehab group together." She glanced back at Jackie. "He had a bit of a setback the other day."

"Is that why he hasn't come up for a couple of days?" Jackie asked quietly and watched as Samara nodded.

"He's been feeling really guilty, especially about letting you down." She turned and leaned back against the windowsill. "He's so scared that you won't trust him anymore." She hesitated. "I told him that you would."

Jackie sat staring down at the glass in her hand and rotating it until the water was circling inside it.

"I think my parents are struggling at times with the idea of Terry and I being . . . together. They want to be fine with it, but my mum, especially, begins to worry when she thinks that there's a chance an accident could happen again."

"That's understandable," Samara acknowledged quietly. "But how do you feel?"

Jackie put her hand up and gently ran her finger over a small patch of her forehead.

"I really don't feel that way. I've lain here and thought about it a lot and I really don't feel badly toward Terry." She hesitated. "I mean, I'm sorry it happened but . . . I don't remember anything of the accident so it's like I don't associate being like this with him."

"You don't remember anything?" Samara frowned. "I didn't realize that."

Jackie shrugged. "I remember turning into the street where the bowling alley is, and then I remember waking up in the hospital feeling lousy. There's just nothing in between, so sometimes I feel more like it's all a dream." She half smiled. "Until my head starts aching again."

"But do you ever think that you might have been killed?" Samara couldn't help asking. "And that it was Terry's fault?"

"Mmm." Jackie nodded. "But all I really know is that Terry was here when I woke up, and he was the first person I wanted to see when I didn't even realize that I was wanting to see anyone."

Samara took her time responding. Then, as she saw the tears welling in Jackie's eyes, she walked over and sat down on the bed.

"He really does love you, Jackie." She shook her head. "He's a great person who's done a stupid thing but I know he can get over it."

"I know he will." Jackie's voice was barely a whisper. "I really know he will, and I will be there for him."

"Then that's all he needs to know." Samara leaned forward and gave her a quick hug. "Just keep telling him that."

She slowly stood and stretched both hands out from her sides.

"And now I need to go home and reply to an e-mail from Sydney."

"Sydney?" Jackie wiped her eyes carefully with a tissue. "Who's in Sydney?"

"That advertising agency that approached me after the exhibition." Samara raised both shoulders. "I hadn't responded and they got in touch with a new offer . . . a better offer."

"So what are you going to do?"

"I'm going to tell them I'll go down for an interview. They're suggesting next week."

"Have you told Rick?" Jackie rested her arms on her knees.

"No," Samara answered immediately. "I haven't heard from him except for a quick e-mail to say he was sorry he missed my exhibition and that he was staying up north for a few weeks."

"Is he going to take a permanent job?"

"He didn't say." Samara shrugged. "Like I said, it was a pretty short letter."

"And did you write back?" Jackie frowned.

"Not yet." Samara didn't look at Jackie. "I was waiting."

"For what?" Jackie responded instantly and Samara smiled.

"I think it was better when you couldn't talk properly. Now I feel like I'm being interrogated."

"I'm just fascinated to see what you do with your life." Jackie smiled as well. "I've been lying here devising all sorts of possible endings to your story."

"Well, I'm glad I've been some sort of diversion." Samara raised one eyebrow. "Dare I ask how the stories ended?"

"It depends whether you want the Adam story or the Rick story or the successful photographer story." Jackie spread both hands out. "But then, you've never been one to read the last page of a book first so I probably shouldn't tell you."

Samara leaned her head against the doorway and closed her eyes briefly. Then she shook her head.

"No, you shouldn't tell me." She lifted one hand in a brief wave. "I'll let you know what happens about Sydney when I visit you at home."

"Okay." Jackie waved back, but as Samara turned into the hallway she heard her voice in a stage whisper. "But I liked the Rick ending best."

CHAPTER TWENTY

"What do you mean you're going to Sydney?" Tracey stared at her daughter as she sat at the table eating cereal. "Where did this idea come from?"

"I mentioned it ages ago," Samara answered quietly. "Some men from a big advertising agency down there came to scout people at the exhibition, and they said my work was exactly what they were looking for."

"So what did Adam think about it?" Tracey buttered some toast rapidly. "Did he think it was a good idea?"

Samara took her time answering.

"He said I had to make my own decisions."

"But did he think it was a good one?" Tracey persisted.

"*I* think it's a good one." Samara was more decisive as she put her spoon into the bowl and stood up from the table. "Anyway, they contacted me again and offered to fly me down for an interview, and so I can decide then."

"And if you like it?"

"Then I'll probably stay." Samara felt a sense of freedom with the words. "I've got enough money saved to stay for a few days anyway, so I'm going to make it my official graduating holiday, and if I get the job I can use the time to find accommodation and everything."

"But . . . where will you live, and what about church?" Tracey shook her head. "I hear of so many young ones going off to another city and just drifting away."

Samara watched as her mother's shoulders drooped, and once again she made herself take the steps across the room and hug her.

"I'll be fine, Mum. The agency office is actually near a chapel, and I met some young adults from the young single adult ward there at the last conference. In fact, one is Rick's cousin."

"Oh, that would be all right, then." Tracey's face brightened, then she frowned again. "What do you think Rick is going to say about your going down there?"

Samara pursed her lips and shrugged.

"I really don't know. It looks like he's got some exciting stuff happening and that he won't have time to worry about what I'm doing. Chasing crocodiles is a lot more interesting than what I do for work."

"That's not true. Rick has always been interested in what you do." Tracey began to spread the butter on her toast again. "Are you're going to tell him you're going?"

Samara stared at the telephone and shook her head. "I think I'd rather wait to tell him if I'm staying. I might be there and back before he comes back from Kakadu . . . if he ever does."

Tracey sighed as she absently cut the cold toast into thin strips.

"Nan and I were talking about that the other day . . . how all the young ones start leaving home. You're off to Sydney, Rick's off in the outback, and even Terry's talking about finishing his engineering degree and working overseas for awhile."

"Well, maybe it's time you went overseas as well." Samara folded her arms. "Isn't it about time you visited your parents? Didn't Auntie Nan say that Grandma isn't well?"

"She's not well at all." Tracey nodded. "And Nan and Adam said the same thing to me . . . and even your father. He suggested we both go for a visit."

"Dad did?" Samara frowned. Due to her father's change of attitude, he would be breaking a lifelong decision.

Tracey nodded thoughtfully as she used the knife to carefully separate the strips of toast on the plate.

"Last night he said that he was through with trucking. The company has offered him a mechanics job at the depot."

"But that's out past Gatton," Samara objected. "That's too far to commute from here."

"Well, that's our other thought." Tracey hesitated. "That I'll leave the motel and we'll buy a small place closer to the depot."

"A cottage built for two." Samara nodded and began to smile. "You don't want Terry and me around at all."

"Oh, it's not that, Sam . . ." Tracey actually blushed. "But we do have a lot of catching up to do."

Samara stared at her mother and took note of the new shirt and trousers and makeup but there was something different . . . a radiance she hadn't seen since she was fourteen.

"Mum . . . do you think you've really forgiven Dad . . . for what he did?"

Her mother kept moving the toast strips around the plate, and then she laid the knife down and folded both hands in her lap. "I had a long talk with Adam about that . . . about whether it was harder to forgive your father . . . or myself."

"And?" Samara held her breath.

"I think . . . both. But I think I've moved on and I think we're moving on together." She hesitated. "But Sam, do you think you can forgive your father . . . or me, for the things we've done? We know we've both made life pretty miserable for you at times."

Samara ran her finger along the edge of the table and back, and then she smiled and nodded. "Let's just say you two had better have an extra room in that cottage for a frequent visitor."

* * *

The job with the advertising agency proved to be everything Samara could want as far as a nurturing environment for a young photographic artist. It was an established company but she could sense the progressive attitude in the owners, and they offered a salary that seemed astronomical after years of living on very little. She accepted the job and decided to stay in Sydney, rationalizing that the airfare back to Brisbane was another week's rent.

She was given a team to work with and a manager who was also a Latter-day Saint. In the first week the manager and his wife invited her to dinner with some other young adults and arranged board for her with two of the girls from the group. She was able to walk to work and that meant passing the temple every day.

At the end of the second day she stared at the phone for a long time before dialing her parents' number. Somehow it seemed to be the final step in separating herself from her old life.

"Hi, Mum." The phone connection buzzed slightly so that the voice on the other end wasn't clear. "Mum?"

"Hello . . . is that you, Samara?"

"Sister Patterson?" Samara frowned. "Is Mum all right?"

"Oh yes, dear." Naomi Patterson's voice sounded clearer. "She and your father are just out looking at houses in Gatton. They should be back in about an hour. How are you, dear?"

"I'm fine." Samara smiled as she always did when she was around Sister Patterson. "I got the job I wanted and a place to stay and friends all at once."

"Oh, that's wonderful, dear. Your mother will be so pleased. She was so worried about you going off on your own into the big, bad world."

"It doesn't sound like she let it worry her too long." Samara laughed. "She's already off starting a new life. When did Dad get back?"

"Yesterday, and they said that the company doesn't need him to do the last driving job because they need him more at the new job, so they have to find a house immediately."

"My goodness, things really are moving." Samara lifted one eyebrow. "I don't think they'll have time to miss me." She hesitated. "What's happening with the motel?"

"Well, even that is working out . . . especially for me." Sister Patterson chuckled. "I'm going to take your mother's place and look after things until the new owners decide what they're doing. It's given me a whole new lease of life and I'm making so many new friends."

"But that's wonderful." Samara felt a warm sensation around her heart and she fought back the tears. "You deserve it . . . you bring everyone else so much happiness."

"Well, thank you, dear." Sister Patterson's voice sounded softer. "And I do hope everything works out for you. Have you heard from young Rick at all?"

"Not lately." Samara smiled. Even Sister Patterson was a Rick fan. "I just hope he hasn't been attacked by a crocodile or anything."

"Oh, wouldn't that be dreadful?" There was a slight pause and then she spoke quickly. "Here, dear, your brother has just walked in and someone else has arrived so I'll hand you over to Terry. It was lovely talking to you."

Samara barely managed to say good-bye before she heard Terry's voice on the line.

"Hi, Sammy?"

She felt a total thrill as he answered. "Hey, big brother. How's life on the Gold Coast?"

"Well, it's definitely not the same without my little sister, but we're managing." Terry's voice was clear and bright. "What about life in the big city? Have they managed to lead you astray yet?"

Samara laughed as she looked up at a picture of the Sydney Temple on her living room wall.

"There's not much chance of that. You can tell Mum and Dad that my boss is a Latter-day Saint, as well as my two roommates, I've already been assigned as a visiting teacher, and I walk past the temple to go to work."

"Wow, I'm impressed." Terry whistled. "And how's the job?"

"Beyond anything I could have hoped for. I'm learning more computer skills and the projects are really exciting. Plus . . ." She paused for effect. "I showed my boss the photo contract from New York, and he must have talked to the big, big boss. They've given me a special children's account to work on, and they're encouraging me to do freelance work as well."

"Well, it's been nice knowing you." Terry gave an exaggerated sigh. "Jackie said we may never see you again."

"And how is Jackie?" Samara laughed at his tone.

"Jackie is doing great considering she's still got about a hundred screws and fifty metal plates in her head. I've told her we'll never be able to travel because she'll always set off the metal detectors at the airports."

"*We'll* never be able to travel?" Samara repeated his words with a smile. "Is that a definite 'we' I hear?"

"As definite as you can get with an ex-drug addict and a head case." Terry laughed, but she could hear the serious tone in his voice. "I don't ever want to be separated from her again, Sam. Jackie means the world to me."

"I'm really glad to hear that, Terry," she responded softly. "So do I hear wedding bells anytime soon?"

"A few months. Although I haven't asked her properly yet," he answered straightaway. "I'm doing well on the rehab program and Jackie should be back to normal by then."

"And I'll have saved enough for the fare back." Samara moved the phone to her other ear. "Do you want me to take the wedding photos?"

"Man, I hadn't even thought of stuff like that." She could imagine Terry running his hand through his hair like he did when he was confused.

"You'd probably better to leave it to Jackie. She's the professional organizer."

"I'll say." Terry's voice had a ring of pride to it. "She was only home a day and she started calling the young adults about a service project. She gets tired really quickly but she sure manages to do a heap of stuff when she's awake."

"That's Jackie for you." Samara sighed happily. "You've got a busy life ahead of you, my brother."

There was a long silence, and then she heard Terry's voice, deeper and more serious.

"You have no idea how good that sounds, Sam . . . just to know that I have a life ahead of me . . . with Jackie."

"That's wonderful, Terry. I'm so happy for you both." Samara stared up at the picture of the temple and swallowed hard. "Maybe we will get to do that whole eternal family thing one day."

"Yeah, and I think sooner rather than later." Terry's voice lifted. "Dad said that he's going to come to church on Sunday."

"What?" Samara actually stood up. "Dad?"

"Absolutely." Terry chuckled. "He said that after talking to Adam he realized how much churchy stuff had rubbed off on him over the years, and so it shouldn't be too hard to catch up to us."

Samara laughed out loud and shook her head. "That sounds so much like our father. 'If you're going to do something, then for Pete's sake, get on with it.'"

Terry laughed with her and then she glanced at the clock.

"Umm . . . I'm going to have to go. I have an activity to go to, but can you give my love to everybody?"

"I will." Terry hesitated. "Does that include Rick?"

"Rick?" Samara's heart skipped a beat. "Is he back?"

"He'll be back next week. Shall I tell him hello from you?"

"Yes, of course." She shook her head. "And you can tell him I'm going out with his cousin, Matt, next Tuesday."

There was the briefest pause, then Terry sighed.

"You know, I think I'll let you pass on that information. I'll stick with hello and your love."

"Whatever!" She laughed at his response, and suddenly it was exactly the same as when they were younger.

"Seriously, Sammy? Do you still have a soft spot for Rick?"

Samara stared at her hands for a long time before she nodded. "Yes, I do, Terry. I think it's always been Rick, but that was part of the problem. He's has always been there for me and I didn't know if there was anybody else. Then when Adam came along, I got swept up in him being my perfect match." She rested her head against the phone. "I know I treated Rick badly, but then he and Adam both went away at the same time and you have Jackie and Mum and Dad have each other. I was left with nothing . . . so Sydney is a good option. At least I can find out if I actually like independence."

"You mean you've gone there to lick your wounds?"

"I prefer to think of it as getting over it." Samara smiled wistfully. "But I realize now that I really haven't. I think that's why I agreed to go out with Matt . . . he looks a lot like Rick."

"So what are you going to do?" Terry was quietly persistent.

"I'm not sure." Samara tucked her hair behind her ears. "If Rick's going to be back home next week then I should try and get in touch with him . . . but I don't know if I can face him. I don't even know what I'd say."

"Well, I can't tell you what to do, but I can say that I'll be eternally grateful that Jackie was there for me. I reckon Rick is worth the risk of a little humiliation." Terry's voice was surprisingly firm. "Don't let your pride get in the way of happiness, Sam. Rick's always been there for you, but you may have to reach out now."

Samara nodded. "I feel like I've been doing a lot of reaching out lately. Adam said I needed to. I hadn't realized how much I'd shut people out." She smiled. "Does that sound confusing?"

"Unfortunately, no." She could hear the smile in his voice. "But I'll be praying for you, Sammy."

Samara didn't try to fight back the tears that began to roll down her cheeks.

"Thanks, big brother. It's good to have you back."

* * *

"I'm sorry to hold you up." Samara slipped into the passenger seat and buckled up her belt. "Are you sure Rick is going to be playing rugby?"

Terry checked for oncoming traffic before he nodded.

"I spoke to him this morning . . . or at least I spoke to Toby, who said that Rick was playing and who then yelled to Rick to check, and I heard Rick yell back that he was." He nodded at his recall of the event and pointed in the air. "And Toby also asked when you were going to come back from Sydney because he misses you."

"Well, it's nice to know that one Jamieson male misses me." Samara took a deep breath. "And you didn't say that I was coming?"

Terry made a zipping motion past his lips and shook his head.

"But I did bring the first aid kit in case it turns nasty."

"You are such a goose." Samara thumped his arm. "But you're a kind goose."

"Thank you, but now I need to know . . . how are you going to approach this, exactly?" Terry scratched his head.

"I don't exactly know." Samara put her hands together. "I have been alternately praying and planning all the way up here . . . and every waking moment over the past week."

"And how does it end each time?"

"It doesn't," Samara answered quietly. "And that's what worries me."

Terry drummed his fingers on the steering wheel, and then he nodded.

"It doesn't have to worry you because you can't plan the ending . . . that will take the two of you." He paused. "But what about Sydney? If it works out with Rick, what would you do about your job? You've only just started there."

Samara stared at her brother and shook her head.

"That was the only ending I could actually come to any conclusion on." She took a deep breath. "I know now that if it came to a decision between Rick or the job . . . I'd choose Rick."

"Wow. You *have* been doing some thinking." Terry whistled softly. "And some changing."

Samara smiled as she stared out the window toward the rugby field. "I guess I had to know if there was a choice before I could make it."

"Well then, I'll leave you to it." Terry swung the car into the parking lot and parked near the end of the rugby field. Then he turned and winked. "Good luck, Sam."

She stood outside the car for a minute, looking over the familiar scene. She'd been one of the spectators at many rugby games over the years, cheering for both Terry and Rick, and some people passing by even now waved out to her. She waved back and then felt her heart do a flip as she heard a murmur of applause begin to ripple across the grounds. That meant the players were coming out onto the field . . . including Rick.

She jumped as the car horn gave a little toot behind her, and she turned to see Terry waving her on in the direction of the field. He held his hands against his chest in a desperate pleading motion, and she stamped her foot at him. When he only grinned back and started the car engine, she turned toward the field.

She managed to work herself in among the large crowd of spectators as the last of the players ran out onto the field. Quickly, scanning the lineup of players in black-and-white jerseys, she felt her stomach churn as she searched for Rick's distinctively tall frame. But then the sinking feeling of disappointment overcame her when she couldn't see it. She stood up on her toes to check near the clubhouse, but there was still no sign of him.

"Is Rick playing today?" She turned around and asked one of the player's mothers.

"I think he's still up north." The woman frowned. "But we could sure use his speed on the wing today."

Samara nodded as she looked back at the field. "We could all use him today," she murmured as she began to work her way out of the crowd. It was beginning to feel claustrophobic among all the bodies, and she felt like she needed air. She stood on the edge for a few minutes, and then she absently picked up the camera hanging around her neck and unzipped the case. It would take her mind off Rick if she took some photos.

"Perception," she murmured as she began to look around the crowd and across the field. "Look at the obvious and then go beyond it."

As she watched the crowd, her attention wandered to a food wagon selling hot dogs and fries. A father had just purchased his little girl a hot dog, and the child was trying to negotiate the length of bread and sausage. Samara began to shoot as the child's frown deepened. She caught the supreme effort of the girl's first bite, followed by her anguished look as ketchup and mustard flowed down her chin and pink sweater.

"Sam!"

She swung around to see Toby running toward her across the grass. She replaced her lens cap.

"Sam!"

"Hey, Toby." She glanced quickly behind him, her heart beating far faster than normal, but there was nobody that she knew.

He reached her at full speed and she had to let the camera swing in order to catch him.

"I knew you'd be here." He wrapped his arms around her neck and buried his face against her. "I told Rick you'd be here."

Her heart skipped another beat.

"But how did you know?" She leaned back to look into his face. "I didn't tell anyone I was coming . . . not even my family."

Toby rolled his eyes as he put a hand on either side of her face.

"I prayed you here, silly." He patted her cheeks. "I knew you'd come."

Samara nodded as he began to wriggle to get down.

"Rick's getting changed." He began to run as soon as he reached the ground. "I'll tell him you're here."

"No, Toby . . . don't . . ." Her voice tapered off as he ran ahead without hearing, and she began to look around with a sense of desperation. As she glanced back at the clubhouse her heart tumbled as Rick walked out in his rugby uniform with Toby swinging on his arm. He looked even taller in his black rugby shorts, and his black-and-white striped jersey made his shoulders seem wider.

As they got closer, she quickly picked up the camera and held it against her face, pretending to focus but not seeing anything.

"It might help to take the cap off." She kept one eye closed as the light suddenly flared through the lens. "I thought you were the professional."

As she slowly lowered the camera, Rick stood holding the lens cap up in front of her.

"Professional fool." She grimaced as she held her hand out for the cap without looking at him. "I couldn't find anywhere else to hide."

"Still hiding behind your camera." He kept the cap in his hand.

"That's silly." Toby tugged on his brother's other hand. "She can't hide behind a camera . . . she's too big."

"My mistake, big ears." Rick let Toby's hand go and began to rotate the lens cap between his fingers.

"Aren't you supposed to be on the field?" Samara dropped her hand then held it out again. "I'll take that so you can get on."

"I'm on second half." He held the cap just out of her reach. "You can have it back if you answer one question."

Samara swallowed hard. "What sort of question?"

"It's a yes or no question."

She nodded and felt the pulse in her neck begin to beat as he looked up at the sky.

"Have you come back to stay, Sam?"

She closed her eyes as the question seemed to hang in the air. Then she clenched her fists. "As long as you want me to."

He was so still she thought he hadn't heard, then he shook his head. "I said this was a yes or no question. Have you come back to stay, Sam?"

She heard the quiet pleading in his voice, and she knew he didn't just mean Broadbeach.

"Yes." She choked on the single word. "Yes."

"I only needed to hear it once." He took a step closer and wrapped her fingers around the lens cap. "I believe you."

"Then what are you going to do about it?" She could barely breathe the question as he lifted her chin with one finger.

"I'll tell you after the game," he whispered against her lips, and then he kissed her for a long time.

"See, Rick . . . I told you she'd stay." Toby began to lose patience as his brother ignored him.

"Did he?" Samara asked softly as Rick moved away.

"He did." He kissed her gently again. "He said you'd be here and that you'd stay."

"And did you believe him?" She lifted her face to look into his eyes.

"I wanted to." He nodded. "But I think I was scared to."

Samara smiled as she pressed her hand against his chest. "O ye of little faith."

* * *

The sun was setting by the time the game ended, and after they'd thanked the enthusiastic spectators who congratulated Rick on the two tries he'd scored, it took several promises of future outings to convince Toby to stay at home with his cat.

"My gosh, that boy is persistent." Rick finally slid behind the steering wheel and waved to Toby as he stood at the front door with the cat in his arms. "I think he loves you more than I do."

"Does that mean that you love me?" Samara felt suddenly shy as they pulled out of the driveway and drove down the street.

"I guess it does, doesn't it?" Rick pretended to look surprised. "Well, I never . . . and all this time I thought we were just friends."

Samara laughed as he reached out for her hand.

"So what are you going to do about it?"

It felt so good not to be pretending or evading the issue that she lifted his hand to her lips and kissed it gently.

"You know, I don't remember having this much trouble concentrating when we were going out before." He grinned as he gently pulled his hand away and straightened up behind the wheel. "We'll be the next ones in hospital at this rate."

He drove south on the highway and Samara began to look around.

"Are we going to Currumbin?"

"Close." Rick pointed as they turned into the parking area near a small bay. "I came down here for lunch one day before I went up north and saw some things I thought you might like to photograph."

"That was nice of you to think of that." Samara glanced at him and he met her look.

"I never stopped thinking of you, Sam." He barely whispered the words but she could feel the intensity of what he was saying, and it made the color course through her cheeks.

"Now you're embarrassing me." She playfully pushed his shoulder, but he only leaned closer and gave her a quick kiss on the nose.

"Good." He sat back and opened his door, holding up his hand to stop her as she went to get out. "Wait there."

She sat still as he walked around the car and opened her door with a flourish, offering his hand to help her out. Again she felt the warmth in her cheeks as she laughed shyly.

"Now you're making me feel like a princess."

"Good, again." Rick bowed low. "All the things I've been wanting to do are working."

"You've been wanting to embarrass me?" she remarked with a smile.

"Only enough to make you notice me." He began to pull her gently down toward a park area, keeping her fingers entwined in his. At the edge of the play area he guided her to a wooden bench and motioned for her to sit down. Then he sat close beside her. He didn't speak straightaway, but there was such a comfortable silence between them that Samara closed her eyes and leaned against his shoulder. Rick put his arm around her shoulder and drew her against him.

"The day I had lunch down here, I had tried to call you early in the morning, but you'd already gone to school . . . with Adam."

Samara stared straight ahead as her stomach suddenly tightened. She felt Rick's chest rise as he took a deep breath.

"I think, right then . . . I was ready to walk away. I had tried to be your friend if I couldn't be . . . more." He hesitated. "But then it seemed like there was just no point trying anymore, and knowing that you were with Adam made it all seem so much more impossible."

She opened her mouth to speak but he briefly pressed his finger against her lips.

"I came and sat down here and some little kids were playing on the playground. I began to remember how good you were at getting the children to work with you when you were doing the photos at the sanctuary and how Adam had helped you." He stroked the top of her hand as it lay on his leg. "Then I started looking at these little kids . . . at their expressions and what was making them laugh, and I began to feel different, like my perception was changing. I started thinking about you and Adam, and it felt like the same process was happening . . . like my perception of him was changing as well."

"How?" Samara asked as she recalled that day with Adam.

"It's hard to explain." She felt Rick shake his head. "All morning I'd been feeling angry at him for taking you away from me—angry at you for being led away by this exotic, older man." He ran his finger along the vein on her hand. "Then I got angry at myself for being useless."

"You weren't useless." Samara objected, leaning slightly away. "I was the one who was ignoring you."

"You were." Rick responded with a quiet chuckle. "And you did it so well that I was completely confused, because sometimes it seemed as if you wanted me around."

"I think I always have." Samara found it difficult to swallow. "I just didn't realize it."

They sat without speaking, and then Rick coughed and pulled her closer against his chest.

"Anyway, I began to think that maybe you two were meant to be together because Adam seemed to be able to give you everything you'd always dreamed about." He hesitated. "He was everything you'd ever dreamed about, and it annoyed me that even I could see it. But then I had this feeling . . . it was almost like I was giving you to him . . . if that was right for you."

Samara nodded and it took her awhile to speak. "I told Adam that night that I loved him." Her words seem to fall into a pool of silence between them and she shook her head. "And I really did think I loved him, but he helped me realize that I loved what he stood for . . . the excitement, the learning, the focus on photography." She hung her head. "I finally figured out that I'd been living a dream all these years."

"But it was a good dream," Rick stated quietly. "He joined the Church and you became a photographer."

"That's what we decided." Samara nodded. "Then I didn't really see him for the next few days. The day you left he showed me the contract from New York and we had a party . . ."

"Yes, I'm sorry I couldn't come to that." Rick looked out at the park. "It was one of those moments where I really wanted to be there, but I was actually glad that they needed me up north."

Samara smiled weakly. "I felt the same. I missed you but I was glad you weren't there."

"Thank you." She heard the smile in his voice. "At least we agree on that."

A seagull suddenly drifted a few feet away, its black eyes darting as it looked at them expectantly. When they sat still it opened its beak and squawked, ruffling its feathers indignantly before flying off into the sky. Samara lifted her face to the sky as it briefly hovered above them and then disappeared.

"I think I'll always have a soft spot for seagulls."

"Random." She felt the chuckle in Rick's chest and she nudged him with her elbow.

"I have my reasons," she protested quietly. "They'll always remind me of Adam."

"Now that's what I need to hear." Rick spread his other arm along the back of the bench seat and chuckled out loud. "Couldn't you have picked a less common bird?"

"No." Samara smiled at his reaction as she stared up at the sky. "The morning after you left, Adam and I went for a walk along the beach, and there were two seagulls flying together . . . a big one and a small one. It was like the big one was teaching the little one to fly, and then after awhile . . ." She faltered and the tears began to flow freely down her cheeks. "It flew way above the little one, as if it were making sure it were safe, and then it seemed to float away into the distance until it was barely a speck . . . and then it was gone." Her voice quivered. "And then Adam said that he was leaving. We hugged and I cried and he just slipped away."

"And then he was gone . . . just like the big seagull." Rick's voice was soft against her ear as she nodded.

"I guess he figured I didn't need him anymore." Samara laid her head back on his shoulder. "I really did love Adam but I confused appreciation with . . . real love."

"So do I take that to mean that you really love me or that you don't appreciate me?" Rick wrapped his fingers over hers. "You don't need to answer that . . . I'm just trying to lighten the moment."

"I know." Samara squeezed his fingers gently. "The thing is that after I went down to Sydney to lick my wounds I began to realize how much I really did appreciate you and that I really loved you. But then I didn't know what to do about it so I sort of convinced myself that I was destined to be a famous, spinster photographer who wandered the world."

"Taking photos of seagulls?" Rick asked quietly.

"And crocodiles." Samara smiled. "And living on memories."

There was another long silence until Rick stood up and held out his hand. As they walked along the grass he wrapped his arm around her waist and kept her close beside him.

"I nearly didn't come back from Kakadu either." He pointed to the north. "I felt safe up there . . . nicely uncommitted."

"So what did bring you back?" Samara glanced up at him.

"Toby." Rick smiled. "I received a very badly spelled e-mail saying that you were coming back from Sydney and wanted to see me."

"Toby said that?" Samara gasped and Rick nodded.

"I didn't even stop to think about it. I got on the plane and it wasn't until I got home that he told me that he'd only thought you were coming back and that he was sure you'd want to see me when you got here."

Samara grinned as she thought about Toby's reception at the rugby game.

"He told me that he prayed me here."

"Then I guess he does have more faith than me." Rick stopped and turned her toward him. "Why did you come back, Samara?"

She stared at the middle button on his shirt and then frowned as she began to twist it between her fingers.

"I think it was something I read in one of the Church magazines about how we can be earthly angels and help people if we're receptive to the Spirit." She patted the button. "I decided that Adam must be my angel. He set me on a path, made sure I knew what I was doing, and then steered me in your direction."

"How did he do that?"

Rick looked puzzled. Samara shrugged her shoulders. "In our conversations he would often point out your qualities, and then . . . after he left me at the beach, I'm sure I heard him tell me that you were a good, good man." She smiled. "It was very faint but it's played over and over in my mind. And then when I saw you walk out of the clubrooms, I felt like my heart was going to burst." She reached up and touched his chest, feeling his heart beating beneath her hand. "Rick is a good, good man . . . and I love him . . . and I don't want to be without him ever again."

She thought she was going to lose her breath when he hugged her so tightly that her feet lifted off the ground. Then she was kissed so thoroughly that the sky actually spun when he stopped.

"We're never going to be apart again, Sam." Rick rested his chin against her forehead. "We'll travel the world together and we'll have heaps of children that you can photograph all day long . . ." He stopped as she leaned back.

"And we'll call our first son Adam."

She grinned as he laughed out loud, then he bent his head and kissed her again.

A lone seagull circled overhead, called out once, and then lifted into the sky above them.

Epilogue

The woman arrived while Samara and Rick were tending the reception desk at the motel. Eddy and Tracey were out for the afternoon, so they were using the time in reception to go over their wedding plans. The bell rang and they both looked up as the tall woman walked into the foyer. She wore a pale beige linen shirt and trousers that seemed to match the salt-and-pepper shades of her short hair. In one hand she carried a small suitcase, and a large bag hung over her other shoulder. She smiled at them hesitantly as she glanced at a piece of yellow paper in her hand.

"Good morning, I'm looking for Samara Danes."

Her voice was precise but with a soft accent.

"That's me." Samara frowned as she pointed at her chest. "I'm Samara Danes. How can I help you?"

The woman smiled again as she set the suitcase down and walked forward with her hand extended.

"Samara, I'm so pleased to meet you at last. My name is Helen Russell. I'm Adam Russell's wife."

It took several seconds for Samara to acknowledge the extended hand, and that wasn't until Rick pushed her gently forward, holding out his own hand.

"Helen, it's good to meet you. I'm Rick Jamieson . . . Samara's fiancé." Again he tapped Samara lightly, and she swallowed and held out her hand.

"Yes . . . yes, I'm pleased to meet you, Helen." She looked down at the desk, then straight into the woman's dark brown eyes. She felt as if she had been appraised, obviously having passed the scrutiny as Helen smiled warmly.

"You are both exactly as Adam described and, of course, the photos couldn't lie." She tapped the shoulder bag. "And believe me, there are plenty of photos."

In that instant, Samara recognized Adam's well-worn camera bag with its many pockets, and she stifled a gasp. She felt Rick's hand behind her back as he peered around Helen toward the open doorway.

"So is Adam still coming?" He began to move from behind the counter. "I'll give him a hand with your bags."

He stopped as Helen held up her hand and shook her head. Samara watched as she gripped the bag handle tightly.

"Adam's not with me." She looked straight at Samara. "He's gone."

Samara felt her throat constrict. "Typical Adam . . . off on another adventure."

"He's not coming back this time, Samara." Helen spoke quietly. "Adam passed away last month."

Samara heard the words, but they didn't seem to make sense as she shook her head. "He said he was going to slow down on the trips, but I guess he just can't help himself." She half laughed as she put a pen back in place on the desk pad.

"He made me promise to come and visit you, Samara." Helen came closer to the desk. "Just before he died he made me promise to bring you this." She lifted the shoulder bag up onto the desk and ran one hand over it. "He said you would make far better use of it than me." She smiled. "I've never been any good at photography." She opened the top flap and Samara found herself staring at the black camera cases Adam had used so much. Very slowly, she reached in and lifted the top one out. It sat heavily in her hand, the huge lens fitting perfectly between her thumb and forefinger.

"How?" Samara managed one word as the camera became blurred.

Helen rested both hands on the desk, taking her time to respond.

"He's been sick for a very long time, Samara." She paused. "He knew he was dying when he came here."

"Dying?" Samara's head jerked up. "He never said . . ."

"He'd had a serious intestinal disease for a long time. Something he picked up in his travels years ago . . . it was literally eating him up but he ignored it."

"He kept coughing." Samara nodded slowly as she looked at the camera.

"That was part of it." Helen took a deep breath. "When he came back to Canada he came to see me . . . to apologize for how he'd behaved over the years. He said that being with you and your family had helped him realize how much he'd missed . . . me."

"My family?" Samara looked surprised as Helen nodded.

"He thanked me for loving him when we got married, and when I said I still did . . ." She smiled weakly. "Well, we were remarried in bishop's office a week later and managed to go back to the temple before he got really ill."

"So when—" Samara couldn't finish as she looked quickly at Rick, who tightened his arm around her.

"About four weeks ago, he collapsed and went into the hospital, but he refused to stay there and I had to take him up to a little cabin he owns in the mountains. He passed away one morning sitting in the chair overlooking his favorite lake." Her tears fell as she pulled a clear plastic folder from the back of the bag. "He was sorting through these photos and asked me to give them to you with this letter."

Samara's hands were shaking as she reached for the folder. Inside the cover, she pulled out a large beige envelope with her name written on the front in Adam's bold handwriting. There were three photos inside, along with a letter. Almost in a daze, she turned the thin packet of photos over and withdrew each one, laying them on the desk. In the first one she recognized herself as a young girl sitting on a rocky outcrop, the shimmering sands and curling waves of Sumner Beach forming a range of silvery grays that blended into the darker sky. She was in silhouette, but she recognized her profile and remembered his instructions to her that day.

"He told me to look into the distance and imagine what I wanted to be in the future." She touched the silhouette gently with her finger. "That was the moment I decided I wanted to be a photographer."

The second photo made her glance quickly at Rick. It was a photo taken at the Currumbin Sanctuary, where Adam had captured a moment when Toby had hugged both Rick and Samara with each arm. Samara was laughing at Toby, but Rick was watching her and smiling, an infinite tenderness in his eyes that Adam had caught perfectly.

The third photo had a background of wispy, white clouds beautifully blended into smoky gray against which two black-and-white seagulls were frozen into perfect symmetry of flight, their wings outspread, their heads tilted at the same angle toward the sky with the slightest reflection of light off their wings.

Helen watched as Samara studied each of the photos in turn. Then she coughed gently. "You know, I think I'll just sit out in the sun on that little bench for a few minutes while you read the letter."

She walked out quietly while Samara stared at the envelope and slowly pulled the letter out. Adam's firm, flowing script filled two pages, and her hands began to shake as she held it out to Rick.

"Can you read it for me?"

He took it gently from her and she leaned against him as he began to read aloud.

My dearest Samara,

If you are reading this letter, I know you have met my dear Helen and that she has kept her promise to me. I wish we could have come back together to see you, but life takes some unusual turns. At least I know that we will meet again someday.

Samara, I wanted you to know how much you have given me since we met at Sumner Beach and you shared your simple testimony of the gospel. The fact that you had the confidence to teach a young, hardened photographer who thought he knew all about life has been a constant inspiration to me.

When I decided to fly to Australia to try and find you, it was a spur-of-the-moment decision. I really didn't know what I planned to do if I found you, but I felt strongly enough to book the ticket. Seeing you instantly brought back many memories, not the least of which was recalling the Spirit I'd felt when I originally joined the Church.

Meeting your family was also an interesting experience, as each one of you seemed to encapsulate part of my life's journey. They say that when you're dying your life suddenly flashes before your eyes, but with me it was more like a gradual unfolding. Terry seemed to represent the young Adam, trying drugs for the sake of it but losing control and not knowing how to get help. Your father was my wandering spirit, unwilling to be tied to people or places in case something more interesting came along, and then unable to rebuild the relationships he'd let go. Your mother seemed to represent the people that I'd left behind or put aside in my quest for becoming the world's greatest photographer.

And then there was you, Samara. You epitomized the spirit of what I wanted to achieve and you were the clay that I could mold into the perfect photographer . . . until I met your family and realized what I had become and what I had missed and what I wanted you to avoid becoming.

I found that I became consumed with wanting to help each one of you see how you could improve your lives because I'd been down that path and knew how you could change . . . how you must change or you could destroy each other. At the same time, you all reinforced my own desire to get myself back on track. Most of all I became concerned with how your testimony had become a shadow of what I remembered, and I knew it was because of all these other things. I wanted so badly for you to get that spirit back.

Samara, you have great talent and you need to share it with the world, but please do not do it at the expense of your eternal happiness. I was able to observe Rick when neither of you was aware of me watching. He is the man I would want to be if I had my time over again, and his concern for your welfare is what I should have shown Helen all those years ago. Heavenly Father has blessed me with a few precious weeks to show her how I feel. You have the opportunity of a whole lifetime. Please don't waste it.

Of all the photos I have taken, these three seem to epitomize the memories I have of you.

Stay strong, Samara, till we meet again.

Much love,

Adam

Samara could barely see the photographs as Rick finished reading and handed the letter back to her.

"He captured it exactly." Rick spoke softly beside her and she laid her head back against his shoulder.

"In words and in pictures." Samara smiled as she looked up into his eyes and rested her hand on the picture of the seagulls. "And we have a whole lifetime together to prove him right."

About the Author

Pamela Carrington Reid is a native of Auckland, New Zealand, and resides there with her husband, Paul. They are the parents of five children. Pamela graduated from Auckland University with a double major in English and Geography and also has a master's in Creative Writing. Teaching at BYU's Education Week and at other venues, she has lectured in personal and family history writing, family and marriage relations, religious philosophy, and fashion design. She has had several articles published in the New Era, Friend, and Ensign, and is the South Pacific editor for the Ensign. Pamela has also written film scripts for the LDS audience, including an adaptation of the movie Legacy. All of her books are set against the scenic background of New Zealand and the expansive South Pacific.